Praise for *Liberty Call*

"Youth, and the sea, and a voyage to nowhere except possibly self-discovery have been a powerful theme in the novel ever since Joseph Conrad, and Dennis Doherty does that tradition proud with *Liberty Call*."

— Tad Richards
NYT bestselling author

"...a maelstrom cruise through the South China Sea in a man's world[,] a raw and honest telling of men living high on the edge."

— Laurence Carr
Pancake Hollow Primer
and Lightwood Press

"Dennis Doherty's superlative novel combines his first-hand knowledge of warships with the compelling character of Walter Schmertz, to tell a sizzler of a story. Animated prose has you turn the pages as fast as the eye can see. Many head-turning events later, you'll feel yourself in a new world, with a new mind. A must read!

— David Appelbaum
fmr editor of *Parabola Magazine*
and founder of Codhill Press

"dazzling (stage-worthy) dialogue with poetically evocative landscape.... constitutes the *voice* of the narration.... The rest is character. And there are many characters that stay with you – above all, the protagonist Schmerz, naval radio operator and Arthurian Knight in disguise."

— H.R. Stoneback
Distinguished Professor
SUNY New Paltz

"an eye-opening story...that is powerful[,] unexpected[,]made all the stronger for its roots in a real-life story."

— D.Donovan
Senior Reviewer
Midwest Book Review

Opening Note

What you are about to read is a deeply personal work and complete expression of its author's exploration of the truth. As a result, we strongly encourage you to explore all of the details and implications of anything you discover or encounter as a result of this work.

Additionally, in accordance with The Mad Duck Coalition's mission of encouraging and providing intellectual stimulation of *all* kinds, we do not—and *cannot*—endorse any of the ideas presented by any member of our flock.

The only things we can—and *do*—endorse are the authorial integrity of the works we publish and the quality of intellectual engagements that they produce and inspire.

Liberty Call

Liberty Call is a work of fiction. In general, names, characters, places, and incidents are the products of the author's imagination or are used fictitiously and any resemblance to actual events, locales, or persons, living or dead is entirely coincidental. However, portions of this book are works of nonfiction. Certain names and identifying characteristics have been changed.

2022 The Mad Duck Coalition ™ First Edition

THE MAD DUCK COALITION, its imprints, and colophones are trademarks of The Mad Duck Coalition, LLC.

For information about our special discounts for libraries, reviews, bookstores, and academic professionals, contact us through our form at thmaduco.org

Copyright © 2021 by Dennis Doherty

All rights reserved. No part of this book may be used or reproduced in any form or any manner whatsoever without written permission from the publisher except in the case of brief quotations embodied in critical articles and reviews.

Published in the United States under Big Ripple Books, an imprint of The Mad Duck Coalition, LLC, New York.

Cover art and design by Mark Delluomo

ISBN: 978-1-956389-06-7

Library of Congress Control Number: 2021946391

www.themadduckcoalition.org

To my closest friends, lifelong shipmates who've shared the long, rough voyage, this is for you. Bravo Zulu, and thanks.

Table of Contents

Overhaul 1

The Need for Speed 7

Morning Light 27

Homeport, Yokosuka 45

Clowns 57

The Devil Inside 63

Radiomen 105

Subic City............................... 115

Welcome 173

Liberty Call

A Novel

By Dennis Doherty

New York

Overhaul

Walter Schmerz and Al Turner stood about ten feet apart on the deck below the signal bridge, slowly working their way toward each other with their needle guns. Walter held his needle gun with both hands as far over his head as he could and moved it in a circle, up and down, all over the bulkhead to the deck. The Stone was at their feet, tearing up the non-skid floor with a deck crawler, kicking at the jumble of pneumatic tubing behind him and pulling it along as he advanced. Bum and the rest of their Tiger Team worked on the signal bridge and antenna platforms, stripping the ship's paint away.

The sun was relentless but the grit was worse, so Walter kept his coveralls buttoned at the neck and occasionally had to stop to clear the sweat from his respirator and goggles. He had on so much insulating gear: underwear, dungarees under coveralls, steel tip boots, bandanna around the neck, respirator, goggles, ball cap, earplugs, Mickey Mouse ear protectors. It was like being housed inside himself against a hail of paint chips and thundering machinery, but Walter's face and ear protection muffled it all to a background rumble.

Walter couldn't tell the noises apart over the insane yakking of his needle gun: an air-powered cylinder with twelve tiny metal rods, dancing back and forth, smacking into whatever they're held against. The aluminum bulkhead stood no chance against it, and the millions of tiny dents its soft metal sent chips flying in all directions and even into the drydock, chattering under the sheer strength of Walter and his needle gun. It started to talk to him after awhile. Pok pokitter pokitting pok pokked, walt waltitty titta walt walt. As was usual for him, Walter continued his work slowly and deliberately, his thoughts coming to him in the staccato voice of the banging needles as his sweat dripped onto them. Al, also as usual, was working faster than Walter was, seemingly enjoying the dirty work, seemingly to say, "My my, isn't this a thing to be doing! Look at me go, tearing up the paint of the mighty Outland on this hot, Japanese, summer day! Land-a-Goshen. Who'd-a-thunk." Al moved the gun up and down at a slanted angel like a chisel, which seemed to help it along, not just letting the needles pop but pushing them into the paint, efficiently shearing it off.

Even The Stone, who they usually had to keep an eye on for all the trouble he caused, was working like a mesmerized maniac, attacking the non-skid as if his deck crawler were a buzz saw. He didn't wear knee pads while he crawled the deck with a bandanna around his head to cover the green marijuana leaf he had drunkenly tattooed on his forehead the night before. He wasn't in the habit of wearing a shirt, so his shoulders were already blistering under the sun, but he didn't care how long they'd still be working in Yokosuka. Everyone knew The Stone had a simple mind, and when the large, black chunks of non-skid flew up and bit him, marking his chest and arms, he'd only bear down on the deck all the harder, tearing it up all the more. Cause and effect seemed to be lost on him, so his sweat would always run black with the dust and black micro-threads that accentuated his otherwise skinny muscles.

As Walter and Al finally edged close to each other, they started to notice something under the paint they were chipping. It was a large, red and white pattern that wouldn't come off under the needle guns' prodding, as if it had been there so long it had become an indelible part of the bulkhead, an ancient painting grown into the pores of aluminum, like some kind of organic stain, or a birthmark. Walter and Al were archaeologists on the verge of a discovery and quickened their pace. They both concentrated on the center of the bulkhead where the hidden design was. The old red and white paint broke and separated into a myriad of dents and pock marks made by the needles, but instead of flying off like the gray coating over it, the color dug deeper into the metal, so as they uncovered it they atomized it, bit by bit.

When they finally came together near the middle, Walter and Al put down their guns and stood back. The painting looked like a ship's insignia as rendered by some crazy pointillist. It was several shades faded, like someone had already tried to erase it but there was too much give in that porous, slightly pitted and rotten patch of aluminum. Walter and Al could still piece the painting together though, between the two of them: a large circle with white letters at the top announcing "DesRon 26", white letters at the bottom that added "San Diego-Da Nang 1967", and between the two in the center was the Outland's emblem, a rascally red devil with a triton.

"Look that!" Al yelled, pointing at their discovery. He lifted one end of Walter's Mickey Mouse ears and began yakking, but Walter only caught every other word or so.

"Yoosta...homeport...Diego..musta...years...think!" He looked like he was laughing but Walter couldn't tell: Al's face was covered with his bandanna, bandit-like.

They showed their discovery to The Stone, who grinned and mouthed something that was probably "Oh wow," or something similar.

First Class Petty Officer Kid—enviably cool, clean, and neat as ever—tapped Walter on the shoulder and yelled into his exposed ear, "Want you in Radio." Walter pointed to the painting, and Kid looked at it, stood there a moment with his hand cupped over his eyes from the sun. It was strange for all of them to see the names of cities and squadrons that weren't their own on their Outland, uncovering the memories of a crew that was gone and part of the ship's life that they knew nothing about.

Walter supposed that the Outland had been homeported in San Diego and the picture commemorated a WestPac cruise and, possibly, the action it saw off the coast of Viet Nam. That proud crew probably got Navy Expedition Ribbons for that one, maybe even Battle Ribbons. It was only later that Walter learned that the Outland had been moved to Yokosuka in the mid-seventies and that it had been one of the ships that took part in the evacuation of Saigon, bobbing unseen in the wings, while, center-stage, desperate people kicked and clawed for helicopter space atop the embassy building, fighting for passage to an unseen and unknown ship, *this* ship.

Walter pictured it: helicopter skids swaying with dogged aviators in green flightsuits apprehensive but nonetheless resolute in completing their mission, hurriedly loading a bucket brigade of panicked, intelligent ants into their green bellies before the onslaught of some terrible and all-consuming disaster.

Walter didn't picture what really happened, he couldn't: a man overboard in high seas couldn't be seen, only the rise and rush of senseless ocean mountains, the million dints of shifting light, and the feeling of futility before such terrific expanse and power.

Walter followed Kid inside the watertight door, then down the passageway to the ship's store where they bought a couple of ice-cold Cokes. Walter sucked his drink right down and burped. "What did I do now, Boss?"

"It ain't what you did," Kid said. "It's what you a-gonna do." His smile suggested mischief.

Walter liked Kid. Walter blew as much of the gray gunk out of his nose and into his bandanna as possible, unbuttoned his coveralls, tied the arms around his waist, and wiped at the grit on his neck and face. "And what is it that I'm a-gonna do, Kid?" he asked.

Kid smiled. "Looks like you a-gonna get yo sea legs, son."

An old adrenal excitement crept into Walter's veins. "Am I going with a battlegroup? Up to the Gulf? Gonzo Station?"

Kid shook his head. "You *want* to go?"

"I don't know," Walter said, and he didn't. But here was his chance *finally*, after two years of shore duty and then coming to a ship during overhaul, to be a *real* sailor and get some blue water under his feet, to get away from the daily paint chipping and start learning his trade.

Lieutenant Moderness was waiting in Radio with The Chief, Leading Petty Officer Starring, and Mallory, a mere seaman who had no business being clean, who was standing a little lost in the center of the room.

"Well well well, Schmerz," Mister Moderness said through his teeth, "looks like you got a chance to get your feet wet."

"Mister Moderness," Walter said, "how come you never talk with your mouth open?"

Kid chuckled, "Yeah, that's right. He always talk like he's mad." He leaned back against the door, still smiling, arms crossed.

Leading Petty Officer Starring was sitting right in a teletype operator's chair, holding his pipe like an actor's prop, absolutely not amused. "You better not address the officers where you're going like that, Schmerz."

"Which is where? I ask."

"Come here, Schmerz," The Chief said from his supervisor's desk in the back with the lieutenant, away from operations but ever in charge. "How you like the yards after two months on Tiger Team?"

"Hey, where am I going—"

"Hey?" he said. "*Hey*? Hey is for horses. You call me Chief. You don't come in here actin' like a old, familiar salt just because you're dirty. You still got to call me Chief. Look at ya. Now, the paint's okay as long as we're in the yards—that's what I call clean dirt—but I don't know about those rolled up sleeves. You don't see no one else with long sleeve shirts, do you? I just don't think they're a part of the ship's regulations, and by the way, you never did put in a request chit to grow that beard. You're gonna have to clean up your act before reportin' to the Cox. You'll be representing our division. That is, you'll be representing me. What do you think, Mister Moderness? I say the boy's so seasick his first week out that he can't even get out of his rack to puke."

"Yeah," the Lieutenant snarled, "but Schmerz is gonna go fucking ballistic when he gets to The Philippines." Starring's laugh sounded like a hiccup. Mallory was smiling broadly.

"The PI? Subic?" Walter asked.

"The Cox leaves tomorrow for weapons testing and ASW exercises," Starring said, "and you and Mallory are gonna be on it—they need a third class and a seaman. You'll stop at Subic for a week on the way back, for upkeep and weapons onload. You're only concern is to get qualified on the NavMacs." It was knockoff time, but Walter felt a new day beginning.

"What's a NavMacs?" Walter asked.

"It's what we're gonna be getting," Starring said, as if that clarified things.

"Goddamnit, Starring," the Chief said, "if you don't know what the hell you're talkin' about then shut the hell up! Don't be ignorant!"

Starring took a sudden interest in the teletype's keyboard.

"You're gonna see it soon enough, Schmerz, and you goddamn-well better learn it inside out 'cause you and Mallory are gonna have the jump on all us, so you're gonna be instructin' the rest of the division when we get it installed. It's gonna modernize this radioshack, is what it is."

Walter pulled a patch cord out of the switchboard above Starring's head, held the plug to his ear and the other plug toward the Chief. "Gentlemen, what we have here is a failure to communicate!"

The Kid unfolded his arms and moved from the door as the cypher lock clicked. "must be Turner," he said, and made a comical bow to the incoming freight.

In walked Al Turner looking like a coal miner stumbling into the wrong world. He crossed his eyes for effect, his creased ballcap brim shedding paint chips like sweat. "Gentlemen," Al said, "good afternoon."

"Petty Officer Turner," Starring said, "why aren't you topside with the Tiger Team? Did Petty Officer Kid give you permission to take a break?" He looked to Lieutenant Moderness.

Al responded, "No, Petty Officer Starring, it was time according to Captain Knockoff, so I figured I'd have a Commander Coke, then visit Rear Admiral Rack for an hour or so catnap before dinner." He pulled his earplugs out and lightly juggled them in his palms. "Hey! I can hear now!"

"What the hell are you doing, Turner?" The Chief said. "Hear this! Knockoff time ain't for ten minutes yet."

"This is true, Chief *Chief*." Al nodded. "But it'll take them that long to get all the gear and hoses put away, which they are now doing. I *have* been busting my little fanny," he said and looked at Mallory, "which is more than I can say about certain non-rated individuals around here."

Mallory glanced up from the operating manual he was pretending to read. "Fuck you too, Turner. Maybe if you knew your rate good enough, I wouldn't have to be down here helping sort all this clerical bullshit."

Al smiled. "I know you don't want to be down here, where you don't belong—"

Kid held his left fist up to his left cheek and poked his tongue into his right cheek. Blow job. He pointed his chin at Mallory.

"Well Al," Walter said, "I'm going on the Cox tomorrow."

"Hoo boy, haze gray and underway! And where, pray tell, is the Cox going?"

"The PI," Walter said. "Subic."

"Among other places," Mister Moderness added, and then repeated "*baaalllllistic*" as he walked out the door.

"Never mind about Subic, Schmerz. You just learn that NavMacs. And, Turner," The Chief said with a scowl, "get your ass back topside and help out."

Al nodded toward the door then back to Walter. "You know, me and Haggard had some wild times when last we were in Subic. Wild times. We were making it with these two girls in my hotel—him and his girl on the floor and me and mine on the bed—and we swapped in the middle of screwing— unscrewed, as it were—and changed places. I kept on laughing, 'cause out of the corner of my eye, I could see his white ass on the bed going up and down and my girl, who was his girl, was moaning and his girl, who was *my* girl, was moaning too, and he kept saying things like, 'Hey Turner, how'm I doing' an' 'Ooh lala, this is the buns.' Fucking Haggard." He slapped Walter's back.

"Well, you're gonna be like a kid in a candy shop Walter, I can tell. When you hop off the Cox, go to Paradise and tell 'em Crazy Al Turner sent you. Be sure to ask for Mimi. She's hotter than anything on The Honcho."

"Yeah," Starring sniffed, knocking his pipe bowl into an empty Coke can. "Subic sure beats hanging around The Honcho. They stopped fucking here in seventy three."

The Need for Speed

The Cox was a Knox-class frigate, the same as the Outland, identical in every way, except of course, that is was fully furnished and adorned, literally shipshape and plying the deep water. Walter's time aboard was short and responsibilities few, only a couple of weeks of exercises in the Philippine Sea, a week in Subic, then back to Yokosuka and the Outland. He had only one task, to get trained on the NavMacs, and he mastered that quickly—data processor, line printers, message screening, high-speed transmission of outgoing messages, and above all else, a satellite link. No more messing with high frequency radio waves. And along the way he picked up everything else he could about shipboard radio communications—ship to ship, ship to shore, transmitters, receivers. He was new to this world, but as a petty officer with two years of shore duty, he felt an awkward pressure to perform.

Walter spent a lot of his free time alone, topside under the sun on the signalman's deck, the fantail, thinking about Iran, submarine warfare.

He was just a radioman from some frigate out of Yokosuka, where protesters of the nuclear shell game—*I can neither confirm nor deny the presence of nuclear warheads, hell, I have no idea*—regularly reminded him of the localized effects of Hiroshima and Nagasaki. President Carter had ordered the Seventh Fleet to keep an eye out for Vietnamese Boat People in the South China Sea who were being preyed upon by pirates, for which the two fifty caliber machineguns had been specially mounted on the Cox, while The U.S. backed Shah had fallen in Iran, which meant he was about to be sent to the Arabian Sea, to Gonzo Station. His Outland would probably head off the moment it was out of the yards, so it made sense that he had been sent to the Cox to learn their NavMacs in the meantime.

Walter looked out to sea and saw the flying fish dancing everywhere, a blurred wave springing into the air, curling back into the sea and subsiding before thrusting in mocking anticipation of the wake that progressed behind. But whenever Walter narrowed his eyes on them, the flying fish became discrete, scattering before the bow, glittering silver and skipping along the surface like flung coins spent into the swells. He wondered whether the entire Pacific had a silver layer of flying fish just beneath the surface, floating idly until a monster stirred them. At which point, they'd leap for heaven, only to

7

Liberty Call

manage a brief horizontal moment above the murk, before slapping at the water and skimming the surface, then, *plop*, hit a wave and sink. The scene was burned into Walter's head, and he wondered if the flying fish recycled each other like the waves did—or more like a fountain, with the same flying fish following him everywhere, jumping for his show and then hastily swimming back to the front of the line to do it again in an elaborate game of deception, just to fuck with him. That is, until the porpoises showed up.

One afternoon, however, on the way to Subic, when the ocean was clear and calm, Walter leaned over the lifeline and spotted something floating beneath the surface. He thought it was some kind of submerged jetsom before realizing that it was staying with them at a whole *eight knots*. It loomed larger as it neared the surface, some billowing sheet of refracting light, tinting the water just above it iceberg-lettuce green. As it rose, its outline grew clearer, more defined, no longer rectangular but sphere long-stretched into a large torpedo, broad and powerful. Walter just barely managed to distinguish its white, mute, and ghostly form that appeared to hover just beneath the water's green veneer. It was shadowing the ship, maintaining their speed effortlessly. Walter called out for everyone to come see his white whale, but as though it had heard him, it diverged ninety degrees from them and disappeared. Those who looked pretended not to believe him, but he didn't care. He turned back to the beluga just as it spouted and began its descent.

Walter could only imagine it in its entirety, following it down as its fluke propelled it with the speed of a frigate, being an air breathing mammal like himself but with the dreamlike ability to swim underwater indefinitely, the entire ocean its living room, unrestricted by air, water, timetable or compass, free. Walter's mind followed it all the way down to where the light could barely filter, where only small dark figures darted by in schools and larger ones moved sullenly, suspiciously. His whale stroked unperturbed toward the bottom, through the dancing streamers of seaweed that reached up from the clusters of rocks and the wreckage of ships. Then there was nothing: the shadows and shapes had converged at the bottom into blackness as the whale's green aura escaped to somewhere even Walter couldn't imagine. But he was sure that creature understood its world.

Enter Subic: empty jeepneys line up on one side of Magsaysay Boulevard, their chrome sparkling in the late afternoon sun. Soon the evening crush of Filipino workers and American sailors would come shambling out of the U.S. Navy base and streaming toward their nighttime connections—home, hotel room, whorehouse, saloon. The jeepneys would get them there.

The Cox had pulled into Subic at midday and the crew beat the crowd into town. Walter, Mallory, and Hasty James—a Cox radioman—walked out past the Filipino and American marine guards, out the base's gate, then over the humped bridge above Shit River that separated the town from the base, so-called because of the sewage that ran in among the children begging from banca boats. Walter didn't know if it had a real name. It probably did. *Shadenfreude River?*

Regardless, the three of them stopped, leaning over the railing to marvel at the kids hollering from the boats. Two shirtless boys with raggedy black hair were just beneath them. "Hey Joe, throw us some money," the longer, skinnier one of them called out, hands cupped around his mouth.

Hasty hitched his pants, reached into his front pocket, then plopped some pennies into the water near their boat. "You gotta dive for it!" He pulled out a few more coins and held them up. "Here you go. This time *dive* for it!" He tossed the coins near the boat, and in the boys went.

A girl noticed the commotion and paddled over. Walter thought she looked like the kind of kid you'd see in a mall back home. Mallory shook that thought when he held up a quarter. "Show us your tits!" She pulled off her T shirt and pulled her shoulders back. Mallory laughed, "you ain't even got none!" He threw the quarter near her boat, and she dove into the mottled sewage. He did a sudden, strange little jig. "C'mon, man. Let's get loaded. Now bear in mind you do that on the street, you'll never get rid of 'em. They'll be dancin' after you all night long."

Magsaysay Boulevard is the main drag of Olongapo City. They walked up to the first jeepney in a long line of them. The street was a low corridor of barrooms that stretched on until it disappeared into a watery mirage of heat at the foot of Subic's hills. Outside the first bar, a small, open-air structure that was literally called Hole in The Wall, Walter watched a young man slide off his stool and walk out to the jeepney.

"Hey Joe," the young man said with an eager grin, eyes alert and hopeful as a puppy at the dinner table. His black hair was neatly greased back at the sides except a single forelock curled over his left eye. His cut-off jeans were worn, sneakers soggy, and T shirt stained, not that it did much to conceal the Mickey Mouse with its middle finger extended.

"Fuck you too," Mallory said and pointed at the man's chest. "The name isn't Joe so you can cut that shit out right now." He had been here once before and told Walter he knew how to handle these people. On the sidewalk, the three had no particular plan on where to go or whether to just start bar crawling.

"What can I do you for?" the jeepney driver said. He ran his fingers through his lone forelock.

"Speed," Hasty James said.

Walter turned and looked at him.

"Speed?"

Mallory agreed to go along with it. "You know," Mallory said, "*speeeed.* Now quit jerkin' us around and tell me do you know where we can get some speed or do I hafta get it from the next guy? Fuckin' Flips."

"Sure man, sure," the driver said. "Anything you want."

9

"Just speed, my man," Hasty said. "We need a dash for the Hasty James liberty special. It's the ingredient, you understand."

"Sure man, sure. I go make a phone call. You wait here."

"And maybe a couple of joints," Walter added.

The driver smiled, sweet and peppy as a Coca Cola with its bubbly eyes and creamy fizz. He headed back for the bar—his hangout—apparently, stopped, then announced, "Just call me Johnny," as though someone had asked, and went in. When Just-Call-Me-Johnny finished his call, he got right in the driver's seat and started the car up.

"Everything's cool," the driver said. "Hop in. I got your shit. We go to my place for it."

"You got it?" Mallory asked.

"My buddy. He's meet us there. Get in, it's cool."

The three looked at each other. Hasty shrugged his shoulders and looked at Mallory. Mallory shrugged and looked at Walter. Walter's nose took in the fog of jeepney exhaust and sidewalk barbecue, and underneath that the scent of tropical dirt and vegetation in open spaces. Shit River and kids begging from it. He could hear women calling to them from the fronts of bars and clubs on the street. "Adventure?" he asked, in general.

They looked at each other. Hasty shrugged and got in the back, and Mallory and Walter climbed in after him. They sprawled on the benches. This was a private ride.

Mallory and Walter were far from best friends, but they were, after all, shipmates. They stuck together much of the time on the Cox because they were familiar faces on a strange ship, accessible. This disarming newness seemed to put them on common footing, and for the first time they formed an odd bond, accepting each other for what they were with interest and without rancor. Except for Hasty James, Walter was all Mallory had.

And Walter considered Hasty, whose real name was James Hastings, a dark, savvy kid from California. He was a capable radioman, and it was his responsibility to train them on the NavMacs. His nickname may have come from his facility in the radioshack, but it more likely came from the fact that he always seemed to be speeding. He had a friend in the Army in Pusan, Korea, who sent him packets of crystal methamphetamine that he called Pusan Rock. During radio watches he'd make head calls where he'd suck a bunch of Pusan Rock up his nose, then return to radio, wide-eyed and maniacal, eager as hell: "Yes, yes, we have communications; we have communications. Communicating sons of bitches! Communicating motherfuckers! Hasty Rock! Hasty, hasty. Hastily handled, with dispatch. In communications, boy, speed is of the essence." Nobody liked Hasty more than he liked himself. In fact, nobody liked Hasty much at all, it seemed to Walter. He was a self-promoter—probably nicknamed himself—and never uttered a word that sounded genuine. He had the quick eye of an opportunist, the kind of guy who, even when he's doing you a favor, makes you think you're being hustled. There was no warmth in his excitement or his humor, as though it was never the moment itself that counted, but something that the moment was reeling-in to him that he awaited with greedy glee. Maybe all of that was just the affects of the drugs. And the first thing he wanted to do when they got to Olongapo City was find some speed, as all his Pusan Rock was used up.

  So they found themselves at the home of their jeepney driver, Just-Call-Me-Johnny. He asked their names and gave a nervous laugh with each one, shaking their hands and holding on for an uncomfortable moment. He said that they were now all friends. "Good friends," as he put it. Fine thing, friends. Friends stick by each other, take care of each other. Without friends you are nothing. What can you do? Where can you go without friends? Friends grow under each other's guidance, prosper under each other's care. Friends look out for each other, protect each other from common enemies. Friends send the good things in life each other's way. That was why Just-Call-Me-Johnny was sending speed and grass their way, because they were friends and had asked for it. And think of how good it is to have friends in other countries who you can write letters to and come visit, a home away from home when you are traveling. Walter, Mallory, Hasty, Johnny—friends.

  Johnny's home was deep in the honeycomb of side streets, and it made Walter a little nervous to think that he couldn't find his way back without him, though it didn't seem to bother Mallory and Hasty, who were quick enough to get in the jeepney. Here, far removed from the glare of the main drag, the buildings grew dingy and haphazard like the wayward palms and leafy shrubs they warred for space with. Random weeds and spores took root unchallenged, blooming along with plants that had once been planned to prettify gardens and courtyards but that now sprawled as chaotically as the dirt streets, rampant flora scampering over fences and climbing up walls, springing through cracks in the stucco and wood that were too weak and untended to check the tropic pull of sun and water.

  Just-Call-Me-Johnny's apartment was in an amorphous, colorless hotel whose asymmetrical curves of stucco bent around an overgrown courtyard like the bulk of a giant hunkering before a campfire of shooting blades and branches. The hotel sat on an intersection shared by a tired looking bar with an upstairs brothel, but the over-the-hill hookers on the balcony showed little interest in hooking in the mid-day heat. There was no constabulary or American presence visible in the neighborhood.

  When they arrived at the home, Johnny's family sneaked into the bedroom and closed the door. A portable black and white TV in the combination living room/kitchen carried a picture of President Marcos delivering a speech to a political rally—they were holding national elections that year. The only things besides the mildew and roaches on the walls were a couple of curling photos from magazines and advertisements for American consumer goods—happy children eating breakfast cereal, a happy family watching color

TV, happy men with their new automobiles. Fungus grew freely around the refrigerator and dripping sink. The room also sported a bridge table, a couple of chairs with torn vinyl and a dilapidated, faded, green sofa.

Walter absorbed it all, fidgeting under Just-Call-Me-Johnny's lecture on the beneficence of friendship, while waiting for his drug connection. When their mutual admiration and the subject of friendship seemed in danger of drying up, Johnny asked if they wanted a beer, and they all cheered.

"Ferdinand," Johnny yelled. "Hey, Nando. Come out here."

A boy of about six emerged from behind the closed bedroom door. "I have guests in the house. My new friends. They want beer. Go get them some beer."

The boy looked shyly but keenly at the three of them, as though looking into them, Walter thought, and weighing what he found, while being ashamed of what they might see in him. He walked over to Walter and stood still, looking at the gritty floor. His head seemed too large for his bony frame, his brown eyes too round and open to hide anything. He was dirty and wore only a pair of boy's briefs.

Okay, Walter thought, that's enough. Go away now. But the boy just stood there, blinking his long, curled eyelashes at the floor. Walter squirmed a little and looked around the room.

"Well?" Just-Call-Me-Johnny said.

They were all looking at Walter. "Well what?"

"Well give the goddamn kid some money for the brews," Mallory said.

"Oh!" He jumped to his feet and reached into his back pocket for his wallet. "How much?"

"Fifteen pesos each," Ferdinand said quietly, looking at the wallet.

Walter gave him a fifty-peso bill. Nando ran across the street, returned with three San Miguels, handed them to each of the men, then darted back into the bedroom without giving any change. They slugged the beer down, which hit the spot for a moment, but they quickly grew restless again. It was hot outside, but it was suffocating in the squalid room with Marcos's voice rising and falling in the background, and with the greasy hospitality of their new friend. Walter thought of the bugs that must be nesting in the warm crevices around the sofa cushions, and his skin got itchy. Something ran down his arm—a drop of sweat.

"So what's the story," Hasty said. "Is your man coming or not? You got a home sweet home, for sure. It's been real nice but we got to be moving along. Women await. The night awaits. Speed is of the essence, you know?"

"He's coming, man, he's coming. You wait. He's my buddy, you see. He got it all, everything you want. Make you feel all right."

"He got crystal?" Hasty said.

"Speed man, like you want."

"Yeah, dude, yeah, but is it crystal or pills?"

"Pills, yellow pills. Very strong. Lots of them."

"Sheeit, pills," Hasty said. "Okay, okay. I guess yellow jackets are okay."

Mallory belched. "Well I hope he comes soon. It fuckin' smells like day old roadkill in here, skunk."

Johnny gave a nervous laugh and yelled something in Tagalog at the bedroom door, which was thin enough for Walter to hear voices whispering inside. He said something again in Tagalog, still smiling but with an impatient edge to his teeth. Once more the boy emerged from the room, still looking downward.

"He goes out to play now," Johnny said. "What you think? Fine boy, huh?"

"Yeah," Walter said. "Great kid."

"You want some more beer?"

"No."

The woman appeared in the bedroom doorway and Johnny smiled at his company. "My wife, man. You like her?"

She was draped in a white sheet, with a naked baby sucking at her breast. She looked at them with a feeble attempt at smiling, and failing that, her face fell into a non-committal blank as she looked at the floor.

Walter stared at her like a specimen, trying to access her eyes, the eyes he had first seen in the boy, as he sat there on the sofa and she stood in the doorway with the suckling baby, though he knew her eyes pulled with some independent and involuntary power at everything within her scope. She was exposed there, frightened, certainly repelled, a reluctant magnet of sad life in a young woman with long black hair and a tremulous face. He felt he could drown before ever finding that center.

"Show them," Just-Call-Me-Johnny said. "Go on."

She pulled the sheet from her other breast. No, Walter thought, you don't have to do this anymore. Her breasts were high and full, swollen with milk. The baby was attached to one nipple and the other pointed away like a lazy eye. No, don't do this. Don't make me look. And he was drawn to her eyes and he looked at her breasts and he wanted to save her.

"Go ahead," Johnny demanded, smiling. "All of it."

She let the sheet drop to the floor and Walter wanted to say, no, don't. I'll love you forever if you just stop doing this. Don't let this happen.

She held her shoulders squarely and stared straight ahead. Her body was smooth and ripe without being too plump, though her stomach swelled above the thin wisp of her groin. Her legs were short and almost muscular. The baby sucked away, oblivious to the spectacle going on around her.

"What you think?" Johnny asked. "You like her?"

Hasty whistled, crossed his legs and threw his arm up on the sofa's back. "How much?"

"How much?" Johnny was incredulous, frowning for the first time.

"That's my *wife*!" His honor was wounded. "I don't pimp my wife. Hey man, like I say, we're friends. That goes for her too. You want her? Okay. I say have fun. She has my permission—and rubbers. Ha! We just relax and enjoy ourself till my buddy gets here."

"Whee hoo. Yes hell!" Mallory said. "Mamma's milk!"

The baby began crying from the bedroom as soon as they closed the door behind them. It screamed, and in the intervals when it gathered air for another gust, Walter could hear the soft bed coils spring and Mallory's heavy grunting. Just-Call-Me-Johnny and Hasty passed the minutes discussing drugs and money. The baby screamed; the springs sprang; Mallory grunted.

Hasty and Johnny talked loudly to overcome the baby's siren-like wailing, and their language was some foreign language—the man whose baby was crying in the next room and whose wife was being fucked, and his new friend the speed addict—talking numbers, prices, quantities, scales, low and high. Walter's head expanded and contracted with the rise and fall of the baby's siren and his ears were tuned to the sounds in the bedroom beneath the cries—the springs and the breathing.

The walls of the slimy cell that contained the woman's life moved closer until his ear seemed pressed to her door, and the shoots and spiky fronds in the courtyard groaned and stretched toward them, reaching for the apartment, climbing the walls and roof and sucking out the air as they moved in to strangle the humans. He listened for Mallory and hated him, hated all of them, including the woman who did nothing to resist. He realized he had an erection and hated them all some more.

Things did not go smoothly with Johnny's main man, Eddy. He was skinny, tall for a Filipino, and relatively well dressed—his clothes were clean and flashy synthetics, wide collar and flared slacks, gold medallion and reflector sunglasses. Eddy was clearly the boss in the relationship, making no phony show of amity with Johnny or with the sailors, and it became painfully evident that they were to be Johnny's big chance to move up in the world. It seemed that he had given his boss the impression that they were going to move large quantities of marijuana and narcotics on base for him. Walter immediately refused, and Eddy glared at Johnny, who sweated and yelled into the bedroom to shut the baby up, which no longer even seemed to stop for air between cries.

Johnny tried to convince them of what a sound, logical idea it was—actually, he now directed his argument solely at Hasty—pointing out the profits to be had in cash and highs, and reiterating his lesson about how friends send opportunity each other's way. When Walter again spoke up and refused, Eddy went to work with his charms; starting with the idea that the military would be interested in knowing where they were and what they were doing, working up to the influential position he and his friends enjoyed in town, and capping it off with the harm that could be caused or prevented to their persons. He was connected. Nothing went on that he didn't know about. The cops were in his pay.

The baby's keening now seemed to be coming from inside Walter's head, piercing his brain like an electric charge, sending sparks to all his nerve endings and throwing him out of his seat.

"I call you!" he shouted, and spat on the floor. "I call you, you fucking cheap hustlers! Fuck! You cocksuckers! Bloodsuckers! Who the fuck you think you are, threatening *me*, you lousy pimps. I'm in the U.S. Navy you little gangsters! Come on Hasty, let's get out of here before I kill somebody. This place is crazy. Look at this cheap place. I'll tear this fucking place apart, stinking shithole."

As he ranted, the situation seemed to become clear to him, once-removed as though all but he was in slow motion, as though his frantic action threw him a step ahead of the others' delayed reaction, giving him time to pick apart and consider every move they made. He saw their bodies fall into awkward defensive postures and their faces flare in amazement as though *he* was the dangerous, alien element in the room. Even Hasty seemed stunned by his rudeness and incredible breach of etiquette.

Mallory stuck his head out of the door and asked what was going on. Eddy and Johnny began arguing in Tagalog with their sides turned carefully toward Walter. Hasty told him to shut up and calm the fuck down, to just wait a minute and be cool until he worked everything out. Walter had already lost the upper hand the second he stopped yelling and started observing again. His violence lost its initiative.

Finally, Just-Call-Me-Johnny came over and put his arm around Walter's shoulder, who shrugged it off. "Hey man, calm down. Be comfortable. This is just business. Everything's cool, everything's real cool. No one's going to hurt you—this is my *home*. You just watch TV and we work something out with Hasty. See that?" He turned up the set so that the pitch of the convention speeches competed with the baby's crying. "That's the President talking. He's a great, great man. See how he talks, all calm and everything? His voice can calm you down. People love him. I'm going to be like him someday—hey, right Eddy? And then you be glad you know me. Because I know how to stay calm and how to make friends. I even name my kid for him."

He patted Walter's back and pattered on as though consoling a petulant child. "This is business; you know how that is. We're businessmen. Got to talk tough sometimes to make a bargain, so people don't take advantage, you see? We don't need to be mad and say bad things, call names. We can make a deal. You watch TV for a minute, and I work something out with Hasty."

"I'll wait outside," Walter said. "It does stink in here. Hurry up, man," he said to Hasty.

He stood in the middle of the courtyard like an irresolute prowler, wavering between going back inside and losing himself in the streets. He could see the kids in the street and the women in the whorehouse, hear the plaintive voices in the apartment, and he prayed for his shipmates to leave the house.

After about five minutes they came out in a hurry. "C'mon," they said, and walked right past him. On the street they walked quickly and talked in a furtive hush. "C'mon," Hasty said, "let's move. We should get out of here. Nice move, Schmerz, you asshole. You cost us our ride back."

Walter looked over his shoulder and got panicky. "I don't know how to get out of here."

"I probably know the way," Hasty said. "Move fast. The sooner we're out of here the better. Your scene almost cost me the ingredient, Schmerz. Almost lost me the deal. I had to buy a little quantity—at slightly inflating prices which *I* fronted—if you don't mind. Had to get a whole oh-zee for ya, Schmerz, and a hundred fifty yellow jackets. That's not bad, fifty apiece. And I didn't get my turn with the babe, either."

Mallory laughed under his breath as they jogged along the dirt street. "I got it twice."

"How was it?"

"Not bad. Love that mama's milk. Dry cunt, though."

What'd you *expect?*" Walter said.

"You're just jealous, asshole. I saw the way you looked at her. You think you're so much better'n everyone else. And by the way, you let yourself get ripped off by little Johnny junior. Those beers didn't cost more than six, seven pesos each."

They turned onto a side alley and could see the evening traffic of Magsaysay Boulevard. The sidewalks shimmered with pedestrian commerce and the jeepneys vainly tooted their horns as they crawled bumper to bumper. Walter took a deep breath at the sight of humanity and the realization that they weren't being followed, and as their legs changed gear to a slower gait, he felt the over-excited motor in his stomach grind down to a low and sickening disgust. Should he have stopped Mallory? There would always be other Mallorys, just as there were other women like her and other Just-Call-Me-Johnnies and Eddies. In bootcamp the Company Commander had reassured them all that out there in the great wide fleet there was a sailor exactly like each one of them. Walter was not comforted by this thought of a doppelganger.

They ducked into the first bar they came to on the corner, called The White House. His T shirt had turned a shade darker from the sweat and there was a dry fire in his guts. Mallory went to the bar while they plopped into a couple of chairs at a table by the window. He returned with six bottles of San Miguel, banged them on the table so that they all foamed over; then he and Hasty picked their bottles up and clanged them together in a mute toast. Walter gulped down his first beer in two breaths and started on the second one. Mallory and Hasty were both sitting erect, grinning out the window. Fuck you, Walter thought, both of you. I don't know what I'm doing hanging around with you animals.

Hasty had that eager look in his eyes and smiled elatedly, his head moving back and forth, following the street scene outside the window like a line judge in a tennis match. "Good shit," he said. "Now we're cooking with gas."

"Gas, hell," Mallory said. "This shit is gunpowder."

"You guys did some already?" Walter asked.

"You betcha, sparky. Did it before we left," Hasty said.

Walter finished off the second beer and thought, I should get out of here. "This just isn't working," he said, and ordered them six shots of bourbon. The liquid burned his lips and mouth, down his gullet and into the trouble spot where it met and began to displace the self-hatred, supplanting the queasy heat with a new, bolder kind of blaze. Yeah, he thought, that's better. Nothing to be done. "Fight fire with fire," he said. "Let me get some of the speed from you, Hasty."

A cellophane bag passed under the table with his share of the pills, then came the ounce of pot. He took two yellow jackets, thought about it a second, popped a third one in his mouth and proposed a toast: "Ferdy and Imelda," and washed the pills down with a shot of whiskey.

With the second shot, the warmth diffused throughout his body, spreading from his core to the outer regions, fingering its way to the boundaries of his skin and mingling with the close air as if they were one element, the way a paper towel dropped on a puddle absorbs the moisture almost immediately but not too quickly for you to see the water crawling over the minute fibers, filament infecting filament in a single liquid moment until puddle and paper are the same density. Sweat dripped down the back of his neck and sogged his armpits. He gave Hasty money for his share of the drugs and then put twenty pesos in front of Mallory. "I order you to go order me another beer. And get me a glass of water too."

Mallory told him to go to hell, so Walter offered to buy him another. He stuck the beer in his mouth with one hand and poured the water over his head with the other. This set the others both to laughing so hard that Mallory spit a mouthful of beer all over the table and Hasty held his stomach, banging his forehead on the bottle in front of him.

"What's so funny?" Walter asked. "It's hot."

"Wah haw!" Mallory said.

"Hee sheesh sheshe!" Hasty said.

"Mallory shook his beer and sprayed it all over Walter. "Wah ha ha haw!"

Hasty shook his at Mallory. "Hee sheesh shesheshe!"

Walter was laughing now too and turned his bottle upside down on Hasty's head. What fun. What crazy guys to go on liberty with. You just can't stay mad at these guys for long.

They were delirious, laughing at everything now, red-faced and breathless, while Walter drifted into himself, locked into his chair by the restraining air, boozed into inertia by the bourbon glow. He got nostalgic for Irene.

Poor thing. What a life, saddled with morose Tom and those kids in their silly Navy housing tract in Connecticut. He wondered what she was doing now, if she still prowled the EM club where she found him. He vaguely recalled the pain in his gut when she brought him home and he realized she was his new chief's wife. She probably got something on the side to replace him. She'd be wet and ready before he even got her pants off, wanting it so bad, and she never failed to come, her cunt grasping him deeper into her, her throat arching with the husky little cries coming out of it. And sometimes she really did cry, saying she wanted to always be with him, her face and chest flushed and her eyes so sad.

He took a slug of beer.

Sad eyes. They all have such sad eyes. Johnny's wife came back in his head. God, he could relish every nook and cranny of her body, from the stout legs to the part in her hair, and all parts in between, as it were. Her eyes knew something, had something that he wanted. And those wispy pubic hairs probably felt like silk.

All the women he'd ever had or wanted began parading across his mind in super-imposed scenes like double-exposed moving pictures, in car seats and beds and parking lots and parks, winter and summer, all kinds. He recalled their breath and their smells, the feel and shape of their bodies during various acts, or merely longing after an alluring face or shape—and through it all the warmth of touching and the life-wetness of sex, the unbearable sweetness of orgasm. Then they were all together in a desperate orgy, sweaty breasts rubbing against his back, stomach, butt and legs, labia on his face and on his cock, and every finger and toe sinking into a warm, wet orifice, above the ground, suspended, surrounded and sustained by women's flesh.

When he saw that his chin was resting on his chest and his eyes were fixed on the floor, he snapped his head up and it felt as though it would keep going until it hit the ceiling. His head and stomach got a liquidy rush as though taking a sudden dip in an elevator. Whee. He bounced in his chair, a Super Ball caroming around the room, his body flying against everything his eyes fell on. Then he went weightless, released from the alcohol and heat, feeling them but detached, above. He was electricity, indestructible, buzzing, floating, profound. A burst of sweetness exploded in his stomach and shot through his blood.

"I'm electric."

Hasty grinned at him. "That's it," he said. "You're coming on. Thought you were nodding for a minute there."

"I think I was. I was dreaming."

"How many'd you take?"

"Three."

"Do another. It's great."

He did, excited as a puppy. He wanted to talk about it. He wanted to go around licking everybody and have them rub his belly. It wanted to do

IT, whatever it was, the main thing, the thing they came here for. His mouth was stuffed with cotton balls dipped in fluoride. He could smell his armpits; he could not blink his eyes. "It's like, when you think about it, all you are is energy. And you die when all the energy's used up. It's all charged particles and atoms and molecules moving around. And your blood moving, and your lungs moving. When you stop moving, when there's no more heat, you're dead."

"Yes, yes," Hasty said. "And don't forget chemistry—keeping the right balance, the proper recipe. It's essential to *feel* right. You're talking about proportions. Your molecules make your chemistry. Put them together and you got heartbeats that're making your feet walk and your brain work so you can transmit message from writing on paper to marks and spaces on wavelengths and back onto paper a thousand miles away.

Wow. Listen to me. Yeah, chemistry. And it all depends on chemistry for your little fingers typing the message, making sure you move fast and think fast. Pusan Rock, dude, crystal meth, energy and chemistry—I'm a fucking genius—moving you through the radioshack like a goddamn wizard, and then yellow jackets, maybe a little grass and just the right number of San Miguels and you're ready for the right kind of liberty and you're talking like a goddamn motherfuckering genius. Hasty liberty!"

"You got that right," Walter said. "We're transceivers. Transmitters and receivers. I see where you're coming from now. So much stuff, so many messages from one tone package, one frequency of electro-magnetic cycles. Wizards, yes. Magic. Alchemy."

Walter understood now Hasty's speed habit and his mania in the radioshack. "All those letters being jumbled, converted to DC pulses, descrambled and printing back into letters and sentences and paragraphs in ink and paper. Always keying the transmitter. Everything you ever felt and seen and did and thought is pulsing through you right now like pure energy, keying, mixing, converting into this kind of pattern that's...*us*."

"We're fucking brilliant," Hasty said, sitting at the edge of his chair and leaning on the table with both elbows. "And don't forget chemistry. The right ingredients make the right pattern."

"That's my point. It *is* right just because I'm alive. I am so much *alive*. Think about all the shit we did today. It's incredible. This place is absolutely in-fucking-credible. There's nothing else exactly like it—this bar, this town, Just-Call-Me-Johnny, that haze gray piece of shit back at the pier. It's happening to *us*, and we are at the center of it. Like, it *is* us because we are alive. We have the energy. Do you know what we're doing here?"

Hasty gave Walter a smirk and growled, "Yeah, right."

Mallory came back and interrupted as Walter was about to answer his own question, but he might have already lost the train of thought; it was moving so fast. He reached for the flicker, but his brain jammed and he lost it. Instead he was back at midnight in the OK Used Car Lot with

Susan McGiven when he was fifteen and she was a goddess of sixteen saying, "You're just a little boy," and then saying, "Yes yes yes yes," and then it was Irene saying it and then it was Just-Call-Me-Johnny's wife.

"Know what I was thinking about?" he said.

"Gravity or science or some likely bullshit," Mallory said.

"Johnny and Eddy and company," Hasty said.

"Women," he said.

Hasty looked out the window. "I remember women."

Hasty didn't make muster the next morning, but Naval Intelligence did. Their man had apparently fallen out the back of a jeepney on its way from Subic City and been run over by the car behind it. He was carrying a dealer's quantity of drugs and was currently in a coma. The local police thought the accident smelled.

Stonewalling the agent was easy for Walter and Mallory, but *what if* had reared its ugly head. He did say that was where he was going, Subic City to see his Filipino "wife," Paz. He said he "valued" her above all others.

They all shook their heads, said "goddamn" and asked how a thing like that could have happened—the answer being, quite easily, actually—but no one seemed genuinely depressed by the news, including Walter, and that bothered him. Where was his conscience? For his part, he wondered if this was because he hadn't known Hasty long, or because he was in shock or because the pills he kept popping had him moving too fast to worry. He was shooting through a world with no atmosphere to slow him, no friction, a vacuum, and he tried to grasp at the thoughts and feelings that might anchor him; he tried to care as he knew he was supposed to, but those things slipped through his fingers and were lost.

The first thing he thought was that Eddy had carried out his threat, but the guilt and fear instantly dissolved into excitement, and he resolved to simply go with the trajectory to its very end. Hasty would have to tell them what happened when he came out of it. But he died the next day.

"Shit happens," Mallory said, raising a bottle to his lips in a toast to their newly dead partner. And Walter felt relieved when he said it, as if that was the answer, as if that finalized the matter and somehow absolved him of any further responsibility. The man was gone; the words were said. Shit happens. It was a guilty, furtive feeling, but his mind was racing too fast to examine it, and each pang became a burn of adrenaline that boosted him farther from the parent emotion.

Walter recounted Eddy's threats and suggested the possibility of foul play, but Mallory insisted that was ridiculous. How could they have arranged that? These Flips were small-time, lightweights. Besides, you don't kill off customers, and the bums made a little money off them. Besides, do you really want to go to war with the U.S. Navy?

That made sense. They were a ship full of customers, a navy of customers, hauling a treasury to pay for services: strategic real estate, port facilities, supply depots, entertainment—food, drink, drugs, sex. There was absolutely nothing that you couldn't buy. *You don't kill off customers.* True, but what about parasites who have eaten your soul, and then, if the host aspires to live like the parasite, well where does that leave things? And nations, Walter thought, and then tried not to think.

The rest of that week in Subic Bay seemed like an imperfectly remembered dream with a scary and nauseating edge to it, like when you wake up and realize you were about to vomit in your sleep, the kind where even the tasty parts make your soul uneasy, the kind that is recalled with an ugly feeling of dumb, animal desperation. Each day he'd pop a number of yellow jackets, work on the ship quickly and meticulously, and head out for the bars. After he slaked himself down with a couple of San Miguels, he's pop another pill and smoke a joint to get that high-voltage feeling, to really get his night's liberty in gear. Once he felt right—when his "chemistry was right," as Hasty had put it—he'd head for a massage parlor and act out the same little fantasy plays every night.

After the parlor scene he'd head back out to the street and find Mallory in one of their beginning-the-evening bars where they would start to drink in earnest. He found that if he just let himself go, if he didn't struggle or think but allowed himself to plunge headlong into experience and sensation, that he was capable of anything. And in this state, he found that he was beginning to actually enjoy Mallory—this was *his* level. And he knew how to have fun, get crazy, forget worrying about things.

During the course of bar hopping Walter would say to him, "Mallory, for a redneck asshole, you ain't sech a bad sort to kill a few beers and slay a few ladies with. Not bad atall." Then Mallory would get misty-eyed and sloppy and say something like, "Schmerz, I know I'm a asshole and I can't seem to help it. But lemme give ya for what it's worth: the world'd be a better place if it was more like you. Hell lot better." Then maybe he'd howl like a wolf or scream "I love you!" at a waitress, veins sticking out of his thick neck and black hair matted to his forehead.

They would move from bar to bar, drinking a few beers in each, talking to all the working women, looking for the perfect one to spend the night with, the one who suited their particular moods and tastes for that night, promising at least one hostess in each place that they would be back for her. Walter was a slobbering bloodhound surrounded by the scent of quarry, addled, intoxicated, awash in the odor of Woman, and he wanted to devour it all: womanhair, womanflesh, womaneyes. He'd fuck and drink himself into exhaustion by two in the morning, then get up a few hours later, pop some pills, head for the ship and begin the daily routine again.

But by the end of the week he had grown used to the speed-induced mania and carried out the routine more with grim purpose than relish. His mind ached with a low-grade fever of anxiety and his soul felt tired, washed of humor or joy, gray as the ship he sailed. Still, the drugs kept his body moving, compelled him on to further experience, insisted on going one step farther each night.

Their last night in Subic, Mallory and Walter got off work early and went into town to hit some bars they hadn't been in yet. Toward the far end of the boulevard where it nears the mountains, they came across a place called Paradise, and he remembered that Al had told him to go there. Mimi. Al was about a girl called Mimi. It had the usual hall full of rooms upstairs, but there was a cool beer garden in the back that was quiet in the early evening.

They sat in the beer garden with their feet up on the table, sipping San Miguels. The girl who got the beer asked if she could join them and they said what the hell.

"You like me?" she asked.

"Why, yes hell, little darling," Mallory said.

"We love you no bullshit," Walter said.

"Very funny. I like you," she said to Walter. "You are cute."

"Wanna play smile?" Mallory asked half-heartedly.

"I don't like that game," she said.

"Fuck it. They ain't enough here to play, anyhow."

"What's smile?"

"Girl goes under the table. Dudes are unzipped. First one to smile buys a round."

"What ship do you come from?" she asked.

"Oh, never mind all that 'what ship' bullshit."

She looked at Walter. "You go bar hopping tonight?"

"Yeah, we're going bar hopping."

"You take me bar hopping with you? Please? Please take me with you."

"How much you cost?" Mallory asked.

She looked at the ground. "Mamasan want three hundred fifty pesos."

"Shit," Mallory said. "I could drink all night and screw all night and still have carfare home, for that much."

"It's because you're so pretty," Walter said to her. And she was, in a sweet way, girlish, teasingly young, with still bright, attentive eyes, her hair in a ponytail and bangs, her pink painted little piggies wriggling on her sandals.

"You please take me bar hopping with you?" she answered. "Please? Mamasan is a nasty bitch. Please? I hate her. We can have fun. I can dance. Please? I do anything for you. I'll suck your dick I'll lick your ass."

"Why, you can do that right here," Mallory said.

She turned to Walter. "Then you stay here and don't go bar hopping. I'm too lonely."

"You know a girl named Mimi?" Walter asked.

The Need for Speed

She smiled and hugged him, licked his ear and said in a playful, husky voice, "Why you want Mimi for? You want me to be Mimi for you? I can be Mimi."

"You're too much of a cutie pie to be a Mimi. I just want to say hello to her for a friend."

"What friend?"

"Get Mimi and we'll find out."

"But I *am* Mimi. Tell me who, please? I don't know about cutie pie. Mimi is my name."

"She's full of shit," Mallory said.

"Know a guy called Al Turner?" Walter asked.

"He is my boyfriend! Where is he? Is he here?"

"She knows Turner like I know the inside of her fat mamasan's asshole," Mallory said. "Never happened. You see her? She *is* a nasty bitch, though."

"I know Al Turner," she said. "I can prove it." She giggled and pointed between her legs. "He is crooked down here."

"I wouldn't know about that," Walter said.

"He ain't here," Mallory said, "but we are. You want to take us topside to see your picture collection?"

"You can see them if you want."

"*Both* of us?" He smiled and winked at Walter. "Can we both go up to your room? You know. In other words, how much for a Mimi sandwich? Hey Schmerz, ever have a Mimi sandwich?"

"Can't say as I have, cutie pie like that."

Mallory went to the bar to pay Mamasan for the sandwich. While he was gone Mimi asked Walter to spend the night with her, to get rid of Mallory after the trick or take her bar hopping with him. She said Mamasan was a nasty bitch and she was afraid of being lonely.

When Mallory had paid for her, Mimi took them both by the hand and up the stairs while Mamasan smiled on them with a fatty squint. Her room was papered with magazine advertisements and snapshots of her and other girls in the company of various American sons: cherry boys, older men, whoremongers.

"I show you my boyfriend, Alvin," she said, and produced a photo album from the top drawer of her bureau while they sat on her bed. She honored Al with an entire page of snapshots.

"What do you know about that," Walter said. All the pictures were taken within the confines of the Paradise—in the beer garden, in the bar, in Mimi's room. Apparently she didn't get out much. There he was with her, his familiar, goofy smile and rippled forehead looking right at Walter. For some reason it made him uneasy. Snapshots of a friend. Homeboy. Here in the middle of this. He had told Walter to come here and now he was winking at him from the photo album of the legendary Mimi. Gotcha.

"Is he a good friend?" she asked. "Is he coming here soon? I miss Alvin. He is so funny."

"I miss Alvin too, that fuck," Walter said, and though he meant it, he found himself growing angry at him. He didn't belong here; Mallory did. Of course, she couldn't really care that much about him; it was just good business. They always do that. Everyone's got to have hope. Write letters, take pictures—write letters, keep pictures, wait, hope, hope for the man who will see something extra special inside them, hope for something special. Isn't that love? And Al cared enough, found her special enough, to recommend her as a good lay. Now his smile was ironic, nodding at Walter's exposed complicity in something unfair and ugly.

He is my boyfriend. Mimi sandwich. She'd lick his asshole for a chance to get out for awhile and go bar hopping, or just to keep his manly self around for the night, Walter thought. Her youthful orifices and organs had already accommodated and endured a fleet of strangers, all for a chance to get out of "thee village in thee province," to be trafficked, to see a little of the world—mostly from the business end of someone's prick—to make a little money, to have a little fun, to win a night's freedom from Mamasan, to please a "boyfriend" into returning, into loving her and marrying her and taking her away to a real home where she can go bowling and play bingo and have nice friends and nice things in her place on Navy Housing.

Mimi beats anything you'll find on The Honcho. Flip whore. *Niggers of the WestPac.* The Japanese import the men as entertainers and musicians; they charter boats to Manila on whoring expeditions, hundreds of conventioneers filing off pleasure ships in their blue serge suits, styrofoam boaters and carnivorous grins, sweeping through the bar districts like conquering hordes of businessmen, riding their penises like toy ponies, wielding their yen like flashing swords that they shove down native throats as they loot, copulating with the population in a flood of semen, then letting the ebb carry them back to their homeland. *They stopped fucking here in seventy-three.*

"I didn't come all this way just to gawk at some goddamn pictures of Turner," Walter said angrily, mad at the sudden fear that consumed him. He was afraid of himself, and for Mimi. He was afraid of Mimi's pathetic loneliness and of his own desperate flight from sadness, afraid that he was falling in love for the same kind of reasons as Mimi. He looked around at the wallpaper and it seemed to grow a shade darker, as if the sun was setting faster than his pupils could dilate, and that seemed a sad thing. His body had been growing inured to the drugs and he couldn't tell if they were keeping him high or not. He swallowed the last two pills.

"That's bad," she said. "Don't take pills."

"I know," Walter said, "how caring. He's not going to marry you."

"What?"

"Anyway, pity isn't the same thing, is it? Anyway, I hate sadness."

He looked in her mirror and saw black rings under his bloodshot eyes and unsmiling lips drawn tight over teeth that were clenched from a week of speeding. "My eyes are dimming. It's not just the pills, you know. They want to stop seeing all the time. They want to stop thinking about what they see."

Mallory turned a page of the album and laughed. "Lookit this."

It was a Polaroid of Al and another man standing naked, with Mimi sitting naked between them, their erect penises in each of her upturned hands. All three smiling at the camera.

"Don't look crooked to me," Mallory said. "Maybe 'cause she's holdin' it."

"Who's the other guy?"

"That's Haggard. I told you about him—Turner's buddy."

Haggard again. And Turner. There seemed to be no escaping these people. He felt as though he was experiencing some else's *deja vu*, as though he was merely the ghost of someone else's life, a gray flashback, an afterthought. Where was the stuff of Walter Schmerz? Where was the substance of *his* life?

"They're no better than you are, Mallory," he said.

"What's that supposed to mean?"

"It means I don't feel like doing this sandwich deal. Look, wanna just take her bar hopping with us?"

"Fuck you. Don't get flakey on me, man. I paid for it and I'm goin' for it."

Walter stood up. "Well, I'm not. Bye, Mimi. It was nice meeting you."

She frowned and held onto his arm.

"What's eating you, Schmerz. Ah, go on, ya non-hacker. Lightweight." He smiled a smile that was glad with mischief. "Better be careful out there. It's a cold world. Look out for the bad guys and don't sit in the back of no jeepneys."

"Nice try," Walter said.

"I'm not kiddin'."

"You said yourself they wouldn't have done it."

"Maybe I lied. Maybe I was just tryin' to make you feel better, long as we was running partners and I had to put up with ya. Maybe they're after you. I had some time to think. You ain't the only one that thinks, Schmerz. I know If I was them Flips I wouldn't just let it go."

"Who is after you?" Mimi asked.

"No one," Walter said. "I didn't notice you looking over *your* shoulder the past few days."

"I don't have to. They ain't mad at me. You should of heard 'em after you went outside, though. They was pissed at Hasty for bringin' you and 'cause he was givin' em a hard time about money and wouldn't buy all they wanted. Said it was peanuts, or some such shit. Some heavy words came down. I said I was just along for the ride, no problems. But when we got out of there, they was some very unhappy Flips. And they was *really* pissed at you—stompin' around like that in the man's home, talkin' about fuckin' people up. Ol' Johnny boy didn't even like the way you looked at his wife."

"*Me?* You were that one that did her!"

"Seems that way, don't it. You know how crazy Flips are. They don't think like us. Said he had his pride. What can I say?"

"Say *sayonara* you lying sack of shit."

Mimi tugged at Walter's arm. "Please take me with you."

Morning Light

Before making the trip to Subic City and finding Hasty's "wife," Walter needed a weapon. In the Philippines, the balisong is called "butterfly knife" in some quarters not only for its winged handles but also for its reputation as weapon of choice for hot-blooded, quick-fingered Filipinas whose lovers butterfly to other attractions. Walter would have preferred something heftier for his protection and sense of security, like a forty-five—at least he knew how to use one, and the thought of sticking someone made him queasy—but butterfly was the best he could find, so he bought one, slipped it in his pocket, peered into every passing jeepney for a glimpse of Johnny, and finally hopped in one for Subic City, scowling at the other riders with his best New York City subway scowl, a look that says, don't mess with *me*; I'm dangerous crazy.

  He kept a careful lookout on the traffic behind him. Hasty had said he was going to the Seaview Hotel in Subic City to see a girlfriend named Paz. He never made it back. Maybe she knew something useful; maybe she didn't hear the news. Anyway, he was happy to be in motion again, to be moving away from Mimi's pathetic room and the streets of Olongapo, winding around and over the mountain to a new destination on the other side. Maybe Paz knew something. Maybe she knew someone.

  He shouted "Subic City!" to the driver even though he knew that was jeepney's route. Except for a close look at the driver and the other cars and the faces of the passengers that got on and off along the way, he noticed little during the half hour ride across until they lurched around the top of the mountain and he could see down into the village. It crops out of the jungle and dangles precariously over the water like an old shelf no longer fixed in place by its disintegrated hinges but by accreted generations of barnacles on a foundation supplanted by a subtly palpitant growth of root and vine, its sinews veining through the cankered structures and twisting toward the lascivious old tongue of Subic Bay. Bush and bay seem to reach for each other like lovers' mouths at either end of a stringy piece of meat, biting playfully toward a kiss at the center, and *poof*. There is only one paved road—the one they came in on—along either side of which are ramshackle wooden buildings and weatherworn signs indicating the pleasures within.

Liberty Call

The balconies and porches are festooned with gaggles of girls, screeching and cackling for business.

As an evasive action, Walter got off at the far end of town and walked back a couple of minutes until he came to the Seaview, a big blue hotel sitting right on the bay. It had a plaster facade and seemed to be built with a vaguely Spanish look in mind, but now it was stooped and tired and had nothing to say. Time and neglect had worn the building to a bloodless blue, and blisters ran along its surface. The courtyard was overrun with large, leafy greenery. Inside, business was slow and the girls at the bar swamped him, then floated resentfully away when he insisted that he only wanted a woman named Paz.

This mamasan smiled and led him by the hand to the veranda out back overlooking the bay. He was giddy and weak in the knees—too much speed and booze and not enough food. He leaned over the railing on the back porch of the Seaview in search of a breeze. The sticky tropical air and accumulated week's drinking made his head reel and his thoughts blurry as they rushed along the contours of his mindscape. The moon sizzled in the dark water below, its shimmering disk occasionally breaking up into electric fragments that throbbed and struck out erratically along the tiny swells, energized by unseen forces. He watched the broken pieces of light slap against the pilings and bounce away, again gathering nervously into a circular whole. It was a quiet evening at the Seaview. a couple of sailors and women sat on the veranda or the ramp leading down into the water. Local men brooded at the bar inside, now and then barking at the loitering girls who had few customers to take to their rooms upstairs. Two potted palms against the railing next to Walter made a languid attempt at dancing, like the perfunctory motions of tired go-go girls, and failing to arouse any enthusiasm, they went limp again as the air closed in.

A woman came out with a couple of beers, put them on the railing and took his hand in hers. She had a patient smile, genuine, happy with pleasure. Her plum-pulp lips were thin, sensual and well-defined, curvy in the middle and dimpling into curls at the ends like tiny springs that buoyed her cheeks and dark eyebrows. Her eyes were still but lively, turning downward in a suggestion of irony and mutual amusement. And her lips and eyes seemed to counterweigh each other, to generate each other, inform each other, so when her eyes widened to greet his, her lips curled up in harmony. She took a long swallow of beer, then rolled the sweat beaded bottle against her cheeks and neck.

"It is very hot tonight," she said, and drew the moist mouth of the bottle gently from Walter's forehead down the contour of his nose to his chin, then across from his right cheekbone to the left, smiling not at him but at her work. "X marks the spot," she said, and touched the tip of his nose with the tip of her tongue, "with a circle and a dot. Tell me what you are looking for tonight."

Here everything would be sweet and easy, a matter of gliding into what he wanted. "Ooh," he said as an electric shudder coiled up from his bowels and seemed to connect to her. "We must be on the same frequency." He closed his eyes and thought that he and she were suspended in a newly discovered energy field that penetrated and held them. They were in the eye of a dream now, alone in the undisturbed center, with Olongapo and the Navy Yard and all their agitated events and characters spinning along the periphery of this moment, a storm roiling in the past and rumbling in the future, leaving only residual thunder and intermittent undulations of their dying shock waves as reminders that they ever did or would exist.

Walter wiped the tickling wetness from his face with his arm and opened his eyes. "It's such a relief here."

She ran a finger along the inside of his forearm and raised her eyebrows as if to say, "and?"

"And peaceful. I'm getting away from people in Olongapo City. You know how to push the right buttons quick enough. God, the air's so heavy but it's nice, like I feel like I don't have to breath anymore. Like breathing in water. Are you a mermaid?"

"Paz."

He sampled a handful of her hair. "You're very pretty. You seem like a very graceful lady. They should call you Grace. I love you no bullshit, Grace."

Her smile was almost condescending. "Oh, so you love me no bullshit. But I am not Grace and I am not a lady. Maybe you love somebody else. My name is Paz."

"I'm sorry," he said. "Just trying to be cute. I guess I'm not very cute tonight."

"You are cute enough, Joe. But you look very tired—your eyes are so red. Maybe you want to see me because someone says I am a nice girl?"

And Hasty spun back into his life. "Yeah, I'm sorry. Someone did say so. But he didn't say you had such presence."

"I don't know what that is," she said, her voice holding the last word and turning it over as though for examination. "Maybe I have some presents for you if you have some presents for me."

"No. I mean presence as in poise. As in *goddamn*. As in, interrogative what the fuck, over. As in I'm smitten."

She looked him in the eyes for a long time, and it felt like she was rummaging around there. "Presents as in poise. You like to play around in words. That means no presents? I think you don't talk like a sailor and try to fool people. I think you are funny."

"Funny ha ha?"

"Funny *ba-loot*. Funny because maybe I like you a little bit. You don't seem like a sailor to me. You are a stranger."

"Funny, because I like you too. This is funniness at first sight. You don't seem like a...I mean, you know...a hostess. Let's talk about auras and chemistry and gravity and such."

Actually, Hasty had said little more than the usual sailor nonsense about her "dimensions," but here was a thing that invited involvement, a certain challenge and expenditure of energy. He wasn't the type to waste time on a woman whose charms and demands derived from something deeper than the cleverness of a ponytail or desperately pink toenails and the diversion of sex. Toys. Candy. No mere ball of catnip, she seemed to enjoy her own company, standing there sipping her beer, enjoying holding Walter's hand, reveling in the bay and the evening, laughing with the pleasure in it—her easy eyes still penetrating into him, twisting deeper, ceding carelessly while taking something for herself, never finally submitting, absorbing rather than diminishing. Did Hasty see that? Or maybe Walter was simply imagining her in his near-hallucinatory state, making her up as he went along.

The back door to the veranda slammed, and Paz looked absently over her shoulder, then did a nervous double-take. Her change startled Walter, and he swung around while reaching in his pocket and gripping the knife. It was Mamasan with a tray of beer for them. She oozed a yellow smile at him, exclaiming what a good choice he had made in Paz, patting his cheek, saying, "very smart girl. Very nice. You think she's sexy, yes? I think she's very nice. All my girls nice, but Paz, umm, so special. I think you must be a very smart boy. Why you don't come before?" He smiled back and paid for the beer—he had already paid for the girl—and she and Paz exchanged brief words in Tagalog, Paz now forcing a coquettish smile, Mamasan maintaining the same creased parentheses around her yellow-toothed grin, and she disappeared back into the bar.

"Do you know a guy called Hasty?" he asked. "Did he come here last Friday night?"

"Sure." She grinned. "We all know Hasty. His main ingredients. You know about that? He only stays in the U.S. Navy for a chance to see us." Then she looked confused. "He told you to come see Paz? What is your name?"

"Walter."

"Walter—I don't like that name. Hasty told you to go out with Paz?"

"Are you lovers?"

"To be lovers you have to love. He cannot love."

"Yeah, I guess I saw that in him too."

"Saw it? You are his friend? He sent you to come here?"

"Yeah, sort of."

"So you know that he cannot love, sometimes. He takes too much drugs, I think. He tells stories that make all the girls laugh. He tries, but he cannot love. I shouldn't tell, but you know anyway. Men are afraid when somebody sees what they are really like. Maybe you can help him to stop taking the drug. It is no good to only love the drug and not the girl. I think men are afraid of who they really are. Maybe they don't even know."

First, the uncharacteristic quality of his taste in women, then the revelation about his sex life. But this part was more than he wanted to know about Hasty. He didn't want him to start becoming flesh and blood now that he was dead and gone. He thought he might perform a service to his memory to a then-abstraction named Paz, but this was something different. He wanted to drop the subject that brought him here, but he had to ask one more question. "Do you love him?"

"You talk so much about love. Don't you know what that is?"

Walter remembered that his own skin had an interest in the matter—there might be people after him—and he realized that no matter how much he told himself that he didn't believe Mallory, that was really the compelling reason for his coming. "Did he say anything unusual to you last time he was here?"

"Yes. He says, 'my friend Walter drives me crazy with so many questions about love. Save me, Paz. Let me feel you up and tell you funny stories about Walter.' Then he cries because he has the sadness. Walter—I don't like that name. I can call you Honeyco. Honeyco, do you come here for love?"

The undertow of booze and speed was pulling him out again, but for now he needed to hold against it. They say that the most important thing when drowning is to keep your composure. He was still a bit paranoid. He felt foolish and confused, thinking something important could be achieved by gravely locating a hooker in a rickety hillside barrio. Then there was that business, that look, between the girl and Mamasan. Maybe that was all it was—business. Let it be love, then, that was located, though that too was a crazy pretense under these circumstances, but with such a natural partner, with such natural presence. His joke of detective work was done before it started, and he had made the gallant trip as messenger from the fleet for nothing. Well, not entirely. He had found a beautiful woman with whom to act out love.

"I suppose I like love," he said. "Actually, I just came to tell you that he's dead. Hasty's dead. He fell out the back of a jeepney and got ran over on his way back from here."

She let go of his hand and her lips slackened. She looked at the water, thinking, and said quietly, "You came to tell Paz." After another while she looked at him and said, "A man inside asked for me tonight. I said I'm with you. Am I?"

"Do you want to be?"

"Maybe I like you a little bit."

"Did I upset you? You okay?"

"I think maybe you are sad. That is why you look so tired? You were good friends?"

"No, not really. Just shipmates. But he mentioned you and I didn't know…so I thought I should tell you just in case. Was he normal, like all right? Did he seem worried or upset, like, did it seem like anything was wrong?"

"Normal? Maybe you shipmate has some trouble? That is why you ask so many questions? I don't want to know. Honeyco, he come here to get drunk and have a good time. That is all. Then he cries because he cannot make love with a woman. It is sad when people die. It scares me when someone I know dies because I am afraid to die. Sometimes he gives us money so we like him. That is all. Not just me—all the girls. Like I tell you, he cries for the thing he cannot have, but he likes to touch anyway, so we let him. Then he leaves." She pulled his eyes back into hers and stroked his crotch with her fingertips. "But that is not your problem, I see." She laughed. "Maybe you have a present for me. We can wrap it in my box."

Walter had been that way since she first touched his face. His skin tightened and crawled in patchy waves of effervescent gooseflesh like that spots of disturbances that the breeze breathes into a still water, that ripple and sparkle on the surface while the surrounding areas smooth over. And he was running hot and cold, which made the slickness on his skin feel more like condensation from the ambient moisture than merely sweat. And she was tickling his insides with her eyes. All right. You win. I surrender.

He put his arms around her waist and said as he thought a movie star might, "I'm in over my head with this thing baby, with you."

"I don't know what you mean."

"I want you. I want to love you tonight."

She pushed away from him with a triumphant smile and pointed at a second story window over the bar. "You are so easy. And we will do it all, Honeyco. There, in my room. But you are a butterfly and I want to be sure I can keep you, at least for tonight. It is still early. First we will tease each other, then we will do it all. We will get drunk with the moon and talk, and I will torture you because are a butterfly. I can tell because you are so easy. You want some more beer? I will pull your wings off. To begin, you must tell me I am beautiful."

"You are beautiful, Paz."

He sat down and stretched out on the deck. She took a long time at the bar, and he could hear her talking excitedly with Mamasan and the woman behind the bar. When she returned, she sat down and placed his head in her lap. "So, Joe, what ship? Where you from in The States? How long you in the navy? Got a wife?"

"Yeah, and what's a nice girl like you? You're my wife tonight, and tomorrow I'll make you a navy widow. What's going on with Mamasan, there?"

"Shh."

She had her hand up his shirt and lazily stroked the hair on his chest. The liquid lapping of the bay and the potted palms' intermittent low rustle lulled his eyes shut where he met the flux sieving through his nostrils, heavy with the salad of meat smoke, jungle flower, sweat, beer, and muck. His mind's eye zoomed away and watched from a distance through soft purple light, then panned back in as visions of each discrete entity there floated by—the pilings, the ripples of moon, the murmur of voices, the parts of Paz. "Oh god," he said, "I want to hear the sound of words coming out of you. Tell me who you are. Fill me with who you are. Fuck me or kiss me or drown with me in the ocean or something, anything so I feel more. More alive. More you. Let's get disgustingly snot-slinging drunk. Give me those lips."

She bent her head down until her lips were against his and her long black hair tickled his cheeks. He brushed his tongue along her lips, parting them, and he sucked her tongue into his mouth. Then he reached up her shirt for her breasts, but she straightened back up. "Too fast. Too fast. Where are you going in such a hurry?"

"I want to feel you. I want to know you, to see through your eyes."

"You will know me. I will tell you and you will tell some things about you. Then we will do it all in my bed, and you will know all there is, simple. First you have to relax. See how warm the air smells here. I love when the moon is on the bay like this. It is so romantic. You have to taste each thing separately and slowly and let them melt into each other and get…bigger, and strong, building up, and then," she smiled and slowly pulled his erection out of his zipper, bending further until the tips of her hair touched it, then swaying her head back and forth, "and then at the top comes love making."

"I'm big and strong right now," he said, but not impatiently. This is happiness, he thought. This is everything I ever wanted. It seemed as though he had everything he ever wanted. He was content there on the deck, happy with everything around him, but happily aching also for further promise. He was paralyzed with a kind of narcotic euphoria, shuddering on the brink of some sap-sweet cataclysm that he could forestall but not prevent by remaining still and void; but it would eventually come, even if he didn't try, if he just laid there and left himself wide open to it, it would come over him. "I think I'm going to have a heart attack. It's wonderful. Rapture of the deep."

She zipped him back up. "Have blue balls instead. See what you make me do? What if someone is watching. You want to hear me talk? I get some more beer and we talk. I will tell you about my life and you will tell me about your life."

So they stayed there as the dark veranda gradually emptied out, and they drank electric beer and spoke magnetic words while he ached at the root, plugged into a world that was coming together as Paz had said it would, the sparkling, purple, whispering night working some kind of magic into them, metamorphosing them into something altogether new and exciting. She stroked his chest absent-mindedly, staring over the bay, and talked of herself. He looked up at her face and thought it was the spark that was talking, each word forming a hallucinatory, iridescent color and shape that bled into the next.

"I'm hallucinating," he said.

"What do you mean?"

"That means you're so beautiful that I can't see straight. It means I feel like I'm not me anymore. I'm a born-again Walter. Like, every cell in my body has changed and become a part of something new. Here I go, I'm bonding now—feel it? My cells are all flying out and bonding with Paz cells and Seaview cells and Subic Bay cells and moonbeam cells. Zing! Feel it?"

She laughed. "You are crazy. I think you are not a sailor. I think maybe you know witchcraft or are a spirit from the devil because I do feel it too. You make me feel it? Maybe you are a prince that will save me. Prince?"

"Wizard. I'm going to make a world where all the elements contain you and me in the nucleus, where nothing ever dies, and we'll become each other and know all that ever has been and ever will be in our world, like gods. And we'll feed each other like the sky and earth, raining and evaporating into each other."

"I like that," she said. "You are also beautiful. You must have a wife—I don't want to know. I have many husbands, too. But I did not want the man who was to be my first husband, a fisherman, so I left the village."

"Now we're getting somewhere. What do you dream? Maybe we share things."

"Sometime I dream that I am falling down a whirlpool and I am very sorry because at the bottom is my death. I see my mother standing at the top and I try to swim back into her, back into her where I am safe. Maybe you can pull me up?"

"I will," Walter said, "but tell me more. Tell me about your dreams. Tell me about the village."

"Just a village. In the village they don't know. They don't know about nothing. Work maybe. Rice, dogs, chickens, pigs, carabao, babies. Stinking fish, fishermen drunk on cane liquor at the cockfights. I would have to live in a house made with nipa and a dirt floor. Make his babies and wash his clothes with the old women and their stupid talk.

"The storytelling in the barangay was good. I liked that. Stories about spirits and witches. They never dreamed of you, Honeyco. I would have nothing there. No shoes. No romance. Every day the same, everything the same.

"Now I have shoes. I have a honeyco. There it was like a castle with no escape, like an island surrounded by the jungle and you can't see out. Here I have the best room, with a window to see all over. I can see the world, can see you coming from so far away. I feel like I can see the U.S. from here. Boys like me because I am so romantic, and they give me presents so I can have nice clothes and perfume. It feels like I know I will go to the U.S. sometime—I don't care if I tell you.

"Here it is closer to the world. I learn a lot. In my room I can see and hear people, what they think about and what they want and the things they fight about. It makes me smart, like I have some secrets, maybe. You will see how my room is. Don't worry, you can be alone there too. The way it works, from the window you get everything, but from my bed it is so quiet. Only me."

"Only you. God, yes. And the chickens and the butterflies and the spirits and your shoes. Tell me more. Tell me more about your world. Or a story, a romantic story."

She launched into her story as if she knew it by heart, had rehearsed it before, and had no doubt given variations on the theme to other men in his position. It began with a relish of mundane detail and blossomed into a magical fairy tale. Walter was in it—the handsome prince, of course, betrothed since childhood and separated by evil forces. The princess's early days were ones of simple joy—of toes scoring patterns in the cool evening dirt as the adults spun stories about the past and about the spirits in the village and the surrounding jungle; of the same toes feeling their way down the rocks into the cascade-fed pool where the women washed clothes and gossiped; of the tang of atis and jackfruit and the stolen sips of fermented coconut juice that spun the world like an over-ardent kiss.

As the daughter of royalty, she looked forward to great things: freedom and romance and riches in an ever-growing world of novelty and adventure. Then a monsoon came that never lifted, casting a gray sameness over her days and an intolerable ague into her soul. She learned from an old woman of the village that her parents—that everyone of the village save the old woman, who wore a crucifix and a magic charm to ward them off—had been abducted by a tribe of wicked monkeys who assumed their shapes and had cast their souls into the geckoes that cried out at night. She was prisoner of these monsoon monkeys, hidden from the world by their magic veil of rain and spared her parents fate only by virtue of her extraordinary beauty. She was to marry the new king's son, the dullest and ugliest boy of the lot, and thereby begin a new dynasty. But with the help of the old woman she escaped to Subic City to fulfill her destiny and reunite with the prince of her youth, who had left the village before the evil tribe's coming, and could never find his way back through the veil.

"Wait a second," he said, "there's some holes in this story."

"Shh, Honeyco. 'You will know him when he comes,' the old grandmother said. 'He will come from over the sea but he will not talk like just a sailor. He will speak of love and magic, like a wizard. He will tell you he loves you.'" Walter guessed that she was first trafficked in Manila before finding herself in this jungle.

She went on for another couple of beers or so, but Walter stopped listening to the story at that point; he just listened to the sounds of the words. He knew she was talking about what their magical life together held in store—there were further dangers and adventures and triumphs, to be sure—but all he could hear was the sound, as though she spoke in another tongue and he had to determine what she said through listening to the quality of her voice, through the modulation of mood and the rising, falling inflection, the notes now spilling happily along some scene of domestic tranquility, now stumbling, stuttering to the wilderness of a pause, perhaps dropping in pitch with the suddenly dangerous pitfall, coarse and grainy as it improvised its way through menace or pain, then casting about cautiously, whispering hopefully, and finally scampering up and finding the track again with a flourish of clear, high, breathless imperatives followed by a smattering of self-laudatory, affirming rhetorical questions.

It was like being treated to a solo performance by the first and only virtuoso on the one and only instrument of its kind. The melody was familiar but the arrangement unique and the playing rapturous—a whole life coming together up from her feet and vagina and belly button and heart and lungs, reconstructed in her mind, squeezed up from her guts, vibrating in her throat, as her eyes—wide and cogent and glinting—turned inward, scanning for images to articulate the feeling of being alive.

"I love you," he said.

"Ah, now I know for sure it is you. Now we go to my room. We can do it all there. We can see it all from my window. Subic Bay."

Her room was dark and heavy scented, like wet lumber and unwashed bodies. Paz staggered a bit going up the stairs and flopped herself onto the bed. Walter sat for a moment on a thin wicker chair in the window and looked at the bay again.

She yawned in the dark. "So, GI, now you want to tell me your dreams?" He could hear her sliding out of her clothes.

"Yeah," he said without moving, letting the view blur into double vision of shapes and shades. "Yeah, okay. But I guess I don't have your imagination. I can't stop thinking about the things that really happen. I mean, at first I just wanted to get away, too. Away from school, dead-end jobs, my hometown, an older married woman. I wanted to get away from going nowhere! I lived in books for awhile, but I was still *there*. So I went, and here I am. I'm twenty-three, Paz. Who do I want to *be*? What do I want to *do*? I want to do good.

The future never happens the way you want it to or the way you expect things to be. You can't know what it's like or who you're gonna be so you're wasting time dreaming about it and making up scenarios, but you want it, want something in it so bad. You can't see it, but each day you got more past to look at and think about. It tells you who you are and who you've been but not who you're gonna be.

Right now I'm dreaming about the long, flimsy white curtains billowing at the big windows in my parents' bedroom on a hot summer night. Covered with talc after a bath, naked on the bed in the cold breeze, kind of anxious for something but feeling good too, like you don't want to move. Waiting for someone to carry you to your own bed. And now I'm with you in this—so far away. But it doesn't have to be, really, I guess. It's still with us. We still go back to these places and live them even though we're together here now.

I'll take you back there with me and put you in the dream, side by side, covered with talc just for the fun of it, because it's there. Just because it tickles us, and it smells like tomorrow. No, we can be the same person in a dream. Remember. We're in a big, messy house on the Long Island Sound—it doesn't have to be so different from the bay here—and the things we know are the parts closest to the bare spots on the carpet where grainy dirt settled between the worn threads; earth-scented holes dug by our dog Zeke under shade bushes in the backyard; mulberries staining the front walk and oozing between those toes; tar bubbles in heat on sloppy patches of the road—little, removed streets where we can sit and pop the bubbles and roll the tar into balls between our fingers; schools of minnows zigzagging at the edge of the ramp by the boathouse, just like here, but they scare the hell out of us because we're so small and they seem so...alarming and mysterious.

And we can begin to tell that there's a pattern to the seasons. Christmas comes in the winter when it snows; Jones Beach comes in the summer when the sand burns our feet. Those are the best times and they're such a long, long time apart. 'When are we going to Jones Beach' we ask in the winter, and 'When's it going to be Christmas?' we ask in the summer. Before the beach we stop at Rye Beer and Soda for tons of soda and beer and ice, and when we get there we hippity-hop on the hot sand and dig with our pails at the surf's edge, and maybe lose a plastic PT boat because we're afraid to go into the waves after it. Dad never takes off his white T shirt but the rest of us always turn pink and blister, sleeping feverishly on the car ride home.

At Christmas we all come down the stairs in our pajamas, rubbing our eyes at Dad's antler of flood lights and the camera going—he always cuts off our heads. There's still a little fire smoldering in the fireplace and big socks and nylons full of candy and fruit hanging from the mantle, and we settle in among the gifts around the huge and gaudy tree as Dad hands them out one at a time. It's over so quick and someone always says, 'Is that all?'

Rituals, man. That's what the seasons themselves are. And now I got you I'm gonna put you right back in the dream with me, in the past, playing in the tar in the summer by the water again, barefoot to barefoot, popping the bubbles."

He got up and sat at the edge of her bed and put his hand on her shoulder. She snorted and curled toward him, breathing heavily. "I'm drunk too," he said out loud, and a single spastic sob came out of him, as sudden, high and squeaky as a hiccup. "Fucking embarrassing. Wish *I* could sleep. It doesn't mean I don't really love, you know, just because I turned out this way." He couldn't turn himself off, as he sat there staring into the dark, biting the insides of his cheeks, talking grimly through clenched teeth. So he knelt beside her bed and dreamed for her. He began by dreaming aloud, speaking from the only-ness of her bed toward the all-ness of her window, and at some point he slipped into a narcotic trance that held him till the morning, during which he dreamt he was talking to her, then narrating his life while simultaneously enacting it, like watching a movie and then realizing that you're actually living it. His subject became interchangeable with his objects until he was no longer himself but the people he conjured up:

Used to play a game with my mother. Not a game—just talk. Take time out and talk, whatever was on our minds, nothing important, not necessarily. So we'd talk about stuff and then after awhile we'd see where we were and trace how we got on the subject. Everything was connected. To a kid that's a revelation. Like we'd be on the subject of China and I was asking why Chinese had slanted eyes—in the third grade I was in love with Julie Chow, I think because her eyes were strange to me—and we got on that subject because my grandmother took a steamer there once, and we got on that because we were talking about trains and the uses of steam which we arrived at because we were talking about sources of power because gunpowder was the topic because I was shooting off firecrackers that day because it was the Fourth of July and the conversation started with American independence. And gunpowder was discovered in China which was where my firecrackers came from because they're illegal in New York. Get it? It all comes down to some Julie Chow in third grade. Or you—it's your eyes I'm seeing all this in now, on the veranda.

What's my point? So that's what it was like on my island when the monsoons began to close in. The world we live in, in which we live. Oh, and it comes to us through the stories of our older brothers and sisters, stories about school and teachers, teaching our own kind of magic, I suppose. And stories of mystery and romance about other boys and girls, stories about the Catholic god and devils that we'd get to know soon—that we'd one day be able to read and know.

We know that Dad's a big success because people always tell us so and because we have everything we want—they tell us that too. He works hard in the city—this big ant farm where everything is busy and seems to have a purpose and know what it's doing or it would collapse and the ants would scatter in confusion. Somehow he finds his way home every day. It's amazing, even when we take long rides—hundreds of miles where we've never been before—he always finds the way home. Sometimes we catch him and Mom naked in bed. She tells us we can be businessmen in the city when we grow up, and we'll be husbands that are supposed to sleep naked with our wives. Not bad. What do Tom and Eileen's kids imagine they'll do when they grow up? Or Ferdinand junior? It was better for me. Still, it's like we all know each other, watch each other on TV, hanging from each other's walls.

Walter ceased his narration to behold the gallery of framed portraits expanding along Paz's endless walls. He realized that he himself was watching from behind a hanging frame. He realized that he was a picture of Johnny's son, Nando, and he stepped out of his frame into the middle of Walter's old life, uncertain and without bearings, at a loss for the proper motions—no matter, he always was, anyway. He is in a car with Mom, riding to the station in the green, appropriate station wagon to pick up Dad from work. The angry crowd of people on the street shout slogans and hold signs saying, *The Enemy Is Only Ninety Miles Away.* Who's the enemy? Cubans. Careful, we might be Cubans, which is really ninety miles from Florida which is really hundreds of miles away from New York. Are we Cubans Mommy? I'm scared. Nothing to worry about Nando, we're not Cubans, we're German hyphen Americans. You're a white boy now.

Then he was John Wayne on TV fighting the Japs—sneaky, vicious, scary, wearing round, wire rim glasses. It's a good thing we dropped the atom bomb, or the Japs would have won the war, Mom. No, not really honey, the war was already won when they dropped it. Don't touch that one—she must know what she's talking about—but it sounds too involved to get into. They must have deserved it.

With the Japs gone, a marine needs new people to fight. Dad says Nando can fight in the Cold War when he grows up. Cold because no one really shoots. If they did, we and the Russians would drop A bombs on each other, and everyone would be killed. At school he puts his head between his knees under his desk for mid-morning air raid drills, not sure if he's doing it right. The mushroom cloud becomes the principal's face telling them that the President's been shot and they must all go home. The teacher is crying. There's sadness all around but it's abstract, you can't touch it, like at church where you're supposed to act sad, and he tries, but it's neat having an unexpected day off in the middle of the week and he can't suppress his glee.

A man visits Nando's house, a fascinating man wearing a shiny army uniform, and he smiles and says kind things. He is a special kind of soldier—better than a marine—called a Green Beret. He is going to fight in a place called Vietnam. Nando hopes Vietnam will still be there when he grows up. Better than a fucking cold war.

But Nando's house is hiding in the backstreets of Olongapo again and the man in the shiny uniform is Hasty James. Nando has a forty-five and knows how to use it. Bang, motherfucker, you're dead. Now it's Walter Schmerz and he's bleeding. Christ, somebody help me, I'm bleeding. Sure Joe—it's Johnny and Eddy—you got any money? We're businessmen. Nando, the man in the shiny uniform is here to fuck your mother. Go get him a beer, you warped little bastard, and stop shooting the customers. And the warped little bastard shoves the bottle down Walter's throat—eat this, you're not bleeding, you pissed your pants—and then another bottle and another until it's all one, bottled hate raping his throat and pouring out again through his unmended bullet hole.

Walter dies and becomes Paz, the nightmare glare of her hovel burning down to a romantic glow; the stabbing pain in the throat rounding off to a sentimental lump of love and desire. They all want me. I'm free; I've escaped. I'm beautiful. I'm love. I relax and incorporate all into my imagination. I am soft and elastic, expanded to liquid. I can swim within myself, go where I want, accept and accept and accept to my depths.

Al laughs and say, well yes, but she's polluted. That's okay, we can use her. He is sitting in a director's chair, speaking through a megaphone and wearing a beret. Did directors really do that? So it was all just a movie he's directing, a made-for-TV summer rerun: nothing new. Nothing wonderful. Nothing frightening. That's entertainment.

Okay everybody, we're doing Walter's life. Nando, you and the boys wait till later. Here, play with Hasty in the meantime. Okay, now over here I want everybody who's angry on the street and sullen in the house. Walt, you're watching TV and listening to the radio where the extras are shouting about the Establishment. Okay, Bum and Kid? You're the negroes in this scene—we still call you negroes at this particular point in time—you're rioting and getting shot by police and attacked by dogs on the news. Now, Walt, you ask Mom why these negroes are doing this, and Mom tells you about slavery and explains about how cruel the white people have been. You think she is telling you more than you want to

39

know without answering the question, why. Too much history. Isn't that cute? Kawaii, ne? Let's shuffle some hippies in, Walt's older brother and company. And Uncle Pete and Dad, you argue about President Johnson's war—I want to hear Vietnam at this point. Unc, you say that the bombing is just insane, and Dad rejoins about fighting the commies and supporting our boys over there. Unc rolls his eyes while Dad throws his Bronze Star and Purple Heart around from the time his destroyer was endlessly—so it seems—being torpedoed while escorting that convoy to Murmansk. Hey, what do you know, Ruskies.

Now Timothy Leary—over here, Tim—gives some acid to Walt's brother Gary, who climbs the obligatory motorcycle to San Francisco. His friends still like to come over and argue with Dad, though, calling him Establishment with a capital E, calling him a German, infuriating the Nazi in him. Or is it the other way around? His father's deli in Brooklyn was smashed up by anti-German, war-frenzied mobs from Jones Beach one Christmas during the Great War. Or something. I like the image—we'll work that part out.

Now they're bubbling back ashore on little plastic boats shooting black fists and peace signs. And up washes King and up washes Kennedy, with seaweed in their hair and foam in their mouths.

Al's montage movie of Walter's life turns out to be a brief advertisement for the real show, which now returns to the black and white screen as he sits on the couch with Dad. It's called the Chicago Convention, starring Walter Cronkite and Huntley and Brinkley and probably Dan Rather and of course Abbie Hoffman and the masses of protesters and riot police—that's police trained to riot. This is a good one, a real free-for-all, like those movies where Romans are fighting somebody that looks like Romans only mangier, maybe—red shirts versus the animal hides—and you don't know what's going on because they're all mushed together, screaming and hitting and stomping and stabbing, and you don't know who to root for, who the good guys are, because you turned it on in the middle. A delegate covered with blood is telling a newsman that the police beat him up on the way to the convention. Mayor Daley is a special guest star, angry and flap-jowled. A phalanx of cavalry cheer and call his name and wave their war-fists. Dad says they're paid to do that. Nixon is the winner.

He turns from the story to notice his toes—a little girl's. Paz again. Is it the village or Rye? Something about a holiday, not here but over there, wherever that is. A new year holiday. He's at the kitchen table in his good dress mixing batter for the men's breakfast, looking at a Sunday magazine picture of bleeding marines being evacuated on a tank from a place called Hue. And Mom turns angrily from the Sunday frying bacon like it's something he did, and says, I hope to god this damn war is over before you're drafted. And he sets aside his half-eaten mango and says, can such things happen? It seems like it could last forever, she says. She turns back to the eggs. She is crying. Her oldest son Carl has just been drafted.

The other brother, Gary, becomes a heroin addict and hangs out with Johnny and Eddy, who have guns. Cool. Mom says drugs didn't used to destroy people's lives. Starts with Marijuana and ends up with heroin addiction. Speed kills. A friend of Gary's dies from a junk OD and Mom goes to the funeral and says he looked just like Walter, only black. Creepy.

Still, he pads about the village combing his pretty black hair and practicing his smile, giggling at the boys as spastic chickens scatter in the dust before his bare, calloused feet, wearing flowers in the jungle hat Carl sent from Vietnam, putting day-glo "Make Love Not War" posters up next to the one of Mets ace Jerry Koosman in their hovel, buying quote literature unquote from the Black Panthers at the well or market or whatever passes for a mall around here. The world is a dangerous and exciting place. Big things are going to happen. My prince is coming.

On a train—he's on a train. It's Carl, back from the war unscathed; no tragic war stories here. Love Train. Peace Train. The Little Train That Could riding over humpy green hills with the radio playing a song called Watergate. Watergate through the Smokies, Watergate through the New Mexico desert, Watergate all the way up the Pacific coast, and all the crazy geeks keep getting on, priests and police that are running the country—Ehrlichman and Halderman and Dean and Liddy. Nixon and Kissinger.

The train keeps chuffing but that monsoon settles in, an oily gray malaise over the landscape. People are shooting at each other on the gas lines, for Christ's sake. There's nothing to take the place of the things from before, nothing to do in the rain but get high and get busted and stuff. Let's hump this baby over to Subic City. Look at it, the country turned inside out, the grass and trees and pretty colors washed away by the rain, dirty on the inside, corrupt. Nothing looks new anymore. There's the family lined up at the station in Rye, New York. You know how a family thinks of itself one way and then it isn't anymore? There are the king and queen, their skins melting away to reveal the monkeys underneath. There's Gary, the ex-hippie, ex-junkie finding god in the rain and hopping a pogo stick of religious sects into the horizon. Carl toots the horn. This train is now a local from Cos Cob to Wall Street. The cauldron of war must have done unthinkable tortures to his mind, indeed. He is a businessman and a prince.

Now they're a slow-moving freight train, a bookmobile, school on wheels. The books all say that it isn't raining but he's soaked to the bone. Their magic isn't working, so he jumps off, drops out and begins hitching west in the greasy April drizzle—nothing but truckers and waitresses and burgers and coffee and diners and state cops and thirty-eight specials shooting up the road signs. No one and nothing to fall in love with. He catches a ride with a Navy recruiter.

Then he rides Irene from New London to Alaska. Kids peeking out from behind bearskin curtains. Tom eating his beer with a fork—Budweiser ice cubes. The kid from Olongapo with the big head and eyes—Nando—jumps out of a velvet painting on their wall. He has a big tear drop frozen on his cheek. He smells sour. Then he is Paz. And it all somehow relates to Julie Chow, each inextricably linked to each like the topics in the conversations when his mother taught him how to think.

Morning light from Subic Bay tapped Walter's eyelids. They opened to Paz's window. He sneaked down to the empty bar in search of liquids, but everything was locked up, and he had the absurd presence of mind to shun the one thing he craved most—water. "How fucking stoic," he said out loud, then felt Paz's hand, warm against the clammy shirt on his back.

"You are talking to yourself."

"I'll do that from time to time," he said, turning slowly around, still bent over like a crooked old athlete whose wounds have fused him into a permanently stooped gargoyle that mocks but acknowledges his past, youth and age welded together along the seams of pain. They were at eye level. "Either I've shrunk or you've grew." He closed his eyes to hide the full extent of his misery. "*Please* get me something to drink, please, or my death will be on your hands."

She found a half bottle of Orange Crush under the bar and handed it to him. He sucked it to the bottom, sticky, warm, and flat. Then he flung himself outside over the veranda and spouted it back into the bay, and that followed by a gush of sour beer, and that followed by agonized bile.

She graciously insisted on waiting with him by the roadside for the next jeepney to Olongapo. He didn't want her to but felt too sick and feeble to be rude, so they stood there, awkward and shy. Then she seemed to get an idea, and threw her arms with dramatic affection around his neck, only sending a shower of red sparks from his head down his spine and by some speedy channel into his stomach, the delta from which they would inevitably spew back into the sea of the world again. "Honeyco, you come see me again? You like me?"

"Sure do," he managed, meaning it. "I'll be back."

"Then maybe you give me a present till next time? There is a dress in Olongapo for only three hundred pesos. I will wear it for you next time. It will be my wedding dress. You have some money for me?"

He had fifty pesos left after car fare, and gave it to her. She kissed his cheek and consoled herself by saying, "Okay, maybe I can get some perfume with this. You give me some more so I can buy stamps and write letters to you?"

"That's it all," he said. "But I still love you no bullshit."

She grabbed his arm again, and this time he was getting a bit annoyed with the jolting and considered making one last dash for the railing before the journey ahead.

"One thing. You make me a promise?"

"What is it?"

"Promise?"

"Promise."

"I was going to tell you anyway. No matter what happened. You promise you won't get mad?"

"I promise I won't get mad if you tell me right now."

"I want you to know who I really am because I like you too much and want to see you again. One thing. My name is not Paz."

"Okay. What just happened?"

"I was going to tell you anyway. You must believe me. Now you know I am honest."

He thought he had handled the shift from romantic lead to paying customer rather deftly, but this one was beginning to throw him as it sank in, and he had the sick feeling that he should get out of there quick before he heard anything more. Maybe this was about more than names. Now she was telling him more than he wanted to know. He stared at her stupidly.

"Do you hate me?" she asked.

"What," he said.

"I am Vivien. Mamasan says you will only pay for Paz, but she knows you are never here before, so she tells me to say I am Paz and be nice to you. But everything is okay, right? You think I am pretty. I can make you feel good. And now you know that I am honest. You like me and I like you so what is the difference, Honeyco? I knew I would tell you in the morning and I did, see?"

Homeport, Yokosuka

Al spun around on his stool, flared his eyes, puckered his dimples and trilled through his pursed lips like a siren. "Lookout Sugar, I'm going to Fred!"

She, Sugar, reached across the counter and lazily lit Walter's cigarette. "Who is Fred?"

"Fred ain't a who," he said, "Fred's a place. It's the next planet you go to after Stinko and I'm on my way. Coming Walter? Perhaps a booster shot of something—vodka. Sugar, my love, might we have two shots of vodka, please?"

"Okay, but then you guys get the hell out of here? It's four-thirty. I'm all cleaned up except for you two. You get out and I lock up and we can all go home and have some nice sleeps. What a crazy night, huh? Here, on me."

They downed the shots. "We don't have a home," he said. "We are citizens of the world. We live everywhere and nowhere. No place is like home. We follow the sun. You know, westward, ho! Follow it all the way around until it's coming up again over the land of the also rising sun. Also rising…also ran. That's the loser of a race. And you know, Sugar, it is a race, this game of life. And so, to Fred."

He roused himself again, as though the shot fired-in and put a new spin on his unwinding mind. "No home. Just a floating steel prison full of homos and sadists and watchamacallits, disgruntled malcontents. Sugar… god, I love this woman. Sugar, you're beautiful. I say this from the heart. You have a face like a…it's just beautiful. God, I love you."

"Go home."

"We have no home!" He batted his eyes and said sweetly, "Take us home with you?"

"Alvin, go away."

"Just me, then?"

"You are bad. I should call the shore patrol."

He hoisted his brassard on his nightstick. "We *are* the shore patrol! We suspect everyone and no one. You see, Walter? No one loves me. No one cares. Fight for these people, then it's Yankee go home. I could compel you, ya know." He somehow waved the brassard around at the tip of the stick without flipping it across the room. "We are the law. Spend all night under the stress of law enforcement, putting our lives on the line for the good people of Yokosuka, scraping drunks off the sidewalk so that my beautiful Sugar won't have to dirty her feet on them, and look how we get treated. Now it's our turn to unwind and they won't even pay us the kindness of a drink." He banged his glass onto the bar. "One more, Sugar. Me and Walter gotta drink up and get to Fred."

"Ay! You are a child, Alvin." She lifted her head from where it had slowly sunk to her hands on the bar during his speech, looked at the bottles, looked at Al and then Walter, swung the bottle from the shelf, splashed the juice in their glasses, then poured half a shot for herself. "Definitely last one. Only because what you did today."

"Take me home?"

"Al, go away."

"For what I did today. Please?"

"Leave me alone."

"Pretty please with a cherry on top? I'm a cherry, you know. Ever faithful to the thought of you. I never in all my life. Honest."

"Finish your beer. I'm closing. I'm too tired for you."

"You see? No wonder I'm going to Fred—wonderful place, Walter. Bigger than here or Iran. Bigger than the Pacific. Bigger than this puny solar system. I've been there, Walter. It's so far away from all this. Can't stand it on that ship; can't go home with the woman I love. Where the hell else is there to go?" Then he changed his tune. "My friend, Walter Schmerz, is a veteran of Fred, and although he is only a rookie, only a baby in the real Navy, a polliwog of a fleet sailor, he already has stories to tell about his strange adventures there, about its wondrous, beauteous sights and strange temptations. Isn't that right, Walter? Tell her Walt. Al held his hands out as if gifting the story to Walter, but continued. "About how plain old things become crazy new things. The seductive moons of Fred. You can even fall in love with a hooker on Fred. Isn't that fucking marvelous?

And we shall get there again. I still know some other bistros on this Honcho that will have us, that will keep their doors open to the shore patrol till the sun comes up. I am a well-loved man on this Honcho." He banged his fist on his chest. "Yeah, and I wouldn't have you now for treating us this way. Why, I wouldn't have you if this was the last bar in Yokosuka. I wouldn't have you if you begged me, if you pleaded with those beautiful slanty brown eyes and kissed me with your lipsticky lips and blew in my ear and attacked me with that body of yours. Sugar, this is your last chance, Sugar."

Walter plunked his empty on the counter and Sugar gave him a pleading look. "C'mon Al. Time to go," he said.

Al stood up, and like a valet, Walter hitched his white web belt around his waist and handed him his garrison cap. "But we only got off this shit detail two hours ago," he said.

He put his hat on sideways. "Home, ha! Very well, to Fred then, where men are men and women are easy, where anything can happen, right Walter? Where all the whores have hearts of gold and lips made out of sugar, Sugar. Hey, The Archies. I'm a fucking poet. I love you Sugar."

He started walking in the opposite direction of the door to the far end of the long, empty bar. "Where you going?" Sugar said.

"To Fred. Where you never have to sleep, and craziness is the plan of the day."

"And afterwards you get underway with a puke bucket between your knees, praying for death," Walter said.

"Where blood alcohol content is high, and aggravations are low."

"And afterwards you hope you never have to meet or pay or even dream about the people and things you pissed on." Walter was halfway there himself.

"Come back here," Sugar said.

He turned around. "Harketh, she beckons at last. Very well, my love, as you command. Where all the bars look like ice cream parlors and all the bartenders are sweet enough to lick." He walked slowly back in the sallow light, spinning each of the abandoned stools at the low Formica counter, and with each spin flashing his eyes under the crooked cap and uttering that childish siren. "Farewell and goodbye, Sugar my love," he said when he reached them.

"Goodnight Al."

"Sayonara Sugar."

"Sayonara Al."

"Hey," Walter said, "it does kind of look like an ice cream parlor in here. Only all the kids grew up and became drunken sailors buried at sea—a sea of booze."

Al placed his palms on Walter's temples and moved his head back and forth, examining it. "I'm looking for the idiot in there who said that. Now shut up Schmerz. You know you really are a fucking bummer. Why don't you go find some two-bit Honcho punks to chase you around so you can tell everybody you're being persecuted by the bad guys. Oh, and then be sure you feel good and sorry for yourself. We almost had a touching moment going for a moment there."

They walked through the curtain in the doorway and onto the street. It was quiet now, just a couple of jukeboxes playing at the all-nighters that still had their neon signs blinking mutely in the gloom. Two drunks stumbled arm in arm, laughing and punching each other in the chest. Some Japanese civilians went by on bikes, going to work, probably. A squad of police stood sucking cigarettes at the corner where the Honcho meets a more respectable part of town, peering up towards them during lulls in their conversation as the two wavered outside of Sugar's bar, Circe's.

Liberty Call

That day had been hell. Walter had only been back a week and it was already their fifth day as a shore patrol team. The Midway came home in the afternoon after a four-month deployment on Gonzo Station. It was amateur night from seven to three. Eight hours of invincible rookies just out of boot camp telling sea stories and bragging in their beer. Eight hours of lonely boys from upstate and down with no one to console them after their bold exploits and deprivation at sea, now more than ever feeling the distance from a beloved Suzi or Toya or Teri or Kimberly or Melissa or Tanya or Donna or Jessica Jennifer Dawn. Eight hours of gangs out to clear the Honcho of riffraff from the little ships now that the Big Boy was home. Yes, after setting the record for continuous days at sea since World War Two, the Midway was back with a vengeance, and it was shore patrol's problem: kids choking on their own vomit in the gutters. Noses kicked in for the crime of being on the wrong faces. Hands slashed by broken glass and heads cracked by bottles or nightsticks. Confiscated knives and brass knuckles. One guy was almost drowned in a goldfish pond at a whorehouse for insisting that another john was about to jump line and go topside with his true and legitimate girlfriend. Walter knocked down the drowner, who must have simply been leaning on the drownee, because he couldn't get back onto his feet; Al fished out the dying man, and when he stopped sputtering and blubbering and coughing and yelling murder long enough to curse them and demand an ambulance and the arrest of his attacker, Al dunked him back in to shut him up, yanked a coin from his pocket and put the call for the wagon through.

They'd pile them into the paddy wagon, hissing and bawling, wave goodbye and then start filling the next van. An hour later the same faces would somehow be back on the prowl. The bar owners were a great help. Greasy little men with sweaty smiles, they come out on the street grabbing anyone who's unsteady on his feet, literally hijacking the drunks, sometimes two on one, pulling by the arms and pushing from behind, jabbering, "Show you good time. Good time. Guls inside. Nice guls. You come inside." When the drunk turns mean because suddenly his money's all gone from buying five-dollar drinks for a sixty-year-old gul, or when he simply passes out on the bar, the same men are out again, yelling, "Shaw patroh, hep! Shaw patroh, you come get this guy. Damn sailor wreck my place." And it's more hissing and tears and dodging bottles, and up, into the wagon, watch your head, maybe see you in an hour when you borrow some more money, twenty for thirty, or forty, come payday. The loan sharks from the ship were no doubt loving it.

Everyone wants to take on the shore patrol. Some saw Al and Walter as simply an annoyance, others as a challenge, and after all, they weren't particularly the toughest men on the street. Walter would have preferred a low-key approach to the job. What were they but fleet sailors like the rest of these slobs, suddenly handed SP brassards and told to keep the peace? Besides, the whole scene was altogether too silly to risk getting maimed. "Never get separated from your buddy or you're in serious shit, and never use your stick unless your life is threatened." That was the job training; the rest was left to instinct. Every GI they met that night threatened their lives. Anyway, there was no restraining Al, and like the man said, Walter had to stick by him. "You take 'em low, Walter, and I'll take 'em high."

At one point, earlier that evening, they made an appearance at Circe's so that Al could strut for Sugar and carry on his courtship burlesque. A gang of firemen from the Midway was trying to run off some airmen from the same ship, and there was Sugar in the middle of the shoving match, screaming herself hoarse and slapping at all of them while the other bartenders cowered behind the counter. As they walked in on the scene, an unsteady fellow stood up from his barstool near the door. He didn't appear involved in the fracas, but Al yelled "Sit down!" Sugar stopped screaming and people turned around to see them, but the oblivious drunk didn't, and started shoving his change into his pockets. "I said sit down!" Al yelled again, but before he could turn around Al had caught him by the collar and jerked him to the floor where his head bounced on the tiles amid a flurry of popped buttons and loose coins.

By now they had the house's attention, and before Al's prop could clear the amazement from his eyes, his victim was pinned to the floor with a nightstick to the solar plexus. "I'll stop his fucking heart," Al said. "You want to make trouble?" he said to the man, who was only trying to breathe. "I'll stop your fucking heart. That goes for all of yas." He stuck his baton inside his belt. "Alright, get us, badass." But badass just lay there blinking as though trying to focus and figure what hit him, and why, and what would happen next. "I said *get up!*" Al lifted him by the back of his pants and his collar and ran him out the door, exactly as they do in the movies. "Anyone else?" It was well executed, Walter thought.

He then strode theatrically from one end of the bar to the other with his right hand on his stick and his left thumb hooked in his belt, threatening to crack heads and run them all in if there were any more disturbances. "Most importantly, the *paramount* thing for you to remember, is that if anyone lays a hand on Sugar or the girls, or so much as upsets them again, me and my buddy are coming after you. And I don't care about the rules. Forget the shore patrol stuff—we're gonna fuck you up." Walter's toes curled in his shoes and he tried to turn his cringe into a grimace. He watched his rear and waited for the worst. There was some grumbling, some anonymous comments, but luckily, they were mostly kids and seemed to buy his bluff. He knew his audience. Except for Sugar, who was impressed, but as it turned out, not properly grateful to Al.

Now, as they stood outside of Circe's hours later, Walter's head ached, and he was tired and still felt sober though he knew he probably wasn't. "Come on," Al said, "let's go to the Magnet. Fred awaits. I'm still only at stinko."

"Fred sucks and I'm not too crazy about stinko either."

"Come on, Walter, what's the matter? I'll buy you a Kirin and let you tell me about your PI gangsters again. They got a cute new hostess at the Magnet. She'll like you."

Walter looked up the desolate street, then thought about walking back to the ship and his rack in the berthing compartment—the crew had just moved back onboard from the barracks. There was nowhere to go. "This sucks."

"Come on, Walter, pal o' mine, cheer up." He poked him in an unsuspected sore rib with his elbow. "What's the matter? We're a team. You mad at me because I was kidding you, 'cause I said you were a bummer? I was just funnin' ya, laddybuck."

He hadn't been kidding, but Walter wasn't mad at him about that. Until he said that, Walter hadn't felt mad at him at all. But now with a boozy pout coming on, now that he mentioned it, Walter was feeling irritated with him, injured by something that faintly ached in the middle of his bones and leached into his blood like an itchy pathogen, that crawled through his veins and tickled on the inside from his navel to his heart till his toes curled again, that reached into his head and chaffed his eyes till they were red and glassy. Something that wanted a name. If there was a name then maybe there would be a remedy—till then treat with alcohol to suppress it, or talk to confuse it. "You're an egotistical son of a bitch," he said.

They went into the Magnet, where the owner, who'd been dragging in drunks and calling shore patrol for help all night, came to greet them.

"Never mind that," Al said, "Where's the womenfolk."

A frowning old crone with an off-kilter red wig stepped up and cracked them a couple of beers. "Ah shit," he said, "you got mossy teeth."

She boxed him on the side of the head and walked away cursing. "Green teeth, and she can't even keep her wig on straight. You see that?"

This was even worse than Circe's and the gloomy street, being alone in the world with Green Teeth and Papasan. Who dreams up these people and places? "Voila gentlemen, I give you the Magnet. Not worse than going home, though," Walter said, trying to cheer himself up.

"Roger your last, mate," Al said. "This place is fivers—comin' in loud and clear. Spittin' nickels."

"Sun'll be joining us before we ever get to Fred," Walter said.

"Join us, aye," Al said. "Join us. In this joint. The sun and the holy ghost. Joint—sounds like the sound the last of the ointment makes squirting out of the tube. That's how I feel—all joined-out. Squish, join, oint, splat. Oops. You don't strike me as a joiner, Schmerzer. I think you really joined us after your baptism under fire in the PI. Anointed by Fred. Came out unscathed and un-clapped. A trip, ain't it. What the hell did you expect?"

"Glory. Fame. Nice uniforms."

"You know, Walter, the sad thing is you think you're kidding. I hate it when you think you're being funny. I'm funny. You are not funny. You're too busy looking for things in things."

"Ah shut up," Walter said. "Hey, give us a shot of vodka."

The old woman banged the glasses in front of them, slopped some liquid around and stuck her tongue out at Walter.

"No," Al said. "I don't shut up. That's not what I do. What I do is tell you quite truthfully that you better unjoin us, boy, or you will be sorry. In fact, you shouldn't even be hanging out with me. Bad blood, you know. Chief's gonna not like you and that's gonna make your life hard and it's gonna bug you out 'cause you're gonna wonder why, as if there was a good reason. And you're weak.

"Know what I wanna be when I grow up? Radioman. Sailor. You do it right and that's what you are and that's all that matters. They can't touch you. They can see you and they can hate you, but they can't touch you. Jealous, maybe, or frustrated." He was rolling the neck of his beer bottle between his palms and smiling at it. "Like they see that I'm the real article, so they think I'm supposed to be a certain way, the way they imagine the real thing is, but I read that book before—I wrote it—*am* it. They're just playing at it. Like you—playing at being a communicator and a sailor. I *am* it. I'm the one who says—no—who *shows* how the real article is supposed to be and it's not what they expect and it's not what they want so they hate me. But I don't care who likes me or what happens or if it's fair or not. So unjoin us when the time comes."

"Who hates you?" was all Walter could say, not sure what he was getting at, but resenting his ability to balance smugness and self-pity on the same drunken thought.

"Sugar. Your sea-daddy. Your mama. So unjoin us."

"You're one bad motherfucker, alright. And smart. Crying 'I'm bad' and 'no one understands me' at the same time."

"Can't touch me. But it can sure as shit fuck with *your* mind. Like a weakness, kind of. I can see it alright. You don't belong. You're an actor; think you're a saint. To you everything stands for something else besides what is just is. You know what that means?"

"That there's a meaning to things?"

"Means bullshit."

"Ah yes, Al the untouchable. You think you're some kind of epitome of a fleet sailor. As if you're the fleet itself, the only one. Everyone gets bugged. You didn't invent anything. Those crying babies we put in the wagon—that's your fleet sailors. Ass kissing troublemakers like Mallory are fleet sailors. You got your Stone—bugged from the get-go. Stone spends his whole life crying about how unfair things are. You're too smart to keep playing this game."

Al tossed back his shot. "Shit son. What you're thinking is that *you're* too smart."

"Stop telling me what I'm thinking!"

"What does your Vivian mean? What does Subic *mean* to you? Did you ever talk to the real Paz?"

"It wouldn't have mattered."

"Bingo. And much as I do love you, Walter, you're the fakest one of all." He held his palms together as though reading them. "You don't have eyes to see. The problem with those other guys is they can't see past themselves, and since they all got pea brains, that keeps their problems small, minimalizes the damage, as it were. When Stone thinks it's a cruel world that's just because of the things that happen to Stone. You can anticipate Mallory 'cause he's always waiting for you to slip, and Starring just because he's dumb and afraid you might actually tell him so to his face and then he'll have to deal with it and break that pose, and Chief 'cause he acts like he thinks a mean 'ol chief is supposed to act.

I got a fix on that—I know that what happens to me does not matter. Now you: Walter's problem is that when he says it's a cruel world he's trying to look at everything and make it fit. Cosmic damage control petty officer, except you don't do anything about it. Just like a Catholic—god's watching—but you have to imagine what it's like to be god and be watching. Sin of pride. You still don't know that what happens to you does not matter. And you think you see beyond yourself and that makes you special. Gonna win brownie points with god. Brown nosing god, for Christ's sake.

People get mad at me 'cause they think I think I'm better. I am: better communicator, better sailor, better drinker. I can take it better and dish it out, too. That's all, and they can't touch me. Nothing else matters or counts. But you got some of these jackasses believing that you're better on some kind of cosmic basis. Because you believe it, too. And that's more dangerous than getting people mad at you. Well, make yourself crazy if you want, just don't go getting superior or holy on me. Now you got me talking shit. Hey Green Teeth," he yelled, "we got another greenhorn here who thinks smart matters for something. Thinks it's gonna make someone care about him."

She spat on the floor from the corner where she kept a spiteful vigil over them. "*Baka. Baka gaigin.*"

"*Yeah?*" Al said. "And your mother's a stupid savage!"

"I like you, Walter. I'm just trying to let you in on something. You think there's a way things are supposed to be and it ain't. You're gonna get hurt. Hang with me if you want…just don't go looking for things to be fair. There's no moral to the story. And then you want to be sure to unjoin us when the time comes if you're still interested in being a saint, because nothing good's ever gonna come of this here. Might be a whole lot of wild and craziness but it won't get you to heaven."

His smile had gone from his bottle to the mirror in front of them in a kind of entranced stare. The filmy light of dawn was fingering through the window, cupping the yellow bulb-light inside so that only half-hearted localized coronas shone at their fixtures like diminutive birthday cake candles, and the fuzzy red walls bled to wash-water gray in the shadows. A long ash from his cigarette dropped into the ashtray and the smoking butt recoiled onto the bar and rolled to the floor where half a dozen other cigarettes burned, their tendrils snaking up around Al like incense burning around a brazen Buddha. He chuckled. "Ol' Haggard bugged."

"What happened to him?"

"I think he went to Fred and never came back. But I'm the only one that knows about it."

"I think I'm getting sick of this guy, Haggard," Walter said, growing queasy at the sound of his name.

Al lit another cigarette. "Either that or Bumfuck, Egypt, but I ain't seen hide nor hair of him for months. No. No kidding, he wigged. Used to be a nice guy. Said Grace before every meal. Wanted to marry the first whore he fell in lust with—I got him out of that—had to show him the importance of variety. And we had some great times, Walter, just like you and me are gonna have. But something was happening to Haggard. He was growing... grim. Yes, yes, that's the word I want. Like all the light of that nice kid I saved from unholy matrimony was going out of him. Like the light inside was dimming. Yes. Only I saw it—that he was going farther and farther away, into his own orbit, just going through the motions. I made a good operator out of him, but he was a communicator only in the mechanical sense, sad man. Just didn't have much heart once he learned one thing and unlearned another, like grace, or getting engaged with people. Something about him you couldn't touch—before and after—and I don't mean in a good way or like he was beyond ya, but like he wasn't even aware of it that it existed for him to not have in the first place. Like part of the program was missing. Not like you—he didn't think he already had something else going on. He just came to realize that *this was nothing*. So he went empty. He forgot how to talk to people, a living ghost. Anyway, he stuck by me."

As he talked his eyes swept left-to-right, left-to-right on the bar immediately in front of him, and his head swayed slightly and unsteadily behind; then he looked Walter in the eyes, bloodshot and leaden lidded, and snatched his shoulders with each hand. "Walter, Haggard was missing something. He wasn't dumb, just missing something. And we filled the missing part, just like putting the brain in Frankenstein, or programming a robot or making Coco the Clown jump out of the inkwell. But it just seemed to make him less touchable, like he wasn't real and nothing was real to him, permanently billeted on Fred and didn't have to drink anymore to get there. I supposed it was my fault. I mean, I'll take the blame since I was closest to him. Finally, every last vestige of him was gone, disappeared altogether. The situation he left under...he just lost it. Wacko. Goodbye. That's all she wrote."

Walter hadn't heard anything juicy about his predecessor's departure—only the good times—but he was chilled and confused about just what

Al was saying. I'm drunk, he thought. Cancer? It sounded like a malignant condition, a mysterious situation, some kind of danger. Al was gripping his shoulders painfully, with what must have been all his might, and he pulled Walter's face up to his.

"What was the matter with him?" Walter said.

Al yanked their faces together and gave Walter a wet smack square on the lips, then jumped back, turned his hat around, flared his eyes and did the siren. "He reenlisted! Woohoo, hoo hoo! Get it! The crazy bastard! Re-upped. Shipped-over. They should make me the morale petty officer, the retention petty officer. It was my fault! I take full responsibility!"

Walter managed not to react, other than to wipe his mouth. Al seemed very happy with himself. Walter would have hated him if he didn't think it would give great satisfaction. No, he could take it, could go along with a joke too, just absorb it and not give Al the pleasure of what he expected, pretend to like it. Walter blew a lazy plume of smoke out of the corner of his mouth. "Yeah, everybody's crazy but you."

"*Au contraire mon* polar bear." He was still excited and pleased with the latest fulminations in his thinking, animated. "You don't listen. Everyone is crazy but *you*. Makes me afeard for your immortal soul. We're all living in the is and *now*; you're living in the way things should be. You're not good, but what's worse in you think you are. You do like I do but you think you're gooder. And you're smart. And nobody cares. And there's no justice anywhere. And there's no shape to anything. And there's no reason for anything. And we're all gonna die. And it's gonna be worst, worst, worst for you, my Walter." He put his head down on the counter.

Walter was beginning to think that they had gotten to Fred after all, and the terrain was hazy but menacing in a dreamlike way, the kind of recurring dream where as soon as you realize you've had it before, everything metamorphoses to new configurations and fills with green shades that you've never seen before but that your mind, that ocean, somehow conceived. A subterranean world, or sub aqueous, with vision smeary around the edges as when you've been too long in a chlorine pool; reduced now to a fishbowl of Al's making, his blue eye looking in, magnified to horizon-size through the mediating glass and water, his words blowing phantoms into the near murk; and you can't run away or wake up. You can only *will* the dream to unfold and expand, to take-in and co-opt all, that you may swim through the glass and into the center of the eye—they being constituent of you—at once contained by and containing all.

He did not think he was better. He knew he was, that he was meant for something, because it did all mean something to him. Not good, but better; not holy or superior, but larger. He could see. He read. Understood politics. Saw his role as a policy tool in the military. We are at war, and we are next in the combat zone. We may very well die for this policy. He was raised by thoughtful, literate people. His father taught him the virtues of manhood. He could be reclaimed.

Al had talked of Walter's string of whores in the Philippines as though they were a sticky roach motel he'd personally set in front of him. He thought the story of Johnny's place was great fun, and that Walter deserved the mind game that Mallory, Hasty, and the dealers had played on him, as though they were all in cahoots. Paz/Vivien was a corker—he wanted to meet her.

To Al, a yankee broadcast system or a ship-shore circuit was just that, though he could set it up and run it as though it sprang from his blood. To Walter it was always something *more*. To him it was the thrill of pulling off a miracle, that such a thing could be accomplished in the world with his own hand: connection, real concrete connection in black and white type, in the sound of a voice miles away converted into mechanical, then electrical energy, encoded and decoded and finally and absolutely connecting. It was him spinning into the atmosphere on high-frequency electromagnetic waves, him marking and spacing through black and red patch panels, him vibrating phone diaphragms, amplifying through speakers, staining rolls of teletype paper at the other end of the network. So to Al it made him a weakling; to him it was inner strength, reserve, the part no one could fill-in or program, the thing that allowed him to tell himself that he too was *more*, and thus was not what he appeared to be, was excused from his actions. He was better, though he had to conform to the conventions of his time and place. Besides, he was gathering experience. Accumulating life until...until he didn't know what...until the big pay-off.

"What makes you think it'll be worse for me?" he asked.

Al beamed at him, almost cross-eyed, and gave his hat another turn. "I know where you're coming from, Walter. I'm a convert."

Clowns

Inside the orange-curtained cocoon of his rack, Walter could feel the bustle of the berthing compartment as it roused itself for another day's work, and he snuggled deeper into the twilit shafts of his dream-mined pillow, happy now with the compensation of sleeping-in after a night of street walking. The clamor of banging lockers and angry voices was modulated through his ear plugs to a rhythmic bass that pulsed a dance of shadows across his lid-screened eyes, insinuating a fuzzy but arresting choreography at the teetering brink of sleep. As muster drew near the dancers slowly faded from the periphery of his attention with a playful diminuendo as he floated back toward deep, downy oblivion and they floated up toward work. Two jarring voices trumpeted loudly nearby, and he was flying back toward the surface. "No!" he shouted up the shaft from inside his pillow. There was a lashing trespass of yellow light all around as he heard his curtain pulled back. Without, his eyes scrunched, and his hands went over them; within, he tried desperately to scrabble back down the shaft.

"Go ahead, ask him. He's up," one of the trumpets by his ear announced.

"No!" he shouted. "Close the curtain! Get out! Help!"

"I think he's awake," it blared. "I saw him move. Do you think he's awake?"

"I dunno," the second trumpet said. "Hey Walter. Hey Schmerz. You awake? I wanna show you something. I need your advice, man."

It poked his shoulder. He heard himself grunt.

"Ugh?" said the first one in a short, guttural note. "White man say ugh? *How.* Go Ahead, Stone, ask him."

"Hey Schmerz," number two said, "I need advice. You're the law."

Walter's eyelids parted and two ugly heads emerged through the gluey membrane of sleep—The Stone and Raynor, an operations specialist, one of The Stone's frequently busted seaman recruit lowlife sidekicks. Raynor had a large, round head with a mop of brown, triangular slivered strands matted down in front, pretty brown eyes, sparkling teeth and baby skin, kind of a cross between Peter Lorre and mom's apple pie.

"I hate you," Walter said.

"Hey Schmerz," The Stone said, "you're the law, right?"
"What the hell are you shooting your mouth off about?"
"I need your help, man. I wanna show you something."

The week before, shortly after serving the fine and restriction meted out at captain's mast for the marijuana leaf tattoo and right upon Walter's return, it was The Stone's birthday. He had the duty and couldn't leave the ship, so to celebrate, after standing his watch, he and Raynor snuck a couple of bottles of cold duck and a couple of joints into the signal shack. Nate Tatum, the lead signalman, found them, of course, after they missed evening muster. Walter saw the pictures—they took turns shooting each other—legs sprawled straight out on the deck, now a bottle to the mouth, now a joint, wearing black raincoats buttoned to the neck with the collars flipped up, aviator sunglasses and paper dunce caps with jangles of crooked, color-coded electric wires stapled to the tops of the cones, streaking up and out in all directions like streamers coughed from volcanoes. Quite creative party outfits. They'd just smiled at Nate when he found them there in their spaceman outfits and the Polaroids on the deck. "We're having a party," they'd said. "What are friends for?" Walter didn't think it was funny.

"Yeah Walter, you're the law, right? 'Cause I need your help, man," The Stone said.

He pulled the plugs out of his ears. Raynor was grinning at him so big that he wanted to hit him, a smile as big as one of those entire screen-sized TV ad actor's after he's told you how happy he is with his new, improved, advance formula, creamier, heartier, nutritious, fiber-filled, fast-acting, doctor recommended smile, government approved, cherry flavored, denture friendly, gentler to your system candy-breath-freshener-laxative smile, now too in mint tablets with the easy to open package; one of those pushy smiles; a big, fat, maniacal, belligerent because robotic, fuck-you-where-you-live smile. He tilted his looming, white-toothed, wide-eyed, greasy-spikes-of-brown-hair-matted-to-his-round-white-forehead smile to one side and belched. "Ugh," he said, "how," and chuckled, his shoulders jiggling self-consciously as though he thought it looked cute, his breath filling Walter's air space with the smell of salami cud.

Walter thrashed at him, trying to free his arms from under the blanket to slap him away. "Raynor, you punk! You butt-fucking juvenile delinquent, get the hell away from me! I'll kill you!"

Raynor jumped back, chuckling, against the bulkhead near Walter's feet. The Stone stepped in. "C'mon Walter, man, cool it. I need to talk to you. You're the law, right?"

Walter started up to get at Raynor, hit his head on the rack above him and leaned back down on his elbow. "I swear to god, I hate this place so fucking much. What are you doing? What do you idiots want? Jesus, I'm a fleet walker, not a fucking sea lawyer. If you want bad advice why don't you talk to one of your buddies. Talk to Turner. I've been up listening to his crazy ideas all night. Now let me get some fucking sleep!"

"I heard that," Al yelled from the recesses of the compartment. "This man has been to Fred. He speaks to you from the belly of the rack monster."

"What are you two clowns up to now?" Walter said to The Stone. Raynor chuckled again. He had his head over Walter's feet, sniffing at his toes like a dog. Walter kicked at him and tried to roll out of bed and grab him at the same time, but he slipped by and around The Stone, and hustled out and up the ladder, laughing, with Walter cursing and clutching at his heels. "I'm gonna kill that fucking little bastard!" he yelled, shaking the aluminum ladder.

"Temper, temper," Al said from his corner. "I need my beauty rest."

Walter rattled the ladder again.

"Shut up!"

"You shut up!"

"C'mon you guys," The Stone said. "C'mon Schmerz, I need to talk to you about this."

"You better get to muster, boy, or you're gonna be in deep kimchee."

"Fuck muster. I ain't never gettin' off this boat till they throw me off anyway. What are they gonna do to me that they ain't already done? That's what I need to talk to you about Schmerz."

"What, Stone, what!"

"Do they think I'm crazy?"

"Who—*they*? They don't think you're crazy, boy, they know it."

"No, I mean, do they think I'm *really* crazy?"

"Oh Christ!"

"Well look at these." He showed Walter the Polaroids of him and Raynor at their signal shack party.

"I saw those already. That may make you an idiot and it may make you a security risk with drug and alcohol related problems, but it does not make you crazy. You try too hard, Stone. Ever hear of *Catch-22*?"

"Well, what if I was gay?"

"Are you?"

"Well, what if they was to think I was a faggot?" He gave Walter a sly smile. "What if I had proof?" He held up the hand with the Polaroids.

"Let me see." The picture was shot close to his face, most of which was whited out by the flash. It was a profile with his mouth locked around what was clearly a large, plastic dildo pointing down at an absurdly unanatomical angle. You could almost hear the prankish, phallus-muffled laugh in the spark in his eye. You could actually see a piece of finger holding it in the upper right-hand corner.

"Who took the picture?"

"Blinkman."

"I suppose that's Raynor holding it? His toy?"

Liberty Call

"You could tell?"

"Well, you're certainly perverts, but amateurs. This picture sucks. Why don't you guys just get it on for real? Or, okay, show the Captain this—maybe it is sick enough. Because nobody would believe you, that's why. You made a joke out of yourself. You've already climbed into everybody's rack in the compartment and they don't believe you're a faggot. They don't think you're funny and they don't think you're queer—just an asshole, you and your buddy Raynor. You could blow each other in front of the whole crew, and they wouldn't believe you. It wouldn't be real. It would be like one of those shows at Tampopos, just doing something unreal for amusement, shooting blanks.

"Your chief and division officer and department officer and XO and captain wouldn't believe it, anyway. But they'd be mad, boy, and they'd get you for it. You'd never get your ass out of here. And you better hope no one else believed it or they *would* be taking you out of here—in a body bag. You remember that poor slob Rivens from supply? They couldn't put that guy anywhere, clobbered him wherever he slept, and he never bothered anybody, probably never even hit on anybody, just a little too girlish. When they finally got him out of here the Captain blamed *him* for being a disruption to the crew—I know because I'm the one that cut his orders to Treasure Island. No one gets what they want. Why don't you just learn to be a sailor. You're not even a good joke."

The smile left The Stone's face and he seemed to really be reflecting on these matters, and he looked hurt, and Walter felt bad, because the truth is that The Stone was the most confused person he knew, and he liked Walter, and Walter cared. But he was going too far—and was going to bring more trouble on himself than he could understand. He was so open to the utter possibility of everything, while the Navy was the narrowest existence he could have walked into with his wide blue eyes, besides jail.

He never said so, but Walter felt that it was a tacit understanding between them—one for which The Stone held no grudge, for which his silence served to bond them more deeply by virtue of its exclusivity of everything outside them, including talk—that it was somehow Walter's fault that he was on restriction and always in trouble, that Walter's failure as a friend and superior contributed directly to his increasing desperation and troubles. He looked up to Walter and turned always to him. He was showing him something—how far he could go, how willing he was in all things—and maybe there was a touch of martyr in him, and certainly some showoff, and always the child; but there was also always in it the game of dare, and Walter wasn't sure if he was expected to try to stop him before the next stunt, but he was sure that he was somehow supposed to catch The Stone before the arc of his gravity-defying ballistics finally ended in the cold, hard ground. There was a special acid in his stomach designed for these thoughts.

The danger lay in exposing your bloody feathers to a treacherous pecking order that could single you out and tear you apart in a random onslaught of hate. The Stone was oblivious to the structure of things, flying frantically about like a bird that comes down the chimney and flutters against the duplicitous windows, or else he flew fast and linear until he crashed into the pane glass sliding patio doors with the flower decals that are put on as a reminder, a pretty warning that everyone else noticed. Either way, he was on the wrong side, and he'd just keep picking himself up and going into the glass.

He perked up again. "Okay, okay, Walter, one last idea and then I won't bother you anymore. Cool?" He held up another Polaroid. "What do you think?"

In this picture he was wearing a black motorcycle jacket, a watch cap pulled down to his eyes, and aviator sunglasses. His smile was scrunched up, showing his teeth, with his lips pulled tight against them, and premature crow's feet around his eyes.

"What am I supposed to think?"

"Can you tell I'm not a Jap national?"

"I can't tell what you're supposed to be."

"Good. But seriously, can you tell I'm not a Jap? You can't tell I'm not one, right? You just said so, so I could be one, right Schmerz?"

"What are you getting at?"

"Going native." He was smiling again as though this was his ace in the hole, the one he'd really been waiting to spring on Walter all along, the final experiment, the culmination of all his creative efforts and setbacks. His triumph. Walter still didn't know if he was supposed to try to dissuade him, or if his being apprised of the plan somehow made it safe to go forward.

"Clever," he said.

"Get it? You can't tell I'm not Japanese." He was so excited he was almost laughing. Simple yet brilliant.

"Native. As in Japanese, right? As in, the Japanese are some kind of natives. Is that it? Is that your idea? Clever."

He nodded in agreement that it was a clever idea. "See the picture? See the picture? It could be anyone. You can't tell it's me."

"It could be anyone that looks like you wearing a leather jacket, watch cap and sunglasses."

"That's right. I'm short like a JN, though they're not as short as they used to be, not really all that short 'cause I've seen lots of 'em that are taller than me, and I'm tan. I mean, they're not really yellow, they're more like… tan, light brown. We call them yellow but they're not really yellow. Like black people. We call them black but they're not really black but brown, and all different kinds of brown. And I can dye my hair black, or keep it like this."

Walter stared at his naked head and had a vision of it careening vertiginously among a welter of dark native skulls like an escaped pinball, then it jerked up into the atmosphere like a loosed helium balloon, and with a wave of nausea he felt that he was the one who let it go, but at the same time it was also he who was unhinged and out of control, that is, Walter was The Stone,

61

only knowing what he knew and being in some way responsible. The nausea of empathy rose and knotted to a hard ball in his chest, and he felt panicked, as though he was damaged, and though he couldn't gauge the extent, he knew the hurt was irreparable, that he was losing something that he would never, ever have a chance of reclaiming. Having let things slip too far, he was now helpless, and he was angry at The Stone for making him feel that way, so angry that he wanted to smash him. The thing was not to let him see it. "Uh huh," he said, deadpan. "And what are you going to do when you have to take this disguise off?"

"I can go to the city, where all the people are...all those people. Go to Tokyo, or further. There's lots of cities to hide in. Millions of people where they can't find you. What the fuck is one person? I'll get a girlfriend and a place to stay and a job and just mix in till they forget about me."

It was cold anger now. That's what he usually wound up offering the boy, and now that he was clearly out of reach Walter knew that nothing he said would connect. He knew that his words could not save him. They could not change the past; they could not prevent whatever he was going to do; they could no more make him see his heart than they could remove the green stain from the middle of his forehead. Walter wouldn't show him his eyes. "Do you know what it is to have an objective sense of yourself?"

"No," he said, curious for an answer.

"They will find you and you will go to jail. You will not mix in and they will find you and you will go to jail. You are not Japanese and you cannot be. They hate you. The Japanese hate everyone. You are just a crazy sailor from Texas. Do you want to go to jail?"

His face collapsed into hurt disappointment and he slowly, deliberately shuffled the pictures into a uniform square, then crouched down by his locker to put them away, and said quietly, "Thanks Schmerz. Thanks friend." As he walked up the ladder he turned back and said, "I'm leaving. I'm gone. Good riddance to all this, and good riddance to you, motherfucker." Then his face changed, softened but serious. "I want to warn you about something, Schmerz. People don't like it that you come from the base library with all those books."

Walter had been accosted on the street once, his arms full of novels, by a large fireman, who said, "What the fuck you doing at the library, radioman?" He was joined by other firemen, and they followed him silently all the way back to the ship. Walter was sure he'd be jumped.

"Do you read books, Schmerz?"

"Everyone reads books, Stone."

"Not here they don't."

"A great American writer once said, 'a frigate was my Harvard.'"

Stone softened further, and his eyes dropped. "Can I ask you something Walter? Honestly, do you ever think about me?"

Walter hesitated a beat, and replied, "Honestly Stone, I try never to think of you."

The Devil Inside

It was still early and relatively quiet, so they took a break in advance and snuck into the vacant shore patrol shack to rest their dogs and have a smoke. Al was in the back making a head call and Walter sat with his feet up on the sill, smoking a cigarette and watching the crowd through the plexiglass window by the entrance of the Alliance Club. A steady mix of GI's and locals were pouring in for Saturday night entertainment, mostly to the disco, but also the hall with the live country music, the two lounges, three restaurants and one video arcade that were all housed within the Alliance's sprawl.

Then Walter saw him, the most conspicuous fish in the stream, whom he had feared—and now wished—was as far gone as two days could take him, that he was long enough out of his hair and into someone else's that he could already afford himself the luxury of getting fretful and sentimental about him, of missing him. "Ah shit!" he said out loud as he sat up, knocked on the window, and quickly pulled the offending hand back like a pet that had leapt out of his lap. There he was in his silly black disguise like some comic ninja biker, knit watch cap on a warm evening, sunglasses in the dark, an All Points Bulletin out for him, and he hadn't gotten any farther than across the street. Walter knocked on the window again, and again immediately regretted it, not knowing what he was going to do with him, hoping Stone wouldn't notice him. He did, and he smiled and waved, glad to see Walter, as though it was any night on liberty. Walter motioned for him to come around to the side door, and he stepped right into the shore patrol shack.

"Hey Schmerz," he said. "Got the duty, huh? How ya been?"

Walter was amazed. He almost said "fine." "Take off that stupid fucking hat and glasses."

He doffed the cap and managed to once again put Walter on edge with that ominous bald head with the spiny green hand in the middle, but he seemed particularly happy with the affect of the glasses, which made him look bug-like and soulless when he talked from behind them.

"Quit hiding behind those glasses and let me see your eyes," Walter said.

"S'matter Schmerz? You don't like my shades? Did ya miss me? I missed you. So, you working all alone tonight?" He seemed to look around the room, and Walter thought The Stone must have caught him glancing at the bathroom door as he wondered what the hell Al was doing in there, because The Stone eased himself back toward the door to the shack; but Walter slid in front of it and stood there with his hands on his hips in a purposeful, macho pose, acting the shore patrol part to disguise his nervousness and to stall until he figured what to do, or better, until someone—Al, the SP supervisor, anyone—came along and set the situation in its proper motion toward official, controlled resolution, one in which he was entirely free of responsibility.

"Stone," he said, "don't you know everybody's looking for you? Where you been? The SP's got your description and they're supposed to take you back. Boy, I don't believe you!"

Stone stopped smiling and looked nervously around. "Oh wow. Thanks, man. Thanks Walter. I gotta get outta here. This is really bad news, this place. Bad shit." He patted Walter on the shoulder. "I really appreciate this."

"Jumping ship, Stone. Unauthorized Absence. Didn't you know? You are UA, understand?"

"Yeah, I really do. I just shimmied down a ratline and was gone like a shot—into the night, ya know? They don't care. So what's the difference? Look, you're my only friend in this place and that's great. The guys on the ship? Raynor, Blinkman and them? I been thinkin'. They're just fucked up, man. They're just kids. But I better scoot, ya know? There's this girl. She's gonna teach me Japanese crafts and stuff, go native. Dye my skin and grow black hair. I wanted to be a radioman like you. If people knew the things that you know the world would be a better place."

"Why?" Walter said. "Why are you here? You can't, you know. You really did want to get caught, didn't you?"

"Unh ah. No way man. You don't understand. Like I said, I gotta meet this girl here tonight. Then I'm history. You'll see, Schmerz."

"Stone. Stone," he said, "you can't go native."

"God, don't do this to me, man."

"Just do your time and give it a try. Fresh start. I'll put in a good word for you. I'm your friend, man. Stick with me and I'll make a sailor of you. Just give it another try. You can *do* it." Walter tried to sound like a seasoned petty officer, but the tightness in his throat stretched his voice trill; he tried to sound authoritative but felt like he was begging.

Stone took off his glasses and bent his bullet head. "Move Schmerz. I like you. Please, man, I'm askin'. I don't want to hurt you."

Walter put his hands up like fenders, praying he would suddenly be reasonable, praying someone would show up and bring the curtain down on the scene—where was Al?—and he was frightened by this wild little creature whose veins he could clearly see tapping their weird and frantic messages along his exposed temples.

"I can't let you go, Stone. I can't."

The Stone might have gotten by if he'd have taken a shot at Walter's head or groin, tried to knock him out of commission in some way, but he merely tried to run right through him, reaching for the door beyond him, and Walter just wrapped his arms and hung on in a kind of passive tackle, hanging on as the fugitive squawked and wriggled forward, dragging Walter a bit as he slid to his man's knees and then to his feet where he locked his arms as The Stone bucked and tumbled to the floor. Walter no sooner screamed "Alvin!" than Al was above them, kicked at The Stone's back and sides and cursing at him hatefully; then he went to work with his baton.

Walter didn't remember the scene in terms of real time; it was an eternal action, something that was always a part of them and will be always a part of them—the past—which, though it makes you, is sealed off like a scene in a paperweight, fixed, visible, but untouchable even to yourself except for the smooth, hard glass that coldly preserves the permanent picture. We may perceive it differently from time to time, we may each attribute different significances to our individual roles in the scene, but there we are locked together in the sealed moment of the weight. All there was in that world of exposed embalmed moment was Walter hanging onto The Stone's fallen legs while Al bashed his head with the nightstick. Walter held on for life, finally pounding at his sides and shouting, "Get him! Get him!" knowing only the twisting, bucking legs and gritty floor while The Stone screamed "Stop! Stop! Stop!" his blood staining them all.

When they brought him back in everyone asked why and looked at Walter as though he'd done something wrong. Al told Walter he just couldn't understand him sometimes. The officers grinned dubiously and shook their heads. The crew cut him both ways, wondering what kind of man would take down a friend like that, and what kind of shipmate would return such an albatross. He saw it now: they probably painted a sign on that ratline saying, "this way Stone" and turned their collective back while he climbed down. Way to go, Petty Officer Schmerz, you jerk.

On Walter's first visit to the hospital The Stone wouldn't talk to him other than to say, "Die. I'm going to get you for this." He was pretty grim looking, with his head swathed in bandages, his face all cross-stitched and swollen a purplish-green like a Hollywood zombie, and his leg is a cast—Walter had fractured his knee with his tackling technique; that is, the floor broke it when he fell with Walter's arms around him. Just a hairline fracture, though.

A few days later, he got up the nerve to try again. The Stone was propped up in his hospital bed, a Bible on his lap and Japanese cartoons on the overhead TV. His nose was scabbed over. Stitches bristled from his scalp like course black hairs among the patches of stubbly blond that was growing out, and the roiling purple and green of his face had settled to a muddied yellow. His eyes were crouched to slits between the swells of his brows and cheekbones that slanted to meet one another. He looked at Walter with an expression that was neither greeting nor rebuff, neither smiling nor angry. Walter chose to read it as amiability muted by pain.

"What up, Doc?"

"I'm the patient. You hurt me. I hurt."

"I was talking to the duck. Is this how you're learning Japanese? Cartoons?"

"I said it hurts."

"Gonna talk cartoon when you go native?"

"You hurt me."

"Here's something to augment your reading," Walter said, handing him a bunch of skin magazines and a copy of *Billy Budd* that Al had leant him.

"Hey." He perked up. "A real book. This is the kind of stuff you read, right? You get this stuff? I don't think I can get this stuff. I don't read much. Just this, nowadays." He put his hand on the Bible next to him.

"It's a sea story—that's something you probably know a little about. The writing's kind of hard because it's old fashioned, maybe, but it's just an old-timey sea story. You can read it. It's about a handsome sailor, like you."

The Stone opened it and flipped a few pages, then began reading aloud at the top of a chapter, his forefinger moving under the words as he read them, monotonously, awkwardly, one syllable at a time: "Life in the foretop well agreed with Billy Budd. There, when not actually engaged in the yards yet higher aloft, the topmen, who as such had been picked out for youth and activity, constituted an aerial club lounging at ease against the smaller stun'sails rolled up into cushions, spinning yarns like lazy gods, and frequently amused with what was going on in the busy world of the decks below.

I guess so," he said, as he closed the book and let it drop to the floor beside the bed. "Whatever that means. A lot of words. I guess it helps if you know what they're talkin' about." He shuffled the magazines and gave a perfunctory glance to each cover. "I'm mostly readin' the Bible now."

"Well, I never took you for a Bible thumper. This a new hobby?"

"It ain't a hobby," he said, sinking deeper into the bed, his puffy face gone fat with his chin pressed against his chest. What Walter had thought might be amiability was his attempt at looking indifferent, and that had quickly given way to his sullen complaint and hurtful pout. For the first time Walter saw him plainly and unguardedly sad. Now he wasn't speaking in accusation so much as resignation, statement of pathetic fact, as though the thing he'd been running from all his life was waiting at the end of the road with open arms, a cosmic "gotcha," an all-embracing "told you so."

"My momma made me read it and I went to Sunday school too. It's The Word. This priest come by and give it to me even though I ain't a Catholic. All you have to do is be interested in the truth, The Word. There's a group that meets in the chapel here. Might go."

"Lots of good stories in it," Walter offered.

"Stories," he spat, getting worked up. "It's *The Word*. It don't have to be hard to read to be good. Truth is easy when you turn to God. I don't know why you have to be mean to me, talkin' 'bout hobbies. I used to think you knew something, Schmerz, like I could talk to you, but you were just foolin' around with me, right? 'You're a handsome sailor.' Shit. Okay for your stories. But you can't take The Word away from me. All the answers, man. All the answers."

"That's better," Walter said, feeling mean, too. "Now you sound like the convert. I suppose you're born again?" He saw his mistake in Stones eyes. "I'm sorry. Would you like me to read it with you, or talk about it? I wonder about god a lot."

"Sure. Make fun if you want. I always been a Christian. I don't even know what you're doin' here. You should try being born again. It ain't easy, you know. *That* hurts, too. Ask your mama."

Listen, if you get right and stay on the Outland, I will always have your back. I'll even cover your back if I see you going the wrong way."

"I tell ya, Schmerz, I got plenty of time to think and figure and read all I need to read, just me and the rack and The Book. And the tiles on the ceiling. All day and all night. Know why, Schmerz? 'Cause it fuckin' hurts! My leg hurts and my ribs hurt and my head hurts all over. Even when they give me drugs I don't sleep. Just think about things and find all the answers in the Bible. Pain's a motherfucker, man. It makes me think about you, too. Yeah, I think about you. Call me a convert if you want. Make fun if you want."

"It's called kidding," Walter said. "It's what we do. I'm sorry about everything. You want to talk to me, you can still talk to me. Here I am. I'm not the one that shaved your head or made you go UA, for god's sake. I thought you might like something to read so I brought you a book. I'm sorry I brought you this stuff, okay? I didn't expect you to lay this trip on me." Why should Walter have to take on The Stone's guilt?

"Yeah, so here you are, alright." His glassy eyes peered at Walter from behind their swollen sockets. "If that's what you think I'm talkin' about."

Walter knew what he was talking about and wanted to take it all back and start over. He wanted to be the person he should have been for him, the one The Stone saw in him and always turned to. He placed his hand on the wounded man's shoulder. "Look, I'm really sorry," he said again, hoping that Stone understood all the ways a person can be sorry.

"I might forgive you."

His hand jumped off. "Forgive me for what?"

"What you did to me."

"The fuck I did!"

"Hey Schmerz," he said, "I got a headache, okay? You might as well go now."

Liberty Call

"I didn't mean offend you. How can I explain anything? You always get me so pissed off, you little fuck. I'll come back when we're both in a better mood."

"Do what you gotta do. I'll be out of here by then." He twisted his torso so that he faced the wall, his back to Walter, and nestled gingerly into his pillow. "Don't forget your book and things. I got all I need right here. My thoughts, my plans, my god."

That was the last time they talked until The Stone saw the Devil. It was after Al and Walter had returned to the division from their shore patrol assignment and the ship became a viable seagoing unit again. Walter got his sea legs and qualification as an underway watch supervisor during the exhaustive see trials and systems tests and finally, the big exam—Refresher Training—in preparation for the great beyond, Gonzo Station, where they would do whatever it was they were supposed be doing to the Iranians—they were still expecting a shooting war, or at least another hostage rescue attempt after the last fiasco.

The Stone wasn't exactly a hermit, but he kept pretty much to himself and always had a straight face whenever Walter caught sight of him. He'd see him sometimes, eating quietly in the mess decks or carrying buckets from the paint locker or watching Saturday afternoon TV in the darkness of the crew's lounge. He'd moved to first division's berthing compartment in the fo'c'sle. He didn't bother anybody anymore and no one seemed to bother him, in part, probably, because he was so serious now, keeping his new-found faith and solemn thoughts to himself rather than becoming a ship's evangelist. But no one bothered *with* him either; he was just another sick sailor infected with religion. No one took him seriously, but no one went out of the way to pester him. That was his status with the crew, a kind of isolated limbo. He went to his Bible meetings on base, and his services on Sunday, and afterwards always seemed to carry back a heavier load than the one he took with him, grimly accepting his burden, trying so hard. His buddies abandoned him, and Al observed that the pity of religion was that it didn't allow for a sense of humor. Alcoholics and nuts were always more fun before they got saved. His prescription for Stone was that Walter take him out and get him snot-slinging drunk and dose him with iniquity and irreverence before sainthood sanitized him, before he was born again in the bright, cold fires of remote, stellified love, before he petrified into an inert image of what should be rather than bathing in the ferment of what is.

But he wouldn't talk to Walter at all, wouldn't even look at him. It was like playing that old kids' game, poof, you're out of my world. The Devil brought an end to the situation and brought The Stone back to Walter.

He waved from across the enlisted club restaurant, rushed forward and took a seat at Walter's table in the bar. He had let his hair grow back out and thin blond sprigs hung over the top of his bandana, and except for that bandana and the emblem it covered, he was looking quite clean cut—not a bad looking kid when he was cleaned up. But his face was thinner and drawn, tired looking; until lately he had always fed on motion and misdirected energy and manic bursts of capricious fancy. Now his flight across the room and his frenetic fluttering about the table as he negotiated the chair opposite Walter was familiar and heartening. He hunched forward, his eyes wild with whatever seemed to spook him and sent him on this urgent mission. Walter was glad to see him crazed again, though his earnestness now served the call of Christ more so than the rest of the ship.

"What do you know," Walter said, "enemies. Have a seat, Stone. How's the weather? Think there's a chance of rain?"

"Hey Schmerz man, I gotta talk to you." His eyes were glassy and red.

"Well willy-nilly and pell-mell. I thought you gave up drinking and other such sinfulness, like talking to me. Come to have it out once and for all?"

He leaned so far forward that Walter pictured his toes trying to hold him to the floor while he reached forward. Walter could smell the booze on his breath. "Yeah, well I just was over to the Knockoff Room talkin' to Turner 'cause I wanted to find out some things about you before…until… well I was mad and things been fucked up between us but I figured I was in my rights for what you did to me. And we was gonna, well like you said for once and all. Never mind that now. Damn Schmerz! I was over to the Knockoff Room talkin' to Turner about you. You know, when in Rome. Know your enemy. So I had a couple of beers with him to find out what gives with you guys, why you just wanna fuck me over like that, and I found out a lot from him, too much, more than I wanted to know." His eyes widened, full with fear. "I saw into him, like, right into him, Walter. I saw his heart, and it's evil. But I learned some things from him too; he made me see some things truly. First of all—"

"Okay, relax a second. I think you're drunk. Just take it easy. So you were coming to settle the score?"

"Forget that. First of all, I forgive you."

"Oh Jesus. Here we go again."

"Yes, Jesus, Walter. He loves you. So do I. I know you're sorry about what happened. I was mad at you for a long time, but I can see clearly now. I learned the power of forgiveness. I thought that maybe you were evil—what you did to me. But you weren't evil, only doing your duty—that's important. It's important to do your duty, to do what's right as you see it. That's how I am. I see clearly now. I see duty and forgiveness and good and evil. That's what I have to warn you about.

"I saw the evil in Turner's heart; he even told me everything. He hates you, Walter. He told me you were sorry. He said you're weak, and that you love me. He hates you for that. But love isn't weakness; love is strength.

It's the power of forgiveness and goodness and duty. It has all the answers. It's god. If god is love, then the devil must be hate."

"Nice Symmetry," Walter said. He could see the whole conversation in his mind—pure Turner. "Okay, Stone, hold that thought. Have you eaten anything? Want to order some food? How long you been drinking?"

"I been drinkin' with Turner. Thought I could talk to him. Get some answers from him. He starts telling me how you're a weakling 'cause you felt sorry for what you did, with this nasty look on his face, this evil look. Then he starts sayin' the meanest things to me, about what a fucked up piece of shit I am and how everyone hates me. How I'm not good enough for the ship or the Nav. And you know how stupid I am. I just keep hangin' out with him, tryin' to convince him I'm a good guy and that I changed, even though I saw into his heart and saw how he hated everything that's good.

"Then I, like, start to see it in his face, like it's climbin' into his eyes and his face from the inside—that nasty look. It was... *hideous*. And he's not Turner like you know him anymore, not just a guy at all. I can't describe it, like he turns into this fuckin' *hideous* voodoo mask or somethin'. His eyes don't blink, they just sort of glow at me, burn white hot. I mean, they fuckin' hurt me, man. And there's this smile that's sort of glowing, too, like it follows you around, laughin' at you and gnawin' at you with pointy white teeth and tryin' to get inside. And then I realized who I was talkin' to. I'm scared. It's still with me, like he said, followin' me around. His face turnin' inside out like that. An evil miracle. Bad dreams come true, Walter, nightmares. I realized who I was talkin' to."

And this was the man who had been playing at crazy to get released. Maybe he had his mind pounded into the pavement one too many times. Walter was getting irritated with Al. He could picture the silly face that had spooked Stone's drunken, deluded, overtired eyes. "Is he still over there?"

"Don't go over there. I'm afraid. He said he'd follow me."

"Is he there now? Is that where you just came from?"

"Don't go in there. I even asked him. I asked him straight out when I saw that face—'are you the Devil?'—and he said yes and that he was watchin' me and was gonna follow me and get me. Schmerz, the first thing is, I forgive you. And I'm sorry, too. Now you gotta help me. You're the only one I trust. You gotta cover my back. Remember, you said you'd do that."

"When's the last time you got any sleep?"

"I ain't slept for days, man. I can't stop my brain; It's goin' a hundred miles an hour."

So this is what a nervous breakdown looks like, Walter thought. Well, Al has his own idea about shock therapy and restoring The Stone's sense of mad disorder. Let chaos blow out the blinding light of god.

"I saw the Devil tonight."

"Come with me."

Al was still there when they walked into the lounge, sitting alone at the bar, watching reruns on TV, laughing in his beer. "Gentlemen," he said. "Seaman Recruit Stone. Haven't seen you in minutes. Petty Officer Schmerz. What are we having? I'm buying."

"Careful," The Stone whispered to Walter.

Walter could play along with Al. "Seaman Recruit Stone, look at Petty Officer Turner and tell me what you see." He looked sheepishly at Al and then back at Walter. "Well, what do you see? Do you see the Devil or do you see Turner?"

"Turner," he said under his breath.

"Ah. Petty Officer Turner, is it true that you told Seaman Recruit Stone that you were going to follow him around, and in some way *get* him?"

Al smiled broadly. "Well, I might have said something about how I couldn't help noticing him, seeing as I have a naturally inquisitive mind, that I watch him, yes, your honor, but I am not a follower of The Stone."

The Stone swallowed. "He said he hated you."

"I object," Al said. "Badgering the witness. I have long been on the record as one who finds you weak and detestable. To say that I hate you is needlessly beating-off a dead horse."

"And you find me weak because...?"

"Truth? You did your job and friend Stone paid and we're all even. You were a baby about it."

"Thank you. Now try apologizing for yourself."

"Fuck you. Hey barkeep, three more, *dozo*."

"You better take the beer, Stone," Walter said. "That's as close as he's gonna get to saying sorry."

"I don't get you guys," he said.

"Okay. Al, what's with all the spooky mind-fuck business? Did you tell our naive friend here, an only child susceptible to the powers of suggestion, that you were the Devil?"

"Oh gee, I didn't know he was an orphan. I didn't put a Judeo-Christian name on it. No, I mean, I may have said I had a heart full of evil and was, like, original sin itself as well as ill-will incarnate, but I never said I was The Great Satan."

"See Stone," Walter said, "that's Al's way of saying that he did bad and knows it. Now drink your beer to solidify our new-found friendship."

"I don't know," he said, staring at his glass.

"What would you do about it if I was the Devil? What if I said I was The Great Satan? What would you do? Make a citizen's arrest? Then what happens?"

"Alright," Walter said, and grabbed a handful of the front of his shirt. "Do the face."

"What? I know not whereof you speak."

"Do the face." Walter shook him.

"What face?" he said, as his eyes lit up like white bulbs, and a maniacal, dimpled, white-toothed grin cut an upturned semicircle from ear to ear while his skin flushed a glowing red. He froze it like a death's head that bobbed loosely back and forth like a balloon at the end of Walter's hand as he shook the hunk of shirt he was holding. Then he whistled through his teeth and his facial muscles slowly deflated back to his normal, life size, semi-drunken grin. "This face?"

"That the face, Stone?"

"Something like that."

"What did you see, the Devil or Turner?"

"Turner."

"Good. I told you that you could trust me. Now drink your beer."

He drank the beer. "I think I'm getting drunk."

"Good. Now that we're all seeing things about the same way, let's clear the air about a few things. Alvin, what are we going to do with our young misfit?"

"Depends. We could try and make a fit out of him. What size are you, boy? You a size four-oh like Walter Schmerz? You a size lifer-and-a-half, like me? Size thirty years and a wakeup? I think not. Depends on what he wants to do with himself. What you want to be when you grow up?"

"I just wanted to have fun," he said. "Every time I try to have fun I get kicked in the guts. Everybody hates me."

"People *are* funny," Al said.

"We're your friends now," Walter said.

He looked up from his beer and the light of happy incredulity at good fortune brazened its way out of his eyes. "Really?"

"It may be he simply lacks know-how," Walter said.

"No," Al said. "He's a preacher. Should have heard him come in here preaching at me before. Preachers know everything."

"I ain't no preacher. I'm just lookin' for the answers same as everybody else. It's hard when even your own people who you trust take you down. It hurts, makes me wanna be mean right back at you. And my momma always said sooner or later I'd find the answers in the Bible. I never got too far from that."

"Uh uh ah." Al wagged a finger at him. "We drank to solidarity. None of that. Now, I got an idea. How'd you like to be a sailor for real this time? I bet we could make the real thing out of you. You got a sense of mission. A man with a purpose like yours would make a fine…career counselor. That's it. What do ya think, Petty Officer Schmerz?"

Walter was happy. He liked this game. He was getting good at it. As he saw it, Stone had given piety his best shot, and it had been the worst medicine for him. They had something better to offer, admittance as an insider to their happy club, and the appeal was better than anything god had shown him. They were freeing him from his momma's fate and the consternation of the Good Book. He jumped that ship as soon as he had the chance, once more down the ratline in search of a world to lose himself in. He gave it all his energy and fervor, but nothing seemed to hold him for long. This way there was no more evil to worry about. He must have been an unhappy little deck ape for some time.

"Yeah," he said. "That's what I was talking about before. Duty. I understand about that now. Like you guys were just doin' your duty. I wanna be like that. I don't wanna be no fuck-up. I can do that. Like I was tellin' Turner before, but he wouldn't listen. I wouldn't be mad if someone'd just explain. But you guys never explain nothin'. I can fight, too, if we have to. That's not against the Bible. But the Bible, it explains so much that I stay up nights tryin' to keep it all in my brain."

"Converts," Walter said. "Stone, the Bible says anything you want it to say. That's the magic of it. You can find anything you're looking for in it, no matter what. So you've always got that. But as Al can tell you, there's only one thing to being a good sailor, and that's the thing itself, or words to that affect. I suggest you channel all your energies into that. Now, here, drink this shot down."

He gagged it down and grimaced, then hiccupped a splashful back into his hand and wiped it on his pants leg. "Uh oh. That's not sittin' right. Oh boy. I don't think I feel so good. Didn't drink for months."

"Good," Walter said. "Now go puke out all that nonsense about devils and answers and tomorrow you'll wake up with a nice cleansing headache. Then we can start converting you into a good sailor." He raised his glass. "I give you the future Chief Stone."

"Career Counselor Stone," Al said.

He stood up and teetered. "I better go. Gotta go puke it all outta me. Schmerz says." He threw an arm around Walter's shoulder, pal-fashion. "So you guys are my friends, right? You guys are fuckin' crazy, you know what? But I like you. We're friends, right? Doesn't mean I have to quit the Bible, right? I mean—"

"More than friends," Al said. "We're shipmates."

"Guy's fuckin' crazy," he said, "fuckin' embarrassing. I musta been drunk. Thought he was the Devil. Fuckin' face. Really. Just keep a sharp lookout for this Turner guy." He wobbled out the door muttering, "Embarrassing. Really had me goin'."

"Joiner," Al said.

"Seeker," Walter said.

"Miscreant."

"Rapscallion."

The subject was women. Walter was thinking of Vivien. Her life actually had to be very dull, dark even, and she was probably a dull and dark woman—what could have formed her into anything else? But she had something. So he took a shot and wrote to her, along with a few dollars for stationary and postage, and explained that he would be stopping in the Philippines soon on the way to the Arabian Sea:

> Some mornings at the gold-washed horizonless ache of dawn in the forge of the infant planet you rise on its rolling and indifferent shoulders, empty of what you thought you were, filled, pierced with the impressions of the other, the else in the salt of motion and infinite play of light on elemental existence. The mere possibility of distinction and division blurs in the ecstatic play of water, air, and organism. This is the joy to efface the perceived plane of membrane, entrancing the waking-rare domain where flukes and fins glide through pickled glades and shadowed forest ridges processing brine in the restless-endless hunted-hunter pursuit of discovery, impelled toward inevitability, now aerialists who screech and excrete from their clutches above, ruffled in molecules and glowing with energy. I held one in my hand once, Saint Elmo's Fire from the clouds, which are the purgatives for all the lessons you thought you knew, and taste like all the ones you really wanted. Midday is always a blue bucking furnace breathing a white, boiling fire. Evenings are somber-sonorous tones of eternity conducted by a clear western disk bathed in red ether.
>
> Oh yes, and mission. Radios. I am a radioman. I am the radioman. Radio teletype, radio telephone. Top secret, antennas, transmitters, receivers, patch panels, patch cords, patch you through to Combat, the Bridge, circuits, systems, frequencies—HF, UHF, VHF, satellites, datalinks, NavMacs, Broadcasts, ship-shore, HiComm, HF contingencies, Exercise Beard Iron fast reaction test get on the horn to ComSeventhfleet, Batterup, Batterup this is Overwork Overwork Exercise Beard Iron my tango oscar romeo is one nine two five how copy over...Christ it's time for hotel juliets...we're losing the tone package go to a lower frequency sun should be going down by now. Go to a low boy goddamnit, the boardcast is taking hits, garbled, getting garbage! Not bad timing, two and a half minutes on a Beard Iron and then we lose the whole goddamn broadcast. Schmerz the tone package is gone. Schmerz it's time for HJ's. Schmerz I lost the broadcast. Schmerz bridge wants to talk to the Midway. Schmerz what do I do what do I do. Batterup Batter this is Overwork Overwork.
>
> Dear Vivien,
>
> I am the radioman. I got a private circuit set aside, tuned to your frequency. Called you from the Japan Sea last night but you were sleeping so I tapped into your dreams. Remember: What dreams. Keep me in your dreams. You're dreaming for two, 'cause radioman never sleeps, port and starboard, in and out.
>
> I am a sailor. I am the sailor. Walk on the water. Nothing between my toes and the ocean floor but a mile of water, straight down. How do fish keep

from getting lost? I dropped a sinker and a mile of line off the fantail and caught a mermaid and the mermaid was you. Remember? Ever lure a sailor onto the rocks? Can you sing? You have to sing for me when we get there.

See you soon, Walter.

She responded immediately, cheerfully chiding him for being so impersonal as to type his letter, bringing him up to date on the people there as though he knew them and they were something shared and that he would care:

Work. Money. Mamasan. Girls. Trickery, bitchery. Boredom. Boys. Hope. Yes, dreams. And someplace to go. Clinics. Shopping in Olongapo. Try to get to church on Sundays, sometimes. I pray anyway. Should I pray for you? Matilda's cat had kittens. Judy stole my earrings. Hate her, I scratched her face. Boyfriends. I have many boyfriends who like me are you my boyfriend? One day we went to the beach it was much fun like a holiday. Swimming and sand castles and chicken fights with everybody laughing. Some of the boys got too drunk. Matilda's children and other children played ring around the rosy and the leap frog. I love children do you? Some days are not so fun. Some days I do not feel well. I do not like anything or anyone, any of this—the customers, the girls, my room. I am not complaining, just tired, maybe. Here is my picture of me walking on the beach smiling in the light of day, not for the camera but for the eye of god, who alone could be expected to recognize and love my special beauty in the obscurity of the world, who alone can eternalize the promise and possibility in a shutter's worth of joy with the miracle of memory, an atom of happiness exposed and suspended in film, whose sleight of fate could circulate the image to one equally obscure and inconsequential but receptive and appreciative, the sun tanning my shoulder, the burnt wind blowing fingers of hair across my face and between my lips, my bare stomach and sides snaking in silhouette against the feral blue, my belly button winking, my toes eating up beach in oblivious communion. Do you have any idea what kind of maddening beauty lays waiting to crawl from under the rock of the world and sting the passerby to aching life? Do you think I'm cute? Maybe there is a picture of you I can have?

Dear Walter,

Yes i have dreams. i dream i turn on the radio and it is you. So you see it works. You are not so silly. Am i? i dream i have a baby and the baby is you too. what does this mean? Do you believe is dreams? i dream i live in a big dolls house and everytime i want the furniture change it just change and everytime i want the new cloths and jewels i just get them like Barbie the doll. And we could go anywhere we want anytime we want. And there is snow i never see snow and we make a snowman but inside it is warm and so we have hot showers. Together. i am sorry. Do you think maybe i am bad? And we are next to the citys if we want to go there. i think America must be *a very grate place. When you come to visit me bring me a gift of channel number #5 perfumm so the others will be jelous to prove that you are my boyfriend.*

Your friend, Vivien Cortez."

The subject was women.

"You're thinking with your dick, Walter. You forget that the world is your bearded oyster. All this pretty shit about your romantic evening with this whore. Man, when you came back you were talking about how she scammed you. You know what made it so special? Your dick was hard. She's tugging you around by it."

"There's something to be said for that," Walter said.

"Besides, all this shit's just something that you're making up in your head now to spice your life up. Wonder who she's fucking now…they all write letters, you know. Keep tabs. They figure that if they write to enough guys someone's bound to take serious interest."

"Again, what's so wrong about that? Isn't that what people do? Do you ever think about where we're going? We're very likely to take an Iranian torpedo right up the ass. This antisubmarine warship bullshit. In New London the sub guys laughed at sonar. We're not going to chase subs. We're going to get in the way of torpedoes heading for carriers. You know aluminum melts?"

"So say we make it, we live. So if someone's stupid enough to take 'a girl serious enough to call 'em girlfriend, then maybe if they're extra special lucky, POW, the big payoff, wedding bells and Navy Housing and a permanent meal ticket and a free pass stateside. Oh, and did she get your picture? They all like to swap pictures. What's wrong with that, you ask? They're hookers, my Walter. They're professionals."

"They're just girls, Al, for christsake."

"Well, I don't see why you didn't take on Mimi. She was good enough for Haggard."

"And you and Mallory, too, but what the hell's that got to do with anything?"

"Nothin' loverboy. Maybe I should meet this special lady. Maybe I should take a crack at her."

"Fuck you."

"Indeed. Okay, Walter, tomorrow it's haze gray and underway for the PI at last, and on to the IO and the Iranian wars. Let us not bicker on the eve of such an auspicious occasion. After all, what's a woman between us?"

"A Walt and Al sandwich."

"Ah, the procreant urge of the universe—I read that somewheres. It always stuck, like peanut butter to the roof of the mouth, speaking of sandwiches. Feed your head."

"If the world was peanut butter, we'd be sticking by each other. I heard that somewhere on a Youngblood's album."

"And we are young bloods, Walter. That's what I'm talking about. Women. The subject is women and their pull upon our young and unresisting blood. And blood's got a lot to do with it. Poets used to call sex death. I think the idea was that each time you die a little more, like you only have so many fucks stored up in you. What did I say?—the procreant verge of the uni-hearse? Now that's called poetry?"

"That's fatalism. The procreant purge of the puny verse. Now that's poetry. You got to have alliteration."

"And a little ration goes a long way in a poet of your caliber. Look out girls, he's a pistol, this one, a fully loaded semi-automatic forty five caliber versifier from the ration nation. Gonna mow you down."

"That's a lot of calipers, and I ain't loaded yet, but you got the general measure of the man."

"You know, Walter, speaking of wordplay, in a language other than our own, Paz has been known to mean peace. Are you going to make peace with Paz when there are so many other pieces to be had? You got your pieces of eight, your Reese's Pieces, your hair pieces, your chess pieces, your pieces of pizza, and most importantly your pieces of ass. Are we not men? You got your field pieces and you got your field mieces. Are we men or mieces?"

"I hate those mieces to pieces."

But do find peace with the pieces. Speaking of which, how's the missives? The one in New London?"

"Irene? She hasn't written in years."

Has she written in English? You haven't been here for years, yet. Know what her names means?"

"One-legged Japanese woman?"

"Stale, Walter. Yeah, that's it. Means stale. White bread. Stale white bread. Peanut butter sandwiches on stale white bread. Monogamy and marriage and kids and death on boring peanut butter sandwiches with stale white bread in Navy Housing or a trailer park somewhere or even a nice home in the burbs, growing old and desperate and cheating on your little spouse and fucking over your little kiddies. Look what it did to her chief the husband. That could be you. Family's a terrible thing. People live lies, Walter, illusions, and do bad things to each other when the dream goes bad, and it always does because you always grow old and die and you wanna take everyone with you. Better to have shipmates. Ah, speaking of which…"

The Stone walked in and was saying hello to Sugar. They were in Circe's again, which Al liked to frequent even more, it seemed, now that he and Sugar were barely on talking terms. His drunken passes finally wore out her patience. She tolerated the rest of them, but Al infuriated her, and she usually wound up kicking him out and telling him he was eighty-sixed and she was reporting him as such to the shore patrol. He'd test her threats, returning time and again, feeding off her anger, at first trying to talk to her, then satisfying himself with talking loudly in her presence until he got ugly

77

and obnoxious enough for her to break down and shoo him out again and plead with us to keep him away.

Walter was glad to see Stone just when it looked as though Al was going to get bitter and put a damper on things. The Stone sat next to Walter and did a couple of spins on his stool. "Hiya Walt 'n Al."

"Seaman Stone," Al said, "you're just in time to join our happy calibration."

"Tell him what we're calibratin'," Walter said.

"We're calibratin' women," he said. "Here's to women. That's the long and short of it. Tomorrow we're humpin' the whale road, PI bound. You should be glad about that. You have a better chance of disappearing there—lose yourself in the jungle, in paradise. Women are more likely to put up with you there, too."

"I ain't goin' nowhere," he said. "I been good. I'm stayin' in the Nav. Seems like now I decided what I'm gonna do, now I wanna stay in the Nav, everyone's talkin' about gettin' rid of me. I been squared-away for a long time. I did good, like you told me. Stayed out of trouble, worked hard. I'm as good a sailor as anyone in first division, so how come no one thinks so? And you said you'd teach me stuff. Hey, ain't I been squared-away Schmerz?" I mean, since they busted me outta communications div you don't see me work no more, but I been a good deck ape. Guess I was never meant to be a signalman."

"You're not packing a full sea bag," Al said.

"Yeah," Walter said, "but what he *has* packed is squared-away for a change."

"Well, what do you know," Al said. "A Schmerz wannabe. A very puppy. Listen here, you want to make a life for yourself in the Navy? You want to atone for your past discrepancies and indiscretions? You want both a career and a lifestyle all in one? You want to serve your country and the free world? You want to be a fleet sailor extraordinaire, and representative of our country's Family Overseas Homeported Program, a walking talking recruitment poster, a symbol: 'Secure Against the Waves,' "First and Best in the WestPac," first in war first in peace first in the hearts of your countrymen, ask not what your country can do for you but what you can do for your country, that when you walk by people will say, 'why, yes yes, that is it; that is it; that is what I always thought it should be'?"

"I guess so."

"We'll make a career counselor of him yet," Walter said.

"Career counselor, eh? I disapprove of the rating. Impractical. A waste of manpower, creating a billet to give pep talks, reenlistment speeches. One must lead by example. One must show. One must inspire. Do we inspire you, Stone?"

"You guys are crazy but I like you."

"Hmm, career counselor, eh? Are you a warrior, that you could give healthy career tips to your brother warriors? Are you a fighter, a warrior?"

"I guess so."

"No guessing! Are you a warrior? A man eating, blood drinking, fire breathing killer? A primal savage, lusting for the death of thine enemies? A living weapon, bent on destruction?"

"Yeah yeah."

"Will you kill who your country tells you to kill, making war on your country's enemies, follow orders scrupulously, do any task at hand zealously, thoroughly, ruthlessly and gladly? Will you stand by your mates, and as you gain in seniority, pass on your wisdom in judicious doses, giving assistance and encouragement to those that look up to you?"

He giggled. "Sure Turner, I can do that."

"What do ya say, Walter? Should we induct him into the holy mysteries of the Knights of Fred? He could have collateral duties as our career counselor."

"Sure. This cherry's ripe. And he has indeed been a squared-away little deck ape these past few months."

"Very well, then." He held out his hands, one on top of the other. "All for one and one for all." Walter placed his hands on top of Al's, and The Stone's went over his. "Repeat after me," he said, but continued before The Stone had a chance. "I, Stonewall T. Stoneman, do solemnly swear to obey the laws and directives of the fraternity of the Brotherhood of the Knights of Fred, and to keep its secrets and holy mysteries within the brotherhood upon pain of excommunication and sudden horrible death; to live the life of the sailor to the hilt; to lead by example; to aid and assist my brother knights in need; to serve in the official capacity of career counselor, offering guidance and a brotherly leg-up to those who are lost or tired; to eschew the Bible, the Koran, the Torah, Buddha, Hindu, Shinto, Billy Graham, Jimmy Swaggart, etcetera in favor of the one true way, the one true Fred; to loan founding brother Radioman Third Class Turner twenty dollars with the understanding that you will receive thirty upon payday n the Philippine Islands. Swear it!"

"I do solemnly swear," The Stone said.

"So help you Fred."

"So help me Fred."

"Then fork over the twenty."

"Okay, that's twenty for thirty. So what's the secrets and mysteries that I can't tell?"

"First and foremost, in *our* lives, everywhere and always, it is this: Brutality Is The Norm. You'll learn how to hold your liquor; how to know if a man has integrity; how to know who you can trust; how to spot a bad idea; how not to trust another's god; how to be the god named Stone. You'll know other Fredists when you see 'em. They'll come to you if you follow the one true path. Think of it—answers, Stone. You'll know when you connect with another Fredist. You'll see it in him; you'll feel it; you'll understand the code, but you must never say what it is. No one can speak it or they betray the mystery. Only know it. Watch Walter and me and you'll know it. Follow us. Fredists."

"Fredists," Walter said. "My, but we're on a roll today."

"Who's on a roll?" a familiar and unwelcome voice asked. Trouble, Walter thought, and looked at the mirror to see Mallory standing behind him. But he tried to stay cheerful.

"Dude!" he said.

"Gentleperson," Al said.

"What's up," Mallory said. "Get up birdbrain, this bar's for radiomen only. Give a radioman your seat."

"Hey, he's in The Brotherhood," Walter said. "You, on the other hand, are not."

"Fuck you," Mallory said.

"Hello," Al said.

"Hello. Fuck you," Mallory said.

"Thank you," Al said. "In walks the KKK. Here we are, wizards and warriors. Strange bedfellows. Well, you're probably wondering why I asked you all here today. Just this: beware the tides of starch if you wanna keep your sheets loose. Lighten up. Now go away."

"Chief said we're having a team meeting. You too Stone. Come on."

"What for?" Walter said. "Knockoff was hours ago. This is our last night before getting underway. And The Stone isn't even on your team, whatever that means."

Mallory smirked. "Chief Parma says we're all in this together, like one happy family. Says we hafta have a big pow-wow before Subic."

"About what?" The Stone said. "I ain't gotta talk to any of you bastards about anything. I ain't in OC div no more. You guys let them bust me down to deck ape."

"Shh, Seaman Stone," Al said. "Remember. Play along. See it through." And then to Mallory, "And where is the rest of our happy family? Bum? Kid? Starring?"

"Let's just say I'm fillin' in for them."

"In what capacity?" Walter said. "You don't even rate."

"Let's just say I'm their eyes and ears."

"Let's just say bullshit," Walter said.

"This is what The Chief *said*," Mallory teased, puffing with the importance of an inside gossip. "The real reason why I'm here, I'm here to warn you all about what's goin' down. Don't you think it's time they knew the real deal, Schmerz?"

"Which is what? I ask," Al asked.

The Stone nodded.

"Bullshit," Walter said.

"Chief said us five are the only ones who knew about what happened in Subic. We gotta go talk to him. Top secret. You do know?" he said to Stone. "I know Turner knows."

"Told me what? What do you mean? I can be here. This is a public place. You can't tell me where to go."

Al was beaming. He seemed to like this. He elbowed The Stone. "Nice try, my fellow knight, but they're on to us. Now we must see this through. Consider this a learning opportunity, Stone. See how the other side lives. Read your enemy. Learn the secrets. We'll refresh your memory and Mallory will fill us in on the pieces that friend Walter left out. Looks like you got your top secret clearance back."

Walter didn't like what was coming, and he particularly didn't like the high-handed way Mallory was bruiting the powers of his office as Chief's emissary, as though he were some sort of papal legatee. He didn't like this unprecedented business of a meeting at all, and he especially didn't like the prominent role he was to play in it. Most of all, he didn't like Mallory.

Mallory was smiling and again told Stone to get up. Stone looked at Walter and Al, and they both straightened up, all for one.

Caught entirely unprepared—how could Mallory have told The Chief about the whole Hasty business?—Walter chose angry denial. "Bullshit." "This is a private party, so you can just take your business and your ugly face the fuck out of here."

"Good point," Al added, "though I'm curious. You're pretty bold, seeing as you're ordering around a sacred Knight of Fred. They're like Masons. You never know when there might be a brother nearby. Could be anyone, and they hate sea-pussy. They especially hate chiefs' sea-pussy."

The threat registered; Still, he maintained the nasty tattletale insistence in his voice and retreated to the old reliable authority of the Chief. "Chief said we had to meet—all of us who are supposed to know. No one else is supposed to know." He was looking at Walter and only Walter now. "Who else knows?"

Walter could only stare at him.

"Does the name Just-Call-Me-Johnny ring any bells?" Mallory smiled, lashing the name at Walter with happy violence, as though whacking him with a coup stick.

"Ah ha," Al clapped his hands together and rubbed them happily. "Blast from the past. Golden oldie. Is *that* all?"

Walter summed it all up in one word: "Bullshit!"

"Who else knows?" he said.

"Just Al—no—fuck you! You tell me."

"Chief does, now. That's what this is all about, I supposed."

"Who knows what?" The Stone said. "C'mon guys, let me in."

"He comes too," Mallory said, nodding at The Stone.

"Okay, Stone, get out of here," Walter said.

"C'mon Schmerz," he whined. "What's goin' on? Knights of Fred, remember? What about the sacred mysteries? All for one. C'mon, you backin' out so quick already?"

"This is only trouble for you. I'll fill you in later—the *real* truth." Walter was looking at Mallory, hating his big face, his pig's face, pink and squinting in a spiteful leer. Walter was growing with anger, glad of the hate that was flowing back into him, the stuff of decisive action, attack adrenaline; no thoughts, just sense recording the moment as his body got light and hard and swift and dangerous, as his soul reverted into steel-jacketed hostility, while the others were tangled in the jerky give and take of awkward talk, frozen in the oblivion of their thinking minds. To Walter, all was now clear, direct, unmediated. *Ratted out.*

He was aware of Al talking. He heard him talking even as he was flying off his stool, even as he cannonballed Mallory in the chest with his shoulder, chasing his backward stagger with his outstretched arms, his hands clutching at his neck. Then he heard the shouts and scuffle of chairs as he caught Mallory's throat and spit in his shocked eyes while their momentum buckled his legs and he sat down hard, grabbing at Walter's wrists. Walter was screaming now. "Get me! Get me! Who's gonna get me motherfucker! Fucking joke's on me motherfucker!" and he was growling through his clenched teeth, gurgling and growling like a dog in a hot struggle while he gripped Mallory's thick neck, squeezing the red into his big face, trying to bust it, burst it, trying to squeeze the stupid, useless life out of it. Mallory threw his legs and torso in the air and they flipped and rolled, one over the other, but Walter had him by the neck. He pried at his fingers, then hit at his face, but Walter had him by the neck.

Mallory rolled on top again, banging the back of Walter's head into the floor and pushing at his chin as though trying to pop his head off, but Walter hung on to his neck, pulling him closer as he squeezed, baring his teeth and straining to rip them into Mallory's face, his chin parrying the palm so that he could bite into that face and suck the life out; and he knew that he was smiling at the horror in Mallory's eyes and he spit at them and pulled and squeezed and juked his head and snapped his teeth at the face. There was a flash of white as Walter's head banged into the floor again. Then, above the shouts of men and Sugar's screams and Mallory's snarls he heard a high, screechy, "Walter!" and The Stone dove out of the still-white edge of his vision, crashing into Mallory and knocking him free of Walter's grip.

It had all been a matter of seconds, and by then people were already trying to pull them apart. As Walter started to stand up he saw that The Stone had sprung to his feet and grabbed a chair to brain Mallory, who was still sitting, looking dazed and holding his throat with both hands in a comical fashion, as if he were choking himself. The Chief materialized behind The Stone while Sugar flew up in his face, cursing and hissing and slapping his shoulders back. At the same time—maybe even before—someone got Walter up under his armpits and wrestled him off his feet, practically squeezing the air out of his chest as he clasped Walter's back to his front, apparently too excited to notice that Walter wasn't resisting. Al Hadn't moved from his stool.

"Okay, okay," the voice behind Walter was saying, its breath on his neck, "just calm down, crazy man, slam on the break. Be cool. Just be cool. It's over."

It had all gone out of him as fast as it came. In a heartbeat he went from the man of action to the figure in a scene of his own creation, from pure, clean, sweet energy with purpose to a character struggling with the setting and predicament he's acted his way into, from motion to repose, vision to reflection. "Buddy," he gasped, "your breath stinks. You can let go of me now please. I'm cool. Honest."

Everything had stopped. They all looked at each other for an embarrassed, blinking moment: The Chief grabbing The Stone's braining-chair with one hand at arm's length, grimacing and turning away from the smoke rising from the butt in his mouth, but it looked as though he found the thing in hand distasteful, like a putrid fish; The Stone in mid-effort of cracking Mallory's skull, both hands above his head, his face astonished that the weapon had caught on the air itself; Sugar rising up at him, her pursed lips poised to spit inarticulate outrage, her hands raised in flat gesticulation of anger, her lovely face twisting into violence; Al looking on, leaning back with his elbows on the bar; Mallory in the center, dumb and pained and silly, sitting up with his legs outstretched and his own hands at his throat. This is the awkward part, Walter thought, wondering what next. Here comes. This is the part I hate. Let's skip over this and get back to normal. Let's have a drink and shoot the shit and be shipmates again. You take back what you did, and I'll take back what I did. Let's right now make this into an old story that we can all laugh about.

"That was fun," Walter said, his voice cracking, head whirling, cheeks burning, hoping he had some kind of appropriate look on his face, hoping no one saw his shaking. "We should do this more often."

"You're every little fuckin Philippino whose ass I ever kicked. You only look a little different," Mallory spat.

Walter maneuvered to the bar, saw two vague beer bottles, knocked the first one over, then managed to pick up the other, his hand shaking uncontrollably, caught it between his lips and swallowed.

"How come you're shaking like that," Al said.

"You try strangling Mallory. Got a neck like a bull. Excuse me." He managed the gauntlet to the bathroom.

The Stone came in while he was washing the sweat from his face and neck and examining the raspberries on his face. "You can count on me, man, You and Turner. You don't have to worry about that asshole no more. You got him scared shitless. Anyways, you always got backup, ya know? Look, I'm stickin' with you guys. Chief Parma says if I stick around awhile he'll forget about it, so you're probably not in any trouble, too. Sugar's callin' the police, so we gotta scoot. I'll just listen to the business and be quiet, man. I won't say a word. I'm on your side, whatever's happenin'."

"Okay, Stone. Thanks a lot, my man."

He smiled, drew a finger across his throat, pointed it at Walter pistol style, then grabbed his hand and yanked it.

"What's this?"

"Knights of Fred handshake. Turner says it's good."

"I like it."

"Schmerz? You gonna tell me about it?"

"Yes. I will."

When he came out he saw Sugar holding up the phone over her head with both hands like a talisman, an instrument of god's wrath, and he quickly joined the exodus of the banished.

Chief Parma herded the four of them out of there and into the back of a particularly seedy second story bar nearby that had no name posted anywhere that Walter could see. He ordered a couple of rounds of drinks and shooed the old hostess away from their dim-lit meeting booth. They settled into the red, well-worn Naugahyde, Al and Stone and Walter scrunched on one side, The Chief sprawling comfortably with his arms stretched out on the back of the seat, and Mallory leaning against the table at his end. The low overhead lamp threw a smoky haze on the table.

"Okay," Al said, "let's get started. Who brought the cards?"

"This is dead serious," The Chief said, "and it could involve all of us."

"Where's Starring, then?" Walter said. "Where's Kid? Bum?"

Mallory straightened up. "Someone's gotta prep Radio for underway, don't they, asshole? Besides, we don't need that idiot Starring, or those niggers."

Walter jerked forward, and Mallory flinched and raised his forearms.

"Alright, alright, save it," The Chief said. "Starring ain't one of us, understand? This is a tricky situation and if that fat fuck was brought in on it he'd only fuck it up. He just ain't one of us. He can't be trusted. And no one else has the need to know, anyway. We here are all who's gonna know. I *mean* that. What I'm gonna tell you is strictly between us and the bulkhead. We got a long, tough haul coming up, and this division's gonna be the best fucking communicator in the WestPac, and to do that you guys are gonna stick by each other and work like a team—Stone, I'll get to you in a minute. I don't care if you like each other, but you're gonna work together and most important, you're gonna follow my orders and do exactly like I tell you. Now, I mean it. Exactly like I tell you or I'll have your ass. First thing, none of this business gets to anyone outside of us, understand? Understand, Turner?"

"Roger that, oh Chief, my Chief."

"Schmerz?"

"I hear you."

"You hear me. Do you *understand*?"

"Yes, I understand."

"Stone?"

"Sure, sure. Top Secret. I don't even want to talk about it. Just Schmerz and Turner and me know."

"Cut that silly secret club shit. This is for your own sake, the sake of the division and your partners, and ultimately and most important as far as I'm concerned, the sake of my career. I could have a couple of people's asses already, right Schmerz? And I'm not even talking about that little dust-up back there. But I like you guys and if I let you slide, it better never get out to no one, 'cause if I go down I'm gonna send as many people as far down as I can, and a lot further. We're talking Leavenworth. Also, I can't afford no casualties, not to no Flip street scum or to the law, just because some of you hip dudes got maybe drug related problems. Right Schmerz? *That* we will deal with after this IO cruise.

"Now, a little constructive antagonism's good for keeping the energy level up, makes for healthy competition. I don't give a shit who likes who, but I want a *whole* radioshack working for me on the Indian Ocean. I want the people I have right here working for me. I want an efficient team, kicking ass and taking names, and I've seen you guys do it before. I want to come away from this cruise with a commendation from the commodore, maybe even ComSeventhFleet. Stone, you will not fuck that up by gossiping around the ship. And there will be rewards for you in turn, special considerations. That's how it works. For instance, I could forget Schmerz's little indiscretion in the PI if he lives up to his four-oh reputation as watch supe. And I mean four months of mistake-free perfection."

Actually, nobody's caught me doing anything, Walter realized. It was "Schmerz this" and "Schmerz that." What about Mallory? Walter had never even spoken up to the Chief before; he was always too intimidated. And what about Al? He was usually the lightning rod. Everyone knew The Chief hated Al, especially since he didn't care. Walter knew he should have come clean when Hasty died.

In a way, he had a right to hang on, for what had happened to him was his alone, a discrete thing subject only to the rules of its own moment, comprised of the myriad intricate accidents that brought the moment into being, unchangeable and irretrievable by retrospect, unrevisable. Johnny's wife standing in the doorway with her white sheet and new baby, the monstrous itch that that vision injected into his blood—that was his. The connection he had made with Hasty and even the momentary camaraderie he felt with Mallory—the incarnations he tried on throughout the speed trip—they were all his to keep. Confessing to his whore-mongering, drug-binging criminal activities would have improved nothing, helped no one, except perhaps job advancement for the guys on the side of so-called law, whatever that is. Well, maybe for the other side, too, because when you remove a crook or kill a low-life you create a little vacuum that sucks the next nearest scum into his niche.

But it would do nothing for the woman in the doorway or for the baby at her breast or for the beautiful boy with the overlarge head and eyes that were out of a cheap velvet painting, or for Walter. Punishment wouldn't undo that moment when they came together and the affect they had on each others' lives. Punishment wouldn't change the events that brought him there, nor make him the kind of person who would do things differently. Punishment would only be bad luck.

But now, the not saying was coming back to punish him in the form of Mallory's revision of events, that which was equivocal, not the real moment. Walter had hung on to what was his, and somehow a perverse version of the thing had come into being through Mallory, and it was now in The Chief's hands. And it was a story that couldn't easily be set right or explained because it *could* be said that he had done wrong; he had no alibis. What can you say, besides, "you weren't there, you don't know what it feels like having all the speed burning through your veins. You weren't in the room, so close to the eyes of the woman that saw things you would never see. You weren't threatened by the punks while Mallory pumped away in her. You weren't confused or compromised by Hasty's death. It sounds so petty.

He was still feeling rocky from the fight, but also hot and heedless, especially as he saw that what was developing was beyond his control anyway, and it was clear to him that he now had a dangerous enemy in The Chief—something that it had done him no good to carefully avoid. He had probably been saving this from the moment they got back from their trip when Mallory no doubt dropped a dime in his ear. In the official hierarchy, Walter was above the one and below the other, but he knew he would have it on his back one way or the other in the coming months.

"May I ask you something, Chief?" he said.

"No you may not."

"If it's so important that we stick together and work as a team like you say, then how come you're keeping the leading petty officer out of everything? What happened to the chain of command? He's our boss; he's got to fit in too, doesn't he? And how are we supposed to run our watch sections when we got seamen thinking that they only have to answer to you? How come you get people working against each other? How come Mallory's here and Kid isn't? And Bum?"

"Alright, Schmerz, that's enough. The others ain't here because I say they don't need to know. I wish none of us had to be here. Once you know, you're in. And you do not bring any of them in by going ashore with them—keep your stink off 'em. This thing is a secret, and it goes no farther than us. Speaking of which, I suggest you start worrying more about yourself and less about everyone else. If you can't handle people who work for you then that's just something you're gonna have to learn to do. It's called military leadership. If you can't stand the sound of the big guns, get off the main deck. No one here's exempt from the rule. My rules.

Now I won't throw any more fat on that particular fire—the one you're getting at—but you just better look out for yourself, son. You can thank him for our being here tonight. At least he had the smarts and the guts to come to me with this information. What did you do about it, Schmerz? What were you planning on doing? I got a whole division to look out for. You have made that more difficult. I don't appreciate that. I don't like it."

He said all this rather amiably, as though the words were a tiresome duty, contradicting his actual attitude, his arms draped expansively from the back of the couch, giving breadth to his chest and gut which thrust out like a badge of rank. His relaxed approach to this thing, which he found so important that he called this weird meeting, and which supposedly made his career vulnerable to their confidence, leant him added authority, despite the fact that he looked at the others with a half smirk that gave the lie to the paternal gleam in his eye when he said, "I got a whole division to look out for."

What Walter couldn't put in words he glared from across the table. He could feel the others staring blankly at him, and knew that he was on his own. They didn't say a thing.

The Chief began again: "Look here. The information has recently come to me that when these two were in the PI they got mixed up with some pretty rough characters. Maybe it's their fault and maybe it ain't. I know you guys get high, and I'm against it. I'm for busting dopeheads, generally. But these days, you bust everyone that gets high and you got no one left to run the ship. This sound about the way you all heard it?"

"You mean the one about the lady Mallory raped and her hubby, Yellow Jacket Jackie?" Al said.

Mallory banged his beer on the table. "She was a whore!"

"Did I say something amiss?"

"This is getting interesting." The Stone leaned in. "I didn't know nothin' about no rapes and no druggists out to get you."

Walter kicked him under the table and mouthed "don't talk."

"The point is," The Chief continued calmly, impervious, "is not to get paranoid. No one's out to get you, Schmerz, but you are proving yourself to be a highly unreliable character, a highly unstable member of the team. The point of this meeting is that we all walk out of here with the same story. Because when we get to Subic you three *will* stick to each other like flies on shit. And Mallory and me'll buddy-up since you all can't be friends.

"Something tells me I heard a different story than your bosom buddy, Turner, there. Like The Stone says, this is getting interesting. The point is, we all have to see it the same and know it the same, because lives may depend on it; my division may depend on it—not to sound paranoid. I may be overstressing the thing, but that's the safe way. I don't give a shit what you guys got going with each other, but in this matter, we are all pulling together. The same goes for in the radioshack. In this, we look out for each other.

"Now, someone was killed in this thing already—his name will not be mentioned. He was not one of us, not one of our own. We have to look out for our own. But this is how serious the matter is. And like I say, none of this gets beyond us or I will have your ass so bad I'll...I'll destroy you. Serious. What's done is done. I wish I didn't know. Now that I know, now that it's out and now that we all know, my entire career is in a sling. But if anyone finds out, I will deny knowing anything. But I will push you down so far, hold you down so long you will drown. Only two people were there, but we all have to have an idea of what to look out for, what we're in for. Mallory, go ahead and tell 'em what you heard."

There was a light in The Stone's eyes, and he was practically jumping up and down in his seat, tapping Walter's arm under the table. "Murder, and shit."

The Chief leaned forward and bugged his eyes at The Stone. "And you are involved. You are involved because now you know. Once you know you can't help but be involved. Schmerz involved you! All I'm saying is to make sure no one else knows, 'cause we don't want no one else involved. And keep a close lookout for your shipmates, 'cause they might need your help sometime. Now shut up and listen to Mallory so you know what you're dealing with."

Mallory gave his spin on the story while Walter Schmerz squirmed. "...then this other guy—the one me and Schmerz are with—he starts talkin' business, payin' out the line, throwin' them a lot of maybes and what ifs and next times and numbers, and I'm tryin' to buy time to think of a way out, and then Schmerz blows the whole thing and flips out."

"You weren't there!"

"What?"

"You weren't even there. You were busy raping the guy's wife, remember?"

"That's low, man. You're tellin' all these guys I'm some kind of a rapist. The man says, 'you wanna fuck my wife while we wait, please?' and she walks over to the bed and spreads 'em. I *paid* her. You're some kind of liar, you know that, Schmerz?"

The Chief said, "Cut the shit and get to the point."

"That is the point, partly. 'Cause Schmerz was jealous and it wigged him. You think I don't see, Schmerz? Anyway, I could hear what was goin' on out there. Momma didn't raise no fool; always keep a eye and a ear out. Besides, I could see what was goin' on from the minute we got there. That place was trouble, with this guy stallin' for his buddy and everybody talkin' about movin' dope. What are you, stupid, Schmerz? You didn't see what was goin' down?

"So that is part of the point. You shoulda seen the way he was lookin' at this broad—couldn't take his eyes off her. You gotta picture it: here's this guy who wants us to stick around so bad he's pimpin' his wife, and he *still* don't like the way Schmerz is lookin' at her, all droopy and gaga and sick lookin'. Love at first sight, huh mister fuckin' holier than thou? Ol' Schmerz missed that part, the important part, after he threw his tantrum and blew the whole scene for us.

"All of a sudden he decides he don't like no one. Here these guys are tellin' us how they own the town, and hero here starts jumpin' up and down, screamin' and cursin' everyone; then he runs out of the house screamin' he's gonna get a gun and shoot 'em all. He freaks, and me and…this other dude are left with these motherfuckers and a fuckin' situation on our hands. They are very unhappy motherfuckers. First they tell us that we ain't leavin' Olongapo, just like that. So this Cox guy starts talkin' fast. Says we can't move the shit on base 'cause we don't know no one there, but if we can get back to the ship and check out how many takers there are, then we can take up a collection and come back and buy quantity for cash. Says he loves speed, needs the money and really wants to do the deal. This way they don't have to front us nothin' and we don't owe them nothin'. That's the way he talked—this guy knew the business and they seemed to like that. They still ain't happy but at least they see we ain't tryin' to rip 'em off and we want more than one get-high's worth. Then as an act of good faith the guy buys a bunch of the speed pills up front, and some smoke-dope for Schmerz, you know, the baby's bottle.

"Well, they still ain't happy—this Eddy brought a ton of shit with him, a fuckin' drugstore—what we got was just crumbs, but whatshisname keeps talkin' and they figure it's better than nothin'. So they give us a couple of hours to get back to the boat and come back with the cash or they're gonna off us the next time they catch us in town, just flat like that. Got eyes all over town. And they said Schmerz was just dead meat one way or the other. They didn't like bein' threatened by no shitty-diapers American sailor. That's when Johnny starts goin' off about how Schmerz used his hospitality and got snotty about his kid—arrogant, he says—and made eyes at his wife, then says he's gonna shoot 'em all. Am I lyin', Schmerz?"

Walter could feel the others' eyes warming him. "Yes. About what happened after I left. Everything's a lie the way you tell it, even when it's true." Even after Hasty died Mallory talked him out of thinking it was the dealers. He had partied in town every night.

Mallory banged his fist on the table and hissed, "What kind of idiot you think I am! The fuck I'm gonna make up a story like that for? I was lookin' out for you Schmerz, asshole. When you split from that Mimi's place I thought you better know. We hit it off pretty good till then, and I thought I was doin' you a favor. I thought we was friends. But knowin' you, I thought you might hit the panic button or report the thing and get us a world of trouble on the other end. You're a very unreliable character. Got us in enough trouble as it is, didn't you?"

"So why didn't the gangster come after me?" Walter said. "If they got *him* quick enough. You were right there with me."

Liberty Call

"To be honest, I don't know. But you're right—I was right there with you. Maybe *that's* why. Ever think of that? That first night was stupid; I admit it. We fucked up. But whatshisname didn't seem too worried, and Christ, that boy sure seemed to know what was going on. Seemed to understand those guys from the inside. Talked their language. I was a little nervous, but it was excitin' too, like playin' spies and shit. So I put a load on and went along with it.

"Let me ask you somethin', Schmerz. After that night when he got it, how much did you see me drink? How much time did we spend apart off base? I don't like you *that* much, pal. I never got drunk and hardly let you out of my sight after that night. But you weren't payin' no attention to whether I was worried or drunk or how I felt about anythin'. Come on, what do you remember?"

Walter was confused. The truth is, he didn't remember many details between the first and last days of that week. Mallory had been friendly, and they had been close. But he really didn't pay much attention to him, even though they were together all that time. He didn't seem like anybody he'd ever care enough about to take seriously. "Bull," he said.

"I never did," Mallory said. "Just drank enough to keep the edge off, then nursed my beers and watched you guzzle. Yeah, I was takin' those little yellow bastards, too, and drinkin' just enough to keep the nerves smooth. I don't think I slept that week. I had to stay awake and keep a lookout for you—remember how much I stuck by you, buddy? I was gonna' tell you after we was out of it and safe, and I was right, too. Look what happened when I did tell you. You throw another fit and take off. Don't know why I bothered in the first place. Don't know why I thought we could be friends. It's like you were tryin' to kill yourself anyway. Then when I try and join in a little fun he turns sissy, gets all crazed and paranoid. Well, fuck you, brother."

"And a good time was had by all," Al said. "Sounds like standard operating procedures for a fool on liberty, ay brother?" he said to The Stone.

"Yeah. Wow," The Stone said. "'Cept ya shouldn't of gone out with a outsider like Mallory in the first place."

"Out of the mouths of babes," Al said. "So what's the point of all this?"

Walter looked around the room and wanted to bolt. Mamasan and Papasan were yammering with some old shopkeeper at the bar. Bruce Springsteen starting singing "Badlands" from the jukebox, and when he looked over there a wrinkled hostess crooked her finger at him. He gulped his beer down and told himself to leave. "Yes," he said out loud. "I'm leaving. I'm out of here." But his body made no motion to go. He was tired. Or maybe he was asking permission.

"Now hold on," The Chief said. "Don't break it up just yet. You can go soon enough. Let me order us all some more beers." He called the hostess over, ordered a million beers and sent her off with a slap on the butt.

"Alright, listen up." He was serious now, all business, their leader, suddenly even-handed and earnest. "I said we had to come away from this with one version of the thing. Now, Schmerz don't seem like he's lyin'; he just refuses to see what's goin' on. That's danger. That's irresponsible. I expect more from a petty officer, Schmerz. I say Mallory's telling the truth and that we see it that way. It's safest to believe in the worst. I want you to buddy-up whenever you're on the beach. If you see anything strange, like if anyone's followin' someone around, I want to know about it, and I want the others to know about it. We look out for each other. I'll see to it that you three are in the same duty section. I'm not *askin'* you to stick together—if I find that one of you hit the beach without the other, I'll pull all of yours liberty. You too, Stone. Chief Boats is a friend and he'll do what I ask without questions, and he don't like you anymore'n I do."

"Man," The Stone said, "everybody be followin' you around in that place. So what do these dudes look like?"

"Who knows," Walter said, still glued to his seat, still telling his legs to walk.

"Like I said," Mallory said, "the Johnny guy's a jeepney driver. Looks kinda like the spick on *I Love Lucy*, the husband. The Eddy guy looks like..."

"Goebbels," Walter said. "In a leisure suit and aviators."

"Gerbils?" The Stone said.

Mallory looked thoughtful. "I sure as shit hope I remember what he looked like 'cause he said *he* never forgets a face. Said to think of him every time a body washes up along Shit River. He looked like...comin' to think of it he did look sort of like a rat, a disco rat with sunglasses."

Walter hated his life. It wasn't tension at their table anymore; it was oppression. He couldn't believe that The Stone and Al seemed delighted with the dirty little covenant that was being put upon them, and it was far from clear what was to be done or what the Chief really wanted done about it. It just seemed that the Chief wanted to draw a circle around them and begin some alien game that somehow pivoted on Walter in the middle. The Chief was working his mojo, stirring it with a big stick. The Stone and Al seemed more than happy to play. For them, the Chief and Mallory were walking into a trap in *their* game and creating a situation that couldn't be better. For Walter, the bottom was dropping out; everything was changing again. For Walter, the responsibility of group knowledge made manifest, the words being said, was anathema.

Perhaps what was most surprising about this meeting was the Chief Parma involved himself and so compromised himself. But his understanding of the dynamic between them all, of where they stood with each other, was keen, and he was now choreographing their steps. His understanding of the institution of chief petty officer within the institution of the Navy within the institutions of governments and laws was apparently his study and his passion, and it was a force beyond Walter's contention. He was the institution itself. He was bringing them together in the configuration of his own making, but more importantly, he was accumulating personal power. What made it frightening and effective to Walter was its apparent arbitrariness.

"You two guys did wrong, and in another life I'd of busted you, but for now I need you. What you did is illegal. It's bad for your Navy. And of course, I don't want any of my sparkies in trouble. Don't give a rat's ass about you, Stone, understand? But you're in all the way now, boy.

"A man is dead. Think about that. A happy sailor no more. He ain't one of our own, and we look out for our own, but all the same he's dead. Serious. Now unless something happens in the PI, which I'm sure it won't, I never want to hear about this thing again. It never happened. Now let's party. Long time since I was out with my boys the night before getting underway. I miss partying with the troops."

And like it or not, their compact was sealed.

Chief Parma had bought an exorbitantly overpriced bottle of bar whiskey for them to drink at the booth, and the others took turns buying rounds of beer. Parma held court, and he really did drop the entire matter as though it had never been mentioned. He sat there pushing the bottle around, telling sea stories about how tough it was in the old Navy and kidding each of them good naturedly in their turn, ignoring the low grade fever at the table and the queer, giddy mood it put them in.

"…Yeah, you men think I'm tough, but you don't know nothing about tough. Nowadays you're not allowed to touch no one, 'cause they'll sue you. Yoosta could kick a sailor's ass right on the ship in front of everyone, especially in front of everyone. Teach you a lesson. Damn if I didn't learn a couple of lessons that way." He picked up the bottle and smiled at the memory in it. "Now we got captain's mast and personnel management and substance abuse counseling and whatnot. Navy got soft. Country got soft. The whores got old and fat.

"Do you realize that right this minute we're sitting in a country that we kicked the shit out of? Yeah, but be careful you don't offend any JN's when you're out trying to get your dick wet. Right in this town—that base— bombed the shit out of that base. You hear where the other day they dug up a unexploded bomb from WW two? I wish it blew up in some construction crew's face. Little reminder of who we are, goddamnit. Now we're defending their country 'cause they don't wanna have a military, keeping them rich, but they don't wanna defend themselves. They treat us like second-class citizens and General MacArthur wrote their fuckin' constitution, for christsake. Can't afford a drink, and the whores all got old.

"Wasn't like that when Nam was cookin', boy. It was hot here then. Alive. Everybody appreciated us. And when we steamed at somebody we *used* our ordinance, and we lost people, but what the fuck is a navy for? Shot our wad on the zips and came back to the Honcho and shot our wad again on the women; money and booze flowing wherever you looked. A fuckin' orgy. I know you degenerates would've appreciated a scene like that. But we had a mission; we were accomplishing somethin', and this was payday when the work was over. Then they fuckin' pulled the war out from under us and then Japan changed. Now you got these jackass protesters crying about ships with nukes. Now they're rich, they don't wanna know about nukes or ships or sailor or even Americans. Ol' Starring's right about one thing—they did stop fuckin' here in seventy-three.

"Now the Navy's soft like everything else. You chumps don't know about death. Nam was death. Once you look into the eye of a shitstorm you'll understand. Now they sue you if you lay a hand on 'em. Yoosta be everything was subordinated to the business of sailoring, 'cause the life of friends and the death of enemies depended on it. Now we've forgotten how to do it. Fucking public relations. Rights of the individual. Individual weaklings. Know what we're doin' in the Indian Ocean? Public relations.

"We'd of wrecked your buddy Stone be now. Not now in this man's Navy. See, chiefs used to have power—the backbone of the Navy. Being a chief meant something; it was a real brotherhood that held things together and maintained the values. Even now, you guys might think it's a joke when you see a new chief gettin' initiated, but it's more than a college boy hazing. It means something. True fraternity. Still. Things we share that a chief can never tell.

"Chiefs used to run the ship. Yoosta be you had trouble with someone you talked it over in the chiefs' quarters and all together devised the proper response. I seen guys made miserable. Miserable. Kicked from division to division, chief to chief, each one making life harder. I swear, I seen guys jump in the sea. Now you got to be more subtle. Can't make it look like that's what it is. I suppose we could do it, though, if we all pulled together. Weed out the bad ones. Hey, lookout Stone! Ha ha."

It was as though he were acting as his own lightning rod now, drawing into himself the cramped energy that he'd put in the air in the first place. Walter doubted if any of them believed he had simply let his mind wander, that he was idling without a point. Having planted the seeds of a new and unpredictable tension, he was now covering them over and tamping them down with his not quite benign patter. They would flourish later.

The bar was dingy and nameless and smelled like urine and cosmetics, the perfume of hostesses who trailed the air of a life spent administering to sleepwalkers, hardened grandmothers who slept on futons in their four-tatami flats with no illusions about human nature or romantic notions about the sexes, women who shopped at the fish markets and bakeries and the Ginza, shuffling loudly in their wooden clogs among the aisles of sandals, brightly colored chopsticks and high-tech electronic equipment, who burned incense at the shrines and wore kimonos on special holidays and dressed the little ones warmly when weather crept in from the god stirred sea, who served dinner on their knees before the TV set, visited and gossiped with friends, took vacations at the seashore and returned to work again where they served whiskey and rubbed crotches in the dark, knowing better than to reveal an inkling with their eyes, perhaps allowing nothing more to enter their eyes than the practical aspects of work, perhaps allowing noting in their eyes at all. And it smelled like the urine of men playing out the flip side of their lives—an inky, narcoleptic stagger through the dizzy processes of vomiting, pissing, ejaculating, pressing awkwardly against the indifferent flesh, muttering stupidly into indifferent ears about the spotty fragments of pain, insults and anxieties of their days and times, drinking more to forget those injuries and that the flesh and ears are indifferent, running from the terror of self-hatred and failing and phantom youth that their one shot on the waking side has turned into, toward the temporary refuge of sugar-crusted confusion and self-indulgent emotions that accelerate the cycle.

And the ghost of Vietnam was there—the last tangible project that one and all were involved in. For the women it was boom town, fast money and maybe riotous fun, naughty times. For the men it was that plus involvement—the thing the world was doing at the time, the big challenge, the arena, center stage, or at least that's the way it usually sounds in veterans' bar talk. Now it was morbid. When you're running on the Honcho, it's the kind of place you usually end up in last, where you spend your last yen and sleep at the bar until sunup, when you grope your way back to the ship you call home.

"Yeah," The Chief was saying, "you boys are alright. I'll tell you what, though. There's some good goddamn communicators on this here ship. Ol' Schmerz here's shaping up okay. Picking up the slack where Haggard left off. He took up with Turner, too. You two guys make quite a pair. And you're working some kind of magic on The Stone, you two are. I can't say as I'm sorry he's out of the division, though." He spoke as if the man wasn't sitting right in front of him, but The Stone didn't seem to mind. He was still happy at being graced as a confidant in the inner sanctum. And he seemed to harbor his own secret that gave him strength—maybe it was only the novelty of his silence. "You know, I always had my suspicions about that guy. He's funny. Gets along great with you two, though." He smiled and tipped the mouth of the whiskey bottle toward them in salute before taking a swig and shoving it at Al.

Al drank deeply, chased it with a beer and burped. "Yup. Everybody gets along great with me. I got it all—talent, wisdom, good looks. I'm on the inside. Keeper of the sacred mysteries."

"Don't start with that shit again," Mallory said. "These three got a little club going. Can't nobody joint but them."

"You can join if you ever get your shit together," Walter said. Quite high now, he talked as though their little joke with The Stone was a thing of substance.

"No," The Chief continued, mulling the matter, "I think it's good what you done. I gotta love that little salute thing or signal or whatever. That's real cute."

"I'm a very cute man," Al said.

"Yeah, you're cute alright," The Chief said, but still without sarcasm or malice, only good humor. "The girls think he's cute. *Kawaii*. Right Schmerz?"

"Yeah, except for Sugar."

Al twisted off a bitter smile at him.

The Stone nodded almost smugly.

Al drank again. "Like I said, I'm a very cute man." He wasn't biting. "Which brings us back to the topic we were discussing before the entire crew busted in on us at Circe's with this business of crime and intrigue."

"Which was what?" Mallory said.

"Your mama."

"The subject was women," Walter said.

"Walter's in love with a PI hooker."

"Fuck you. Anyway, she puts Sugar to shame. You might say it's a crime. At least I like women who like me back."

"Yeah," Mallory said, "but I boned her first. Lousy lay."

"Not her. Walter's in love with a PI hooker in Subic City whose name isn't Paz. Lots of people boned her first. She writes him letters."

The Chief redirected: "I've heard some guys say they thought Turner was sea-pussy, being so cute and all. Maybe that Sugar chick thought she could sense something about you, seeing as you're always in the company of Schmerz, here." He pushed the bottle to Al, who took another slug.

It was happening again. The spotlight zeroed in and the footlights flicked on and hummed, stewing Walter in their heat as the curtain went up, hushing the stirring murmur of the crowd. Was he expected to dance or sing? Was this comedy or drama or mystery or melodrama? The air was heavy with the exhalations of expectant, congregate lives; second-hand, viscid air; used, depleted air so thick you had to suck to breathe.

Al kept smiling, ignoring something, and seemed to take a bow in acknowledgment of the audience's appreciation of his coming performance, taking his kudos in advance, throwing himself off the stage and into the audience's lap. "Please, fellas, it's just platonic. But if I was sea-pussy I'd be the best goddamn piece any of you ever had."

The Chief shushed what Mallory was starting to say. "Yeah, ol' Sugar probably figured if she took on you she'd have to take on Schmerz here, too. Where you joined at?"

"We're joined to you, Chief Parma, nut to butt, and we've been taking it up the ass since we've known you. I assume because we're so pretty."

"Yeah, you're cute. They used to talk about you and Haggard, too." The Chief maintained his tone of amused barroom chatter, gossip among pals, as though Al would find it equally amusing. "Said you took Haggard's head off and screwed it on again backwards. And now you're buddy-buddy with Schmerz, got him talking like you—another Turner-striker. Gotta hand it to ya, Turner."

"No," The Chief said, "I'm not calling these guys queer. It's just the *perception*, is what I'm saying. Why, Turner'll pork anything that calls itself female—eight-to-eighty, blind crippled or crazy, if they can't walk he'll drag 'em. Any split tail. Right, Turner? I mean anything. Right Turner? Gives new meaning to the word motherfucker."

Al gave Parma a twisted grin and nodded that he saw where things were going.

"Uh oh," Mallory said," stand by for heavy dirt."

"Amen," Al said. "That's right, Mal. And you know, in France *mal* means shit, as in malefactor, or the shit factor. But in Navy talk it just means a good for nothing."

Stone snickered.

"Manly men," The Chief said. "Like I said, I know Schmerz ain't queer 'cause of all the whores he wants to marry. And I know Turner ain't queer 'cause he likes girls so much he'd fuck his own mother, so he's okay. Ain't that right, Turner?"

Al picked up the whiskey bottle and tongued the rim, then swallowed, his eyes fluttering. "Here we go, huh Chief?"

Mallory seemed to know what was coming, too. "Was it good?"

"Jeez," The Stone said. "Wow. Man oh man, you didn't." He giggled. "Say it ain't so," he said, hoping it was.

Al slowly wiped his eyes and then his mouth with an open hand, and it looked as though he was actually trying to suppress the smile that was spreading across his face. He chuckled and hiccupped a drool of whiskey onto his lips and wiped it with his forearm. "Not at all, not at all, Chief. Was saving it for the right time. Now we got all this newfound brotherly love and camaraderie-ship, why not?

"Simple, really. It's simple. And natural—you all know deep down that it's natural in an Oedipal sort of tradition. I mean, what are you all looking for, when you really think about it? Got to get back to The Garden, right? Back where we came from and where we're going to. No, never mind that part. It's wasted on you.

"I'll cut to the juicy part. You just want the story." He flattened his hands and the table and straightened his arms like braces. "Simple enough. One fine sultry summer evening when I was eighteen—remember Saturday nights when you were eighteen? One Saturday night I come home from a party. I'm high as a kite; been smoking killer weed all night, Sensamilla, and I'm practically tripping, too high, so I come home. It's late and the house is dark. Dear old Dad's away giving a lecture or a paper or some such good shit, I think. Therefore I am. Get it? He's a think tank guy. Very bright but very boring. Ever know a think tank guy?" He looked at Walter. "Well, you can imagine. Anyway, I tiptoe into the house figuring Mammy's in bed asleep, but I'm too high for sleep so I turn on the living room TV and begin to zone out on reruns of *Get Smart*. Then I hear this weird sound coming from the kitchen like the cat's being sick, this kind of choked-off squeal like the stray, off-freek signals you sometimes hear squawking across an open receiver.

"So I go to investigate, and when I turn on the kitchen light, what do I see but *mi madre* sitting in the dark at the kitchen table with an almost empty bottle of vodka."

The Stone slapped his knee. "You did it on the kitchen table!"

"Listen. So I turn on the light and I kind of jump—I'm flying on this weed—and there's Mom like a ghost out of the dark. I sit next to her and ask what's wrong, but she can't really talk—she's gagging on tears. She just takes my hands in her hands and looks at me with the sad, wet face, kind of hiccuping and rocking back and forth. And I'm tripping-out on the way she looks: everything's hanging down; her hair's hanging straight down; the bags under her eyes are pulled down so hard it's like fingers are actually doing it the way you make a scary face, or maybe they just look that way because her eyes are red all around; and her cheeks and jowls are hanging straight down and the corners of her mouth are frowning down and gravity's pulling all the lines in her face down."

"Ugh!" Mallory said.

"Then I see her bathrobe's open and I can see one of her big tits hanging down."

"Better!" Stone said.

"I keep looking at it and it sort of swings out when she rocks forward. There's something hot about that—the way it looks warm and heavy.

"'What's wrong?' I keep saying. 'What's going on?' But she's not making any sense, just keeps sputtering and rocking, sometimes saying my father's name and sometimes saying my name, and things like 'oh baby, my baby,' and something about how old am I or how old is she. She's holding my hands in my lap, saying 'do you love me? Do you love me?' and I'm saying 'yeah, of course I love you,' but I can't look at her red eyes so I look at the breast, but now the bathrobe's looser and the other one spills out and they're both swinging."

Stone said, "yes!"

"These hefty, pendulous pendulums, and I feel myself getting warm all over and I can't believe it but I want to touch them, thinking how weird and exciting it would be, thinking I used to suck them and thinking that I actually might remember it. Then I realize that as we're rocking her knuckles are brushing against my crotch and my dick's getting hard."

"I know about that" Chief said.

"It feels good so I just let it—I can feel the heat coming up against our hands in waves, and so can she because she's rocking a little faster and putting a little more pressure on my dick with her knuckles. I'm imagining it's those fat, heavy breasts with those chewy old nipples, stubby like eager fingers or something that are rubbing me. 'Do you love me?' she says, and I realize I haven't been breathing, so I start breathing but can only manage short breaths and I'm getting dizzy and kind of queasy, probably from the dope. 'Yeah, I love you,' I say.

"Then she does it and it's so good I can't believe it. I think I'm going to faint from the short breaths or have a heart attack or something. She unsnaps my jeans and carefully unzips them, and when she does. I can feel the heat escape—I actually feel it hit my face. I sort of lift my hot little butt off the chair with my hands, and she slides my pants and then my shorts down around my ankles. It's just her and the one-eyed worm, face to face. I probably groaned, and I heard myself saying, 'do it, do it,' and I opened her robe all the way and squeezed and lifted, squeezed and lifted—those old titties were on fire. She took my cock in her hands so slowly and gently that I was almost bouncing up and down to make more friction, but she went with the motion so it wouldn't rub, just holding it lovingly, just sort of cupping it with one hand and cradling it with the other."

Walter was getting uncomfortable, and pushed his chair out to make the sound of leaving. Maybe the others would catch it. "And man, she did love it. I was practically bucking in the chair and hanging onto her tits, and she was whispering, 'beautiful, beautiful, beautiful. Such a beautiful. Oh, my beauty.' By then I was begging. 'Please,' I said. I must have said please a dozen times before she finally got on her knees and went down on it, first just kissing and nibbling it and running her tongue up and down under the shaft. And when I said 'oh no, I'm gonna come.'"

"Come!" Stone shouted.

"She said 'oh yes' and slid her mouth all the way down on it. Soft and sweet and warm and wet—doesn't matter who it is. She slid all the way down and all the way up, and each time she got to the top she said a word—'now' suck, 'now' suck, 'now' suck—like she was chanting on my crank. After a few of these I let go her tits and sort of wrapped my arms around her head, and I mean I exploded. I erupted. I pumped it into her, holding her skull up against me and groaning and twisting, pouring it down her throat, and she was just 'ummm' like it tasted so good, like she was drinking nectar, elixir of the gods."

Throughout the story he sat perfectly still with his glazed eyes staring blankly in the direction of the tabletop, his lips fixed in a distant half-smile. The effort flushed red mottled stains to the surface of his cheeks, and his ears glowed. He jerked forward for the bottle, his eyes focusing back in on the immediate, the sudden violence of motion breaking a brief spell over the booth, a pornographic reverie, and Walter wondered if he'd been gawking as the others were—even The Chief had begun to look a little dreamy, a little sentimental. "Yup," he said, letting the whiskey vapors out of his mouth with a smack of the lips and a sibilant ahh, "that there was some of the best sex I ever had. Hot little mama. And the great thing about it is that it's right there. You don't have to go out for it. Plus, older women love it; they really do, and they're so grateful."

That last bit came as a relief to Walter at first; it sounded like vintage Al putting everybody on, and he wanted to believe it was a put-on. Even as a joke it made him uneasy—what kind of a warped person could make up a thing like that?

"Get outta here," The Stone said with an awe that sounded like astonished admiration. "I don't believe it. Throat-fucked his own mother. Incredible."

"How can you live with yourself?" Mallory said.

"Not done," Al said. "There's more. Care to here it?"

Walter didn't want to hear more, whether it was true or made-up or part of both. He grabbed the bottle in his hand. "Come on, Al, that's enough. Save it. Let's get out of here."

"Shh Walter Schmerz. Shh Walter, my Walter. How far you want to go? Don't wanna save it. Been saving it for you; now I wanna share it. We're having fun now. Get's better."

Now that his concentration was broken he was suddenly and completely trashed. A minute ago he had sat transfixed, perhaps because he was marshaling all his energy, for he spoke lucidly and vividly as though he were channeling it as purely as possible. Now he was playing to the audience, a sloppy clown full of silly body language and funny faces.

"So that was all fine and good," he said, "but now I got this horny old lady's head on my lap, and, like, I shot my wad, you know?" He cocked a finger pistol at his head and sputtered his lips. "You know that let down feeling—postpartum blues or post coital depression or whatever you call it? And after all, it is Mommy we're taking about. So it's kind of an awkward moment and I try to get up, only she can't get up. Too drunk. So I hold her up for a minute trying to figure what to do, and finally I decide to just take her to bed and let her sleep it off."

He raised his eyebrows and sighed a theatrical shoulder shrugging sigh. "Now, as you may know, real people are hard to carry, so I have to kind of half carry her and half drag her up the stairs, tripping over her robe and her tits flopping all over the place. Not at all like the song—she ain't heavy, she's my mother. Heh. And she comes to again and starts muttering these lines right out of old movies, shit like, 'no, we mustn't. What if we're discovered,' and 'this is *too* bad,' and 'be gentle with me.' She probably even called me naughty."

His voice rose to a high cartoonish honk as he picked up the pace. "So we're finally there and I dump her in the parental bed and she's sprawled out all tangled in the robe and blankets and she spreads her legs and goes, 'Take me. Fuck me. Do me. Ravish me.' I mean, *ravish* me? Let's just take a look at what we're ravishing, here. This red-eyed, drunken, fat old lady with greasy gray hair in her face, doing the backstroke in bed with her tits slung over the sides like waterwings. She's licking her lips and swinging her knees back and forth and running her hands over her fat stomach towards her cunt. Then, lo and behold, she is playing with herself, working her fingers in and out. *Ravish me.* I mean, gag me.

"We must remember that I'm still high—not an excuse, I'm just saying. You know how when you're stoned you sometimes get fixated on things, and I'm zeroed in on those little old fingers diddling away on that big old muff and her moaning 'fuck me' and boy was it kinky...*Chief.* Bet it tops the kinkiest sex *you* ever had. What *did* you do, anyway? Guess it wasn't worth remembering."

He broke off to light a cigarette, and Walter could see he was gathering himself up again, was getting that glazed look in his eyes, concentrating on the story and dropping the comedy. Walter wanted it to stop and banged his beer bottle on the table to break the spell, but Al just blinked and continued in the kind of hushed, confidential voice people use to tell ghost stories.

"Anyway, the subject was women, and that hole, that object, was suddenly the hottest thing I ever saw. Man, I wanted it. I wanted to get in it along with those fingers. I wanted to be it. I was hotter than the time before. Ripped off my clothes and my dick was standing up, slapping against my belly, so I just climbed right in. Fucked it, took it, did it, ravished it. While I'm sloshing around there in the Grand Canyon I feel her tighten up and start to tremble, then shake, and I figure she's about to come big time."

Someone knocked a bottle off the table, said "shit!" "But I look at her and see that she's crying. Well, not crying so much as slobbering uncontrollably, huh? Which makes me even hotter. I get straight up on my arms so I can watch and do pushups into it at the same time, pumping like a jackhammer. You know how it is when you're that stoned, how one thing becomes another, dreamlike, and now I feel like it's the crying that I'm fucking, like I'm humping her tears and her stinking vodka breath and he fat old age and it's the hottest hardest fuck I ever threw at anything. I came all over all of it. Best orgasm I ever had. Yesiree, give me dirty, nasty, rotten, low-down sex any time. Ravish that shit."

Whether it was true or made up—it might as well be true for you to imagine it like that, for it to live in your mind. Walter was angry. He was drunk. "Then what happened?" he said, using his standard response to bad jokes. "Then what happened, *asshole*?"

"Yes, hell," Mallory said. "You're a sick puppy, alright."

"You betcha, Sparkie. Can't touch me. Try and top it if you want, but I say it takes the prize. I say I win."

"I thought you said it was gonna get better," The Stone said. "I like the part about the blowjob better. So what was yours, Chief Parma?"

Before he could answer, Al said, "Thank you for that careful and considerate critique, Seaman Stone, but that's probably just your latent homosexuality speaking. And don't ask Chief for his secrets. He'll tell you something lame out of Penthouse Forum, but his real trick is how he manages to slip it to a whole division—all at the same time—and keep it up indefinitely, right Chief?"

"It's no trick," The Chief said. "Just takes stamina, something you seem to have run out of. You're starting to sound as drunk as your old lady with the vodka. Better be careful, momma's boy. That's how you wind up a catcher instead of a pitcher."

Al pushed off the table and got to his feet, planting them as though on a rolling deck. "Thank you. Well boys, like the man said, if you can do nothing else, might as well just lie back and enjoy it. But as I still have a Honcho to run and have so far hit only two bars—it would be inappropriate to get underway without a hangover—I shall be on my way. You no longer amuse." He smiled at Walter. "Join me?"

"No," Walter heard himself say. A minute earlier he had wanted to drag Al out.

"Wait up, Turner," The Stone said. "I'll come with ya."

Al put his arm around The Stone. "Right you are. Come along and we'll continue our orientation into the distinguished society of Fredheads. Right." He cocked a finger at Walter. "I understand, Walter. Perceptions."

"Then what happened?" Walter was saying. "Al, then what happened?" He was tugging Al's shirtfront, partly for emphasis and partly to hold himself up. He didn't know if he was being earnest or sarcastic, and he couldn't really make out Al's face at that point; he just kept grabbing him and asking what happened next. "That's the point, you know. You always have to face what happens next."

They were standing on the Honcho side of the intersection across from the main gate of the base, cars whizzing by both ways along the thoroughfare between bars and base, the whoosh and blare of their momentum a watery rush that seemed to cut deeply beneath the curb as though they were plowing through troughs rather than paved lanes. It made Walter reel, as did the dizzy blink of neon and the reek of corndogs and the welter of bodies wafting liquor and vomit and sweat and cheap cologne. The bodies would pool together at either end of the traffic light, then the pools would bleed into one another when the light changed, the individuals trickling through to the other side, pulling free to the safety of the far curb, the exchange complete just as the haltered cars lashed forward to reclaim the road, their eyewhites knifing the sullied air.

After Al and The Stone left them, they were the source of much wonder and fun, and before The Chief could find amusement in Walter again, he lit out on his own and found a safe place to drink and brood in anonymity. There he thought about mischief and confusion and how we are all so rotten to each other.

It was later that night and he was slushing his way home on rubbery legs guided by the narrow tunnel vision of drunken eyes. On the sidewalk near the crossing light he began to get caught up by the crowd of night roamers and jostled toward that steep curb with the shark-like cars below. He grabbed the streetlight and there was Al standing before him like an apparition. He had outlasted The Stone. "Hey," Walter said, and shoved him from behind. Al spun around and hammered him in the chest. Walter fell back against the lamp, hitting his head, then fell forward, grabbing Al's shirt. "Then what happened?"

The cars stopped and the pedestrian tides hemorrhaged together and momentarily emptied the curbs while they stood there hanging on to each other.

"What? *What* do you want?"

"The next hour. The next day?"

"Told you about these things. Warned you."

"Now."

"Now it's deep water. Blue water sailing."

The drunken revelry surged around them again, then burst forward to exchange places with those rushing out to be drunk.

"What about then?"

"Became a sailor, laddybuck. And here we are."

"Because of that?"

"Idiot. What it was all about—the party and everything, drunken mom—going away sendoff. Left that morning."

"Your mom. What about you mom?"

"Why? Wanna go out with her? Suppose she's riper than ever now. Story turned you on, didn't it? You were thinking of your own mom, maybe."

"I don't know what. I don't know anything about your life. Only what I imagine. I want to know." Walter was yelling against the human throb of bodies that again swelled, flowed and ebbed around them. The rhythm stirred an angry nausea in his bowels, now seasick at the assault of busy motion and the shifting pavement. "I can't think. Everything's moving too fast to think. To touch the meanings."

Al spat on his foot. "Meanings."

"None of it's true, right?"

"Fool."

"Then what happened?" Walter was shaking him.

"Then? Had to come up with something, didn't I? Playing with a nasty fellow. Only afraid I didn't go far enough."

"So you're just putting everyone on."

"Whatever."

"What really happened, Alvin?"

"Whatever makes you feel better. The hell you care? It's a story."

"I have to know."

"Which will make you like me better, friend?"

Walter was shaking him again, and he was trying to peel the fingers off his shirt. "You can't...can't just be that way. People care, you know. Want to understand. What makes you so...why can't you be human?"

Walter cursed him—maybe the words could blast away his facade. They could not. "You really are a motherfucker! How can you live with yourself?"

Al shoved him up against the post and dove back into the wave of home going GI's. Walter waded after him. "You mean, how can *you* live with *me*, Walter," he shouted over his shoulder.

"I want to understand you. I think I understand..."

Al's eyes and teeth flashed as he spun and shot a fist at Walter, and his head exploded in white before he could duck. His legs couldn't find a proper position, his knees locking and unlocking, his feet flopping at the pavement, but he failed to hit the ground. He thought that he couldn't find that either, but Al was holding him, shaking him around by the shirt as his eyes flew around, they too trying to find something to hold onto, but the world was liquid and silvery, slipping from his touch like mercury. "A fucking story, you jerk! Why can't you get it? Go along for a change? Got you! Got all of you! You don't cut it in *my* nav. Go home, Schmerz, you're a loser." Walter could feel Al's mouth chewing on his ears as he spat the words into his head before diving back into the Honcho: "You *wish* I did it! It's what you want. *That's* the story you want, you fake!"

Walter coughed up what blood he couldn't swallow, stood there sputtering and gulping with his hands cupped over his bent face, catching the blood and then flicking it onto the pavement, almost as though it was something to do, a distraction until he could compose himself and figure out what to do, until the shock wore off and he could think through the blinding interference of pain that his nose was sending into the rest of his head. The sting gave rise to a swollen numb buzz over his face and an insistent ache in the temples, and he became dimly aware of interested passersby at the periphery of his consciousness. There was a hand on his back, and he knew that men were crouching by his side—at some point he had squatted to his haunches, lost balance and sat down with his head still in his hands.

"What happened here, buddy?"

He tried to look at them but couldn't lift his eyes above the billyclubs and brassards. "He hit be."

"Who? Where'd he go?"

"I dote doe. Sub guy. Sub druck guy." He laughed at the sound and spit a wad of blood. "Ooh, by face feels so fat."

Somehow he talked them out of making him file a report or go the hospital; he supposed they didn't really want to be bothered. So they saw him

103

safely and amiably inside the base where he assured them he was fine, and he staggered headlong back toward the ship. On the quarterdeck, the officer of the deck had some misgivings as to what to do about Walter, and some choice words about his appearance. He finally decided that "Schmerz is his own problem," but pulled his ID card for good measure, just in case he'd gotten into trouble and there were repercussions.

Walter poured himself down the ladder and along the passageway, splashing from bulkhead to bulkhead, cascaded loudly down a second ladder into the compartment where he was hushed by sleepy sailors, cursed them all violently, fell into his rack, and died.

Radiomen

Somewhere in the distance someone was singing, high and sweet, a sad and comforting melody. Must be his mother getting breakfast ready. He wondered if he was late. Was it a school day? He didn't want to go to school. Wanted to stay in bed forever and dream. *Maybe it's a Saturday. Maybe when I get up I'll run to the ballpark and play baseball till dark, till you can't see the ball until it's heading for your nose—ow!—till parents come out on the porches and call the kids to dinner in the loud, particular music of our names, the warm safety of the familiar and the unacknowledged freedom of a home to resent returning to, of a family dinner to rush through to get back to the kids and the fireflies and the night games of tag. Maybe I'm not even in school yet. Maybe I'm still in my crib waiting for Gary to come throw me in the air and hang me upside down by the ankles, scaring me and making me laugh. I hope that's it. Or maybe I'm in a motel room with Irene, and that was her singing, sitting cross legged on the bathroom counter while she makes herself up before going home. Soon she'll come to the bed and give me something to remember her by, maybe the right kind of kiss, or more. I love Irene. I love her so much that I won't look. I won't see her leave. How can life go on with her constantly leaving like this? How can anyone live without that kind of love? Life without it, without possessing and being possessed, without coming into her body, and her tremblingly, stabbingly making me hers, all I want to be…she being the only thing in the world worth being, and married to the wrong man and always leaving me with "I wish" and "imagine" and "what if" and "I want to come with you. I do. Let me come. I beg you to let me come." And not coming with me. Robbing me. Life without that is inconceivable; I won't look. Or maybe I'm back in the Philippines with Vivien. That would be sweet. That is what I want. No one has a heart of gold. But I could live with eyes like that, could live in eyes like that. I could look then and not be afraid they'd go away. I'm not afraid of her life. Only a woman, no more, no less. Her crime—that, and poverty in the Philippines. What's that make me? Lucky. Her lover. Because I love the song she's singing like the cool well water that gushes over her body that doesn't so much clean as rinse and refresh. The communal pump of home that washes over her life, the life that's in her eyes. And what am I to her, a specter, an idea, pleasant distraction or a bit of business—not that, I can tell. After all, she's singing. But am I just another, a reminder, a replacement, another uniform link in the Great Chain of Men? It's important that it be her. Only her. Particularly her. Insistently, willfully, consistently. Because she is her, sweet her.*

Liberty Call

Such a nice place to be, although the music now seemed to reach him not through his ears but through tiny electric wires that entered his closed eyes and proliferated just under his scalp, crisscrossing each other as they wound around his head and tightened, humming that innocuous air that was growing increasingly annoying as it grew louder, and as it grew louder, so did the wattage in the banding wires turn up and burn, each thin line stinging along its discrete orbit of his head, the entire network mapping now a solid description of his skull in orchestrated burning, cutting in from his scalp and welling beneath his eye sockets, searing into his brain, the music now an electric flute piping him to his doom. His brain was beginning to smoke. He could smell it.

Walter cracked open an eye. Worst case scenario: the berthing compartment. The music he heard was Waddo the postal clerk singing a Lionel Ritchie song. The lights were on and people were starting to bang lockers and shuffle up to the showers in their silly flip-flops. "My brain's on fire," he croaked, and closed his eyes again.

The thing was coming. Eight hours on, eight hours off. One long harassed moment until the next port. There is no sense of time underway; night and day are arbitrary phenomena that catch you off guard. When you think a week has gone by it's been only two days. It's best not to count. Perhaps it would be different working topside under the sky, but in radio there are only the fluorescent lights and syncopated flickers from the crypto gear and the chatter of teletypes and ghostly moans emanating from the radio speakers and orders barking from the bridge and paper flowing, unfolding and transmitter breakdowns and frequency shifts and fast reaction tests and circuit changes and order to give, responsibility and unceasing pressure and your legs hurts from the constant rolling and your mouth is foul with coffee and cigarettes and that would all be okay if you could only get enough sleep.

And things with Iran were hot since the hostages were taken. The volume of message traffic had bloated. Battle lines were being drawn. More ships into the Arabian Sea, into the Persian Gulf itself. The Iranians sent P3s and second-hand U.S. destroyers out to recon the fleet, each appearance prompting a flash report from the forward picket. The Russians accelerated activity and the usual cat and mouse games intensified. Rumors abounded among officers and crew. Everyone was caught between the dread of battle and the excitement of involvement, secretly longing for action. But not now, now that it might happen.

Contingencies. Al told of the time they were making a simple R and R cruise from Yokosuka to Pusan and got mugged in Sasebo, where they loaded some spooks and a van on board and spent the next month chasing a Russian aircraft carrier all over the North Pacific. "Bravo Zulu. Keep charging." Everyone got gedunk ribbons. Contingencies: Russians, pirates, Boat People, Iranians—mopping up from their nation's previous adventures. Walter Schmerz juggling it all in the fluorescent hysteria of radio central on the USS Outland, frigate.

Looking ahead, beyond the Philippines to Indian Ocean contingencies. That was a mistake. Heavy weather. Considering the state of his oncoming hangover, there was sure to be heavy weather. That was a contingency. Hell, his whole life—he certainly didn't belong here doing these things. The Chief had said that if Walter were in charge the division would run on autopilot, and he was probably right. If Walter were in charge the frigate might just not sail at all. A regular stay-at-home, minimize the contingencies. Getting underway made him sweat.

Walter fully opened his eyes and saw Bum directly across the brief alcove on the middle rack, his head stooped, a stocking over his afro and a cigarette dangling from his lips. He wanted to say, "Stand by for heavy weather, Bum. Get the word out. I'm going back to Subic City because I have to, but I'm going alone. Keep them away from me. Look out for your shipmates. Make them stay at home this time." He swung his feet over the side of the rack and fished under the mattress for a cigarette—a ludicrous, rote gesture with his head on fire, sickening. But he lit the nauseating thing and glared at Bum, who looked back at him, tired, unhappy, but managed with some amusement: "Boy, look at yo eyes. You a fuckin' mess."

"I thought my brain was on fire. I thought I could smell the rancid, burning flesh of my own gray matter, but it was only you. You stink."

"Not this morning, Schmerz. I'm in no mood."

"Bum, you smell bad."

"I said don't start this morning."

"I mean, you really stink."

"Yeah? And you ugly. You seen a mirror lately? Who messed up yo face for ya?"

"I want you to correct your odor problem. Why do you have so much trouble attaining the proper smell?"

"Attain this," he said. "I want you to correct yo face. Look atcha, red-eyed bitch. You know how much I'm gonna hate seein' that fuckin' face every day?"

"Bum, I think someone took a shit in your rack last night. Maybe you should check your skivvies."

He grabbed his crotch. "Check this."

"I'll slap you down."

"Slap this down. You ain't big enough to slap me, ya skinny fuck. You got no ass in yo pants. Looks like somebody already slapped you upside yo head. You better get what's left of yo ass up to the radioshack or RM number one Starring will have it all, bitch."

"I'm telling Radioman First Class Shit-For-Brains that you're an unsanitary menace to this berthing compartment."

"And I'm telling Petty Officer Shit-For-Brains what you just called him. You can't get away with that."

107

Walter looked in the mirror and saw his damaged, tenderized face. Seeing it that way made the throbbing double in intensity. His image in the mirror seemed to warp with the rhythm of his pulse, shrinking and swelling in time with the expansion and contraction of every broken blood vessel in his skin. His nose was swollen and clogged, the nostrils blood-encrusted. His eyes looked as though they were set in deep purple sockets, bruises belted across his cheekbones and arched from the bridge of his nose to his temples like a botched Egyptian makeup job, painfully comical. Most disturbing were the red eyes, the whites entirely suffused with the bloody tincture of the night before. He was surprised that he could still see with his eyes so affected. He felt he could see in them what was coming, and that he could do nothing.

Despite the buzzing of machinery and the bustling of Starring and the two duty radiomen taking care of last minute business, the air was subdued, still and dense with smoke. The two Hicomm speakers hissed a steady complaint while Tug Control directed the outbound task group traffic. The broadcast was clacking away on the three teletypes and a bank of green and orange bulbs blinking in unison said that the crypto was up and purring in sync.

Nate Tatum checked the plan of the day while his three signal strikers sprawled on the deck, mutely fidgeting, smoking, and drinking Cokes. Mallory and Blinkman sat in the tapecutter's chairs with their ball caps pulled low, assuming airs of surly indifference. Bum sneered at Starring as he pored over the equipment status board, shaking that fat red pinched face, hypocrisy and affectation slanting every word that squeezed between his trim mustache and mahogany pipe. Kid ran around setting up circuits and doing radio checks. The cipher lock clicked and there was a crash against the door as it re-locked. It clicked again. This time it gave an approving buzz and the heavy gray vault yawned open as Al Turner spilled through. His loose, untied boondockers clomped on the deck. His shirt was still unbuttoned and untucked and his ball cap sat on the back of his curly blond head. He smiled broadly and announced loudly, "Good morning everybody."

All looked up for a moment, then returned their interest to Coke can, cigarette, speck of dirt on the deck. Starring glowered, suppressing his distress—Al, who had the power of being in his bones what Starring could only play at—always presented him with dilemmas of leadership.

"Turner, you're drunk."

"Thank you."

"You're a fucking mess, mister."

"Roger that."

"Straighten up that uniform before the Lieutenant gets here. Fine example for a petty officer. You're going downhill mister. Are you wearing that cap or is it following you?"

"Certainly."

When Al's eyes met Walter's his forehead rippled and his ears jumped back. "Wow," he said. "My my."

"Yeah," Starring said through teeth clenching his pipe, "looks like you've been a real influence on Petty Officer Schmerz. For awhile it looked like we had a real sailor. Not another fuck up."

"That the Outland fighting spirit," Bum said. "Red-eyed bitch took on the whole Honcho last night. Ain't that right Schmerz?"

Al batted his eyes coquettishly at Walter. "And do we know the story behind what happened here, Walter?" though it must have already been evident that he was safe.

"A drunken fucking asshole blindsided me when I was trying to help him."

"Looks like he didn't want your help." He walked past Starring and plopped into Walter's lap, threw one arm around his neck and gingerly pinched his cheek. "Well, good morning anyway, Walter. How are you?"

"I hurt, as a matter of fact. My head hurts." He was comforted to see that the hand now draped over his shoulder was swollen, the knuckles red and raw. He squeezed it hard and Al jumped off. "And a very good morning to you, Alvin. How are we today? Stinking, I think."

"I had a dream about you last night in the YurNavSucs Hotel."

"And where, mate, is the YurNavSucs Hotel? Are we inventing again?"

"It's that tall, thick hedge around the Fleet Support office. Very comfy and discrete for those times when you just can't get back to the ship. I've just had a lovely stay."

"And what happened in this happy, happy dream?"

"Well, I dreamed I was in a bombing crew and you were the general giving the briefing and you were pointing to the Philippines on a map."

"Do tell."

"You pointed at Olongapo City and you said, 'Gentlemen, here are the buns,' and Olongapo was shaped like a woman and you were touching a big X on the ass part."

"How nice. And what are we going to do when Lieutenant Moderness finds out that we're stinko?"

"I wonder does Captain Kangaroo ever go ballistic?"

"Let's ask him." The cipher lock clicked and Lieutenant Moderness walked through the door.

"Attention on deck!" Al shouted, knocking his heels and saluting.

"Alright, cut the crap." Mr. Moderness did not seem in the mood for an early morning ride. "Starring, get them together. Everyone here?"

"Yes sir. All present and accounted for. Our friend Mister Turner just made it."

"Tattletale," Al said. "Never trust a man whose last name is a present participle. Good morning Mister Moderness. Nice day for an Indian Ocean cruise." He grinned.

109

"Morning. What's with you? What's the story with Turner, Starring? And what the hell happened to Schmerz? Belay that. Don't tell me. I don't want to know."

"Petty Officer Turner is drunk, sir."

"You drunk, Turner?"

"Mister Moderness, I never get drunk. I am not now drunk. I'm shitfaced!"

"He doesn't have the first watch?"

"No sir. He has the mid watch with Petty Officer Schmerz, but I think we better break up that act. They think they're a couple of clowns."

"Do not," Walter said.

"Shut up!"

The Lieutenant gave them the official version of their mission in the Indian Ocean, flat, routine, with an ill-tempered irony in his voice. He was poor officer material, protecting himself with sarcasm as though he didn't care about anything, so you'd never know how he really felt. That was his way of trying to be a regular guy, as though he found everything distasteful, like the average bluejacket. They all knew they were in for some kind of action. They all knew a crisis was coming.

"Are we going to attack Iran?" Blinkman asked.

"Negatory," Moderness said. "Just like I told you. First, Subic and supplies. Then we're just going on exercises, showing the flag. And the sigs should keep an eye out for Vietnamese." The part about Vietnamese sounded particularly aggravating to him, as though he were being asked to go buy a quart of milk in the middle of the Superbowl. "We're saving Boat People these days—as you probably know, those shiny new fifties are for killing pirates who've been feeding off these people."

"Hey, pirates," Al said. "Now that's something. Now this is getting exciting. Can I get on that machine gun? I'd get a kick out of shooting some pirates."

"You're enough trouble just shooting your mouth."

"I never get to have any fun around here."

"I got your fun," Bum said, once again grabbing his crotch.

By the time their watch came around Walter was incapacitated. His head was raging and every time he took aspirin he merely retched it up again while failing to empty his stomach. He was shaking, in a cold sweat, and each time the ship rolled in that infinity of roiling, haphazard insult he swore the next slap would be his last. Each wave of nausea brought him to tears and blasted his mind from his brain. When he could think, he was convinced that he was seriously injured, even dying, but he didn't care, was too weak. He supposed he did have a bit of concussion, between the workouts Mallory and Al gave him, his head got knocked around enough. He stayed slumped at the supervisor's desk while Al did all the work, carried the watch for him, conducting the seamen in their duties even as he reached over their shoulders, performing their tasks for them in the interest of time, changing the crypto on time, tuning transmitters, tearing messages off the broadcast and routing the traffic, offering words of encouragement and assurance that Walter was going to live through the night. At one point The Chief came in and screamed at Walter until he climbed to his feet and went through the motions of some minor duty while riding out the panic of a head spin. The Chief threatened to write him up for bringing this condition on himself. Then he threatened to write Al up for somehow being in conspiracy with him. He threatened to pull their liberty in the Philippines. But somehow, after the last night, it all rang empty. Walter did not care. "Atta boy, Walter," Al said. "Just go with it. Go all the way into it and it'll see you through. Don't let 'em touch you."

When The Chief left, Al touched Walter's shoulder, slumped over the supervisor's desk, and said, "Look, Walter, everything's running smooth. I'm gonna make a head call and get a cup of coffee. You're in charge. You've got the con. Got it?"

Walter grunted.

Al shoved the shoulder. "Got it?"

"Yes!" He put his head on his forearms and listened. He thought he could hear the ship steaming on the surface of the globe, where rushing blue brushes the black vault, the breaking of the waves, or was that the rushing of blood or a ringing in his ears? He could hear the eerie whirring of open frequencies like a theremin in a horror movie, punctuated occasionally by stray dits and dahs of continuous-wave code trespassing into the wrong high frequency lane. He thought of the black vastness of the space these waves travel through. Then he heard the human sounds—these young men he trained handling and checking equipment, stubbing butts into Coke cans, tearing off printed messages from the ever unwinding giant spools of teletype paper, and he began to fall asleep to the music of the printers, typitty-typitty-typing. The metal keys slapping the paper were indeed set to time, the time mediated through a crypto machine to make them ugly and unintelligible, then into transmitters and out into perhaps thousands of miles of space on a particular soundwave frequency, then into another station's receiver, and from there decrypted back into beautiful and intelligible language and music—To: USS Outland.

And suddenly, the dream broke. The slapping wasn't rhythmically timed. The music was ugly. "Shit!" he yelled, jumping up, forgetting his body and his head. "Bum! Broadcast!"

"Taking hits, Schmerz! Nothing but garbage from the entire fleet!"

Walter grabbed an oscilloscope and jacked it into an unused received. "Get me a clean freek, Bum! High! Go Higher—it's late at night! He found a gorgeous dance of unmolested wave eeling along the scopescreen, ran to the patchboard over his desk and plugged the broadcast into the new receiver. "We're in. Get me a time-check on another receiver! Crypto's still busted."

Bum did so and said, "Take it!"

111

Walter patched the crypto into the timer: "At the tone the time will be two o'clock. Zirp." He clicked the crypto on the heartbeat of "zirp" and watched the lights blip back into harmony. The teletypes' clatter fell back into cadence. Noise, that hijacker of system had released its thrall. A garbled heading of mad random type ceded to the gallop of text at the center of the scroll. From the universe to your eyes only:

```
From: Comseventhfleet
  To: USS Outland
Subject: Exercise Beard Iron
```

It took Walter a moment. Really? "Holy motherfucking shit!"

"What is it?" Bum said.

"Test! *The* fucking test!" The radioman's crucible from the commander of the entire fleet.

Walter tore it off the broadcast and time stamped it for proof of receipt, then grabbed a handset and got on the Hicomm radio: "Batterup, Batterup, this is Overwork, Overwork, Exercise Beard Iron! Repeat, Beard Iron, Over." And then came the sweet, cool voice of comfort and joy ghosting through a thousand mile of Pacific static: "Overwork this is Batterup. Roger. You are loud and clear—fivers."

And roger that, Walter thought. "My Tango Oscar Romeo, two zero one!"

He hung up the phone and said out loud, "Oh Commsta Subic, relay to Commander Seventh Fleet, message received. By me, Walter Schmerz, please note, at two oh one, two oh sweet fucking one in zulu time during high frequency contingency test on the tick and hum of operator excellence and the march of the stars with the pitch and yaw of frigate purchased seas, a coup for duty and honor and hope."

The lock clicked and Al stepped back in. Walter said, "You took friggin' long enough."

"Ran into a guy. Anything happen while I was out?"

"Only lost the broadcast. First message after that was a Beard Iron," Walter said.

"Bum said, "Hey Turner, what's beard iron mean?"

"Means better hope never to get one when you're in charge. It's a naval term, Bum. What's that hair on your face called? We're the only service in the military that can grow one. Wear it proudly, son. And what color is iron? It means that by the time you're able to do what Radioman Second Class Schmerz just did, you'll probably have a gray beard. How'd you lose the broadcast, Walter?"

"What do you think? Static, interference, noise."

"Beware of noise, Walter. It's the radioman's greatest enemy. Always beware of noise. Know what I'm saying?"

The reappearance of Al brought Walter down from the airwaves and back into his body like a falling elevator. He doubled over and vomited yesterday's shit-on-a-shingle all over the deck. "Get a mop and clean that shit up, Schmerz," Al said.

Subic City

"There it is," Nate, the Leading Signalman, said, "Paradise." Walter looked through the big-eyes at the khaki colored hills rising straight out of the soft, Subic blue inviting cushions on either side that made your heart hitch with the prescience of consummate sensuality. The hills looked smooth, almost textureless, like the airbrushed skin of a pinup, burnt brown in a youth spent splashing in the surf and sunshine, flashing her black eyes and white teeth at passing admirers, laughing in husky delight at flatteries with her high cheeks pushing pleasure into the eyes, and curvy lips drawn tight against those so practical teeth; a youth spent walking among the beach's nipa palms, a lattice-like dappling of sunshine filtering through the fronds and playing upon her bare, airbrushed brown, round shoulder as she walks from you, her hair liquidy-black, her buttocks swiveling on the spring of her calves; but a youth spent also, perhaps, in the shadow of Catholic admonition and knowledge of poverty, and her blush maybe partly in shame at your leer, and defiance too, in knowledge of the practicalities of life—*need*, and the leverage of her smile and body, of the dirt, disease and joy it brings forth. Then you know that there is more than hospitality in the pinup's eastern smile, and more than seduction, that there is a cruel understanding, a mute accusation, a mutual exploitation. And the sight and smell of the land *is* like that of a strange woman, for you've been at sea for ages and the hills rising like knees at either side of your head are as hospitable as any land but exotic because of their brown smoothness, and the insistent land-smell that intoxicates your nostrils and accelerates your blood is recognizable in its genus but original in its variety, particular in its perfume, sweet to the verge of rottenness and the more exciting for it.

The mountains opened, making way for their ship, enticing them up into the bay. Not engines and propellers, but allure and aroma powered them irresistibly toward the center. Walter swung the telescope forward. Ahead in the distance in a direct and inevitable line from the bow was a triangular mass of jagged brown and gray, of steel, concrete and glass. The base was still too distant to discern individual shapes or motion. It was still an abstract blur. But soon they would be in it, a part of it.

"Paradise tonight," Nate said, as Walter backed away from the big-eyes and leaned over the signal bridge. Below, on the fo'c'sle, a gang from deck division swore at each other as they shined the brightwork and prepared lines for mooring. Behind them the hills continued parting slowly, almost imperceptibly, wrapping around them. The ship cut the bay willfully, but the foamy white flaps quickly closed as the wound filled and was covered again by steady, smooth blue. The bay said nothing and the engines hummed and Walter thought they were really being carried by some tropistic attraction. The hills were silent and the water was still, but their own push forced the Philippine breeze to sigh against their salt skin, pressing their clothes, snapping their bellbottoms and cracking the flags as if prodding them into an idiot dialogue with the white sun. The hills spread, unfolding and undulant, and said nothing.

Walter's excuse for being on the signal bridge was to do a maintenance check on the signal shack's watertight door—he was OC division's damage control petty officer. He didn't know why there was a watertight door on the highest deck of the ship—if the seas ever knocked on it they would have already sunk—but he used it as a pretense to get under the sun and escape the oppression of radio central. He envied Nate's near autonomy as leading signalman, up there on top of the ship with the sea and sky, with his flags and lights, even sleeping in the signal shack when the warm weather permitted. He was aloof from the personality politics of the division and eluded most of The Chief's petty tyranny. So Walter watched the bay open and the base draw near, for he didn't have the radio watch or duty the first day in, and he wanted to see paradise.

The tug boats came out to greet them and a bos'n mate called away the Sea and Anchor Detail. The sound-powered phone in the shack issued a squiggling squawk and Starring, at the other end, summoned him to Radio for muster. Back to bedlam. He swallowed and felt the queasy, sour lemon lozenge at the bottom of his stomach that always reappeared at the sight of the heavy, cipher-locked, haze-gray door marked Top Secret, Radio Central. Once in the catharsis of work he was fine, a frenetic demon like his fellow radiomen, but at the sight of the door he steeled for confrontation and the lozenge would dissolve in his stomach's acid, releasing yellow dread, loathing, and finally, resignation.

Mallory sat in the tapecutter's chair typing outgoing messages and Blinkman was mechanically tearing messages off the broadcast. Nate's signalmen and the off-watch non-rates sat out of the way in the corner, smoking and drinking Cokes. Starring was posing in front of the status board, pulling on his pipe and smoothing his mustache. Another pipe stuck out of the back pocket of his too-tight dungarees that always seemed to bell prematurely at his ankles. Bum and Kid were talking quietly by the corner near the signalmen, out of harm's way. Harm was The Chief.

When Walter came in Starring glowered at him for effect, though at the center of his eyes was only the general hopelessness of a lifer and the immediate distress of a confused and frightened sailor. He was too ridiculous to be scary. When he tried to be imposing, he was merely mean. But he was the LPO; he had to act tough. Walter glowered back. He was a non-com too, and fully feeling the part now, especially with an audience, especially since he felt he had weathered just about anything that could be dished out and come through rather smartly. Besides, he knew where power and authority in the division came from, and that was now bellowing from its desk in the forward starboard corner behind the UHF phones.

Starring motioned his head toward where the sound was coming from and said importantly, "Chief want to see you."

The OOD called through the intercom demanding something be done about the state on the bridge's tug circuit and added, "Combat says they can't communicate with the beach. What the hell are you guys doing down there?" Starring went to work on the problems. Al was the object of The Chief's current rage for having lost a couple of broadcast numbers on their watch while they were off the satellite during a high frequency contingency test. None of the messages, it turned out, were addressed to the Outland, but that didn't matter to The Chief. Walter waited his turn, feigning indifference like the others, as the man roared above the machinery.

"You goddamn idiot! Don't you tell me about radio wave propagation. I was standing mid-watches when you were in diapers. You're not so fucking smart. Just remember who's running this radioshack. It's mine. I'm the Chief. That's my name to you—Chief. You're lucky I don't pull your liberty and make you wait till Australia before you even see a woman again. Now get the hell out of my sight before I change my mind."

"Thank you," Al said.

"You're a fucking mess!"

"Roger that."

"Don't you roger me! I could have your ass. And another thing, I should run your ass up to captain's mast for turning over a watch without properly inventorying your pubs. Goddamnit, that's a breach of security. What are you? Coverin' for your friend, Schmerz? Do you understand the severity of this?"

"Aye aye, Chief. Firstly, I didn't sign for it, Schmerz did. Secondly, I merely handed over said completed pub inventory to yon Mallory, who—"

"And you left your station before the watch was properly turned over. Jesus Christ..." He was about to continue when he spied Walter. "Schmerz, get your butt over here."

He went.

The Chief opened the publications inventory book and pointed at Walter's signature. "This is your signature for the last watch's inventory?"

"Yes."

"You *did* inventory all the pubs?"

"That's why I signed it, Chief."

The Chief called to Mallory, who looked up from his typing. "Mallory, what did you say was missing?"

Mallory looked at Walter and said, "ACP 113, Chief."

"You checked them all?" The Chief asked. "Schmerz says he inventoried them, which means he either lost a classified publication during his watch or he is lying or you—"

"Unclassified," Walter corrected.

Mallory looked at Walter again with a sneer of contempt, a dare, and said matter-of-factly, almost cheerfully, "It just ain't there, Chief. No ACP 113." Walter wondered if he had the nerve and sheer spite to have thrown it over the side. "I can't help it if Schmerz has problems running his watch," he continued, his tone growing angrier as they glared at each other. "I may be a lowly seaman, but I know what I don't see, and I know what I do see around here, too. Which is—"

"Alright," The Chief said, "Schmerz, you are responsible for that goddamn pub. That's classified material, boy—*all* pubs are classified material—and you signed for it and you are responsible for it. Now you find that pub or you are in a world of hurt. You signed yourself right into a breach of security."

Walter reached up to the book rack over The Chief's desk and began pulling the books down as he bent over and around The Chief, who refused to budge an inch out of the way. From the middle of the stack he pulled a slender volume marked *Allied Command Publication 113*.

"Here," he said, and dropped it on the desk in front of him. His cheeks were hot and he was almost shaking.

"Good," The Chief said. "Now put them back."

Walter looked at Mallory, who had again turned toward him. "Well fuck me," he said. "I'm damned. Just goes to show how easy things can go wrong. I could of swore it wasn't there."

"That's it," Walter said. "I don't care who your sea-daddy is—"

"Never mind about that," The Chief snapped.

Mallory returned to his typing, and The Chief returned to the subject of Walter's imperfections, checking off his own inventory of transgressions as a professional and as a man. He received a chewing out for offenses against his person, against the division, the ship, and the Navy. He was informed of his good fortune that he'd still get liberty, be knee deep in Filipinas and have a jolly time even though he was a sorry excuse for a sailor and a lousy example for a petty officer. As Chief worked into his subject his voice rose higher above the radio din, his dark eyes bulging and beer gut thrusting and heaving, when over the PA came those most glorious words: "Moored. Shift colors."

As if the touch of land instantly softened him, he relaxed back into his chair and mellowed his tone, summoning Al back to the corner with them. "Alright, listen up, you two. Everything I said back there in Yokosuka still goes, and I'm holdin' you to it. Now for further details. Here's the deal. I will be at the Hard Rock at six p.m. You and The Stone—I said you were to stick by each other—you *will* check in with me there at six. Ain't my kind of place, but it's busy and crowded and nearby, kind of safe feelin'."

They looked at each other with disbelief. "No, no," he said. "I just want to be assured everyone's okay and that everything's goin' smoothly. All like I said. You will keep a lookout for the bad guys, you will report anything that seems weird or out of the ordinary; you will watch your backs and report to me. On time. I'll decide how I'm gonna play the particulars from there. Who knows, if everything's copacetic maybe we can forget about the whole thing. In any case you will standby for further instructions. Understand?"

Walter's heart popped like a pus sac, fouling his stomach and gagging his throat so he couldn't speak. Al stood at parade rest, bouncing on his toes, a tight-lipped smile zipped across his face.

"Nothin' to worry about men, you'll see. Relax, Schmerz, I'm sure you'll get to see your girlfriend. Now am I understood?"

"Aye aye, Chief," Al said, smiling.

He rose and spoke loudly, for the benefit of all hands. "I'll deal with you two later. Starring, take care of muster and tell The Lieutenant I had business to attend to," and Chief Parma was gone—to the chiefs' quarters, into civilian clothes, probably the first one off the brow and onto Magsaysay Boulevsard.

"You want a shoeshine?"
"You want a good time?"
"Hey Joe, you like my sister?"
"Can I buy your watch, mister?"
"Psst, dope, good smoke, *speeed*."

The swirl produces the murmuring intonation of a constant pleading song. Augmenting the smoke from cheap jeepney exhaust is the smell of barbecue vendors roasting their wares over twigs and refuse. They sell skewered chunks of monkey meat, chicken and dog. Each is slathered with a syrupy glaze that produces a queasy-sweet aroma that almost complements the atmosphere of corruption.

There are bars along either side of the street as far as you can see: country-western bars, rock bars, discos and holes-in-the-wall. The monopoly of bars is broken only now and then by the intrusion of pizza and massage parlors with clucking women queuing on the front steps. Anyone would have to go somewhere for an icy San Miguel, clothes sticking like wet paint in the tropical heat and the sweat slicking back the hair.

Again Walter felt like quarry in the midst of a consuming hunger. There always seem to be more girls in the bars than customers. They hover in the background, then close in and beg you to buy them chewing gum, flowers, photographs, and of course drinks at inflated prices. They throw themselves in your lap and ask you to dance. They revile you for your stinginess, then try to coax you with sad stories or promises of delight. Some have names and some have numbers tacked to their chests. They throw their noses in the air, call you "stuck up" and march off. You laugh at the game. They'll be back. They have nowhere else to go, and neither do you—and after a few more beers you'll see yourself as the hunter. You are locked in the dance of an original moment, born of a chain of action and consequence that has conveyed you to this moment, that compels you to dance, that informs your blood that it must boil with the moment. Your entire past decreed and your every nerve demands that you steep in it, that you simultaneously create and learn it, moment begetting moment, like instant passion and procreation with your own life—here with Al and The Stone, in certain circumstances, in a certain planet, in a certain country, in a certain town, in a certain bar, called The Paradise.

"I'm divastated, I tell ye. Simply divastated. Sure, and it was Haggard and meself against the world, so it seemed in them days. And when we wasn't a fightin' the good fight and a-brawlin' between ourselves, weren't we lovin' up all the femininity in the self-same Paradise, as well as kissin' off the last golden drops of many a bottle, like the final gongin' off of old worthy sailor friends, crossin' the brow for their last time? Formidable, we was. Many a dead soldier and deflowered daughter in our wake in them days. Drank the house dry, if I dare say so meself. True. Yes, formidable. I'm simply divastated."

The Paradise wasn't quite as Al remembered it. It was subdued and lonely and somehow empty, despite the coven of working girls nosing around and flying impatiently back and forth. Perhaps it was the wrong place to start. Mimi was gone from the old haunt, to Al's chagrin, and the other girls didn't seem to compensate, though they all insisted that they could be Mimi if wanted. She went missing one night and never came back. And Haggard was missing, too, Walter could tell. Al was let down, and Walter got the awkward feeling that The Stone and he were part of what was wrong with the scene, that they weren't the people he wanted to be with; he thought how rarely we appreciate the actual moment that we're in. There was always something better in the past or coming from the future. Odd that Al could be nostalgic, sentimental. For The Stone it must have felt wrong because he had lived it through Al's memory, expecting craziness with buddies and wild sexual shenanigans. Nothing was happening. He was bored.

Walter was waiting for the right time to go missing, himself, hiding his still-bruised eyes in a *Stars and Stripes*, peeking out from time to time, looking occupied while he searched inside himself for resolve.

"Simply divastated."

"Oh shut up," Walter said. "What's the difference if it's Mimi or not, really?"

"What do you wanna do now?" The Stone said. "This place ain't so hot. Let's go somewheres that's hoppin'. Music or something."

"Sad to say," Al said. "Might as well. What'll it be? Muster in at the Hard Rock?"

"We really gonna do that?" Walter said.

"Don't you want to see what happens next? Could be fu-un. Wasting our time here with no Mimi, that bitch. Kind of changes everything. But I tell you what, men, no reason why we can't get extra specially crazy tonight. I mean, we can get truly naughty if we so desire. Just have to pick up the pace. We got a case of the doldrums, here."

"Man. That Chief's weird. He's fuckin' with us, and shit. Wow. Fun? They got music?"

"Live bands. Dancers. Lots of action. But more than that, they got Chief Parma, who could be our key to a successful liberty. Let's see what he has up his sleeve. After all, it could be *our* chance to fuck with *him*. We have secrecy on our side, friends all. We have what he doesn't know. Surprise!"

"Without me," Walter said. "On principle. You're just making an excuse for giving in. I don't give a damn what he's up to. And like you say, he can't touch us, really."

"C'mon Schmerz. Let's moto. What're we waitin' for. Let's rock and roll. Let's party where there's action."

"Join us, Walter. Don't you want to see what happens next? What he's got in store for us?"

Why should he? He was on his way to see a real woman who supposedly was waiting for him, not just a gyrating number on a bikini to be had for the price of a bar fine. He was afraid to find out what Parma had in mind, and why should he want to see someone he hated? "Well, just for awhile," he heard himself say. He was waiting for the pull of it, the feel of being locked into life, a matrix, like crypto gear in sync, with the liquid electric signals fluxing through him, his green lights flicking in silent harmony. But being fragile, easily disrupted, some inner hesitation—noise—had thrown him out of rhythm, and he was now processing only confusion.

They walked back through the bright twilit and exhaust-choked air, back toward the base where the Hard Rock tickled the urgent liberty-minded eye with its hot blinking pink neon monolith at the mouth of Magsaysay where the jeepneys lined three deep, as if to say they would start the night all over again. Along the way Walter daydreamed of his impending reunion.

She says nothing. Moonlight glistens off the dark, careless bangs across her forehead. Her nostrils dilate almost imperceptibly to take in that extra catch of air, highlighting the quaint curve of her nose, and needing more air still, her lips part with a faint wet tick of her moist teeth. She exhales warm against his face that same breath that for a moment had buoyed her just so. Her skin is coffee milkshake and her eyes a tart, creamy surprise of floating brandy filling. Her eyes swell with emotion and plead for understanding. He smiles, amused and generous.

Such a cozy picture, but what if her eyes don't swell with pleading and emotion? He could feel the sweat under his arms lathering up his deodorant. His underwear was bunching and twisting its soggy way up his body as they walked. He wiped at the greasy shine he imagined on his face. Now it felt dirty from his hands. He pictured his bruises smeared all over his face, yellowish brown streaks. What if she's turned off by the bruises and pink eyes. Forgot about that. His healing eyes itched and he rubbed them. He wanted to ask someone if his face was dirty.

"Walter," Al said, "is something funny or do you have a gerbil stuck up your ass?"

"Is there newsprint on my face?"

"Let's see. You've been rubbing it so much, if there is you've probably rubbed back to yesterday's news. Yes, you've gotten all the way down to last year's *Stars and Stripes*. Can you read him, Stone?"

"Like a book, man."

"See, Stone made a funny. And what's the headline? 'Friends to run Olongapo. Swear to remain inseparable.' Yup, guess that means you can't go mess around is Subic City. Prophetic paper, I'd say. That why you're smiling like you just ate a faceful of balut and pretending to like it?"

"Just thinking. And I *am* going to Subic City."

"Then we're duty bound to come with you. Escorts, as it were."

They had halted him to read his face, and they were now standing in the road amid a fleet of idle jeepneys. Some of the drivers were slouched in their seats; others gathered, smoking and spitting and looking around like furtive truants.

"Hey, lookit all these jeepneys again. Should we be lookin' out for that guy in 'em?"

"They *all* look like Ricky Ricardo," Al said too loudly, standing there, conspicuously searching the faces around them.

"Let's drop it. Anyway, that's my business, not yours. You understand that, Stone?"

"Yeah yeah Walter. but I'm not afraid of these punks. Just point the guy to us and we'll take him out, all of us. I know how to deal with enemies." He too spoke loudly, taking his cue from Al. "Hey how about *that* guy? He look like the guy you described?"

The man sat in his car as though he were driving, a bare suntanned arm out the window, his hand gripping the roof, a concentrated stare straight ahead as his jaw muscle worked over a wad of gum. He was even bouncing slightly in his seat to some nervous inner rhythm. Walter was sure he must have heard them, but the side of his face didn't change.

"Well, actually he does. But I don't think it can be." He made a motion toward the club, anxious to extract himself from these particular surroundings—no point in tempting trouble—but Al and The Stone tarried, pleased with the attention they were arousing.

They all looked like Johnny to Walter. He was seeing him everywhere. He wasn't exactly afraid, but he kept a sharp eye out and stayed alert, going over all the drivers and holding them up against his image of Johnny—too often they checked out on too many points until the original image got confused with its more immediate counterparts and the comparisons of features got jumbled in the exchange like overlapping transparencies or dial-a-change faces; this one had the hustler's smile and appetite in his eyes; this one had the nervous shock of hair; that one had the square, T shirted shoulders and too good looks, the white teeth and smooth jaw. And his memory of Johnny incorporated their traits—didn't he slouch like that? Was there that girlish swivel in his walk? Did he wear a cigarette behind his ear? He was thin, but didn't the veins on his arms protrude from his wiry muscles like that? Like he had rubber bands tying them off? Finally, they all became one big composite Just-Call-Me-Johnny. But he kept the feeling tightly closeted in an emotional compartment labeled "intense curiosity," and when he wasn't nonchalantly—so he thought—studying the drivers, he was keeping his eyes straight ahead while watching the street in all directions with scatter vision, unfocused on any one thing but attuned to everything, like you use tracking animals in the woods, alive to any color or movement or sound that breaks the flow around you. In this case the flow was not the rustling leaves and the twittering drama of birds, but that hive of human activity. And he didn't have a clue as to what he was looking for.

    Al walked up to the first driver The Stone had pointed out, whose jeepney was standing in the street in front of the Hard Rock. The Stone followed close behind, his body in that attitude of readiness, his fingers curled together at the end of his distended arms like they'd just dropped something heavy but didn't know it yet. Walter looked around them and his heart picked up tempo the way it always accelerated when Al got an idea about fun and swung into action. This was the wrong time for his games. The man looked everything like Johnny, or not. "Hi," Al said. "What do it be like, my good man?" The Stone craned his neck from behind Al, and Walter could imagine the blood-flushed grin on him.

    The driver turned his face to them, a mask of slack indifference. He nodded warily." You want a ride somewhere?"

"That and more, my fellow. So much more."

"Whatchu mean? Whatchu guys want?"

Stone stepped up. "Tell him what we want. Tell him what we mean."

Walter motioned toward the club. "I thought what we wanted was to go inside. C'mon, for Christ's sake, let's go. What're we doing?"

"Relax. I just want to talk some turkey with this man for a minute. What's your name, buddy? My friend was just saying that you looked like an old friend of his named Johnny. Are you Johnny? Would you like to do a little business?"

"Sure. Whatchu want, man?"

"Well, Johnny, we want to party like hell. We want an old-fashioned slam bang get crazy for tomorrow-we die-in-Iran kind of time like we used to have in this town. But it seems kind of flat, you know, Johnny? We want to put the fizz back into it. And you know how we can do that?"

"You want nice girls?"

"More than that. There's always girls. We want to get sky high. We want to get closer to the edge. We want speed."

"All right!" The Stone said, bouncing on his toes, clenching his fingers together and raising his fists to his chest like he was retracting his landing gear and breasting into the blue yonder.

"Oh shit!" Walter said. "Al! Goddamnit! What're you doing? Let's get out of here."

"Yes indeed, Johnny. We're friends of Eddy? Know the guy? A skinny guy that's something of a local big shot? Last time we were here he sold us a whole mess of speed."

"Let's get out of here, Al."

The driver seemed to study Walter for a moment. "I don't know."

"Sure you do. You know—*Eddy*. The speedmeister. Here's the deal. We're gonna be inside partying. You get us some yellowjackets, say about four apiece, and we'll pay you when you get back. I'll give you a ten-dollar commission on the price. In fact, get a couple for yourself—I'm buying. In fact, why don't you call it a night and come hang out with us? Bring the wife. How is the ol' wife, anywho? And if you see Eddy you tell him to come join us, too. We miss him."

As Al talked the driver broke into a slow grin and moved his head from side to side. "Ten dollars?"

"And all you can drink. But act now. This offer won't last. Out of town, please call collect. Void where prohibited."

He put the car in gear. "We see. Maybe. Ten dollar first, the rest when I come back."

"Now we're cooking," Al said as he fished a bill from his wallet and gave it to the man.

"Who are you guys?"

"We were here a few months ago, a few of us bought some speed and kind of got out of control, but it's okay now, we all made friends. Ring any bells? Just tell him Walter is here."

"Maybe. We see." The driver did a U turn into traffic and disappeared up the street.

Al turned to Walter and smiled. "Get it? All for one and one for all."

Walter wanted to kill him.

"I get it," The Stone said. "We're with you Walter, man."

Walter wanted to kill them both.

Walter led the way through the pink doors into a blacked-out hallway where he was startled by a sudden smiling ghoul's face lit red by a flashlight under the chin like you do to scare children. "Welcome," it said, and the light was turned on his eyes, blinding him. "Fifty peso cover." They fumbled with the change as he held the light on their hands. "This way, please." The flashlight took them through another set of doors into a darkened ballroom where the end of the beam danced on a rickety little table with folding wooden chairs.

"Hey, Tinkerbell!" Al said. "Clap your hands if you believe in fairies."

The room hummed with the impatient motions of a hundred young mariners working on the first buzz of the evening. Tobacco smoke was so thick you could wring the juice from the air, and it burned the eyes, which were still blinded in the centers with spots from the flashlight. But soon they adapted to the level of obscurity to utilize the thin light and absorb the room. Working women lazily orbited the small clusters of men, milling in the lanes between random groupings of tables, turning heads, exchanging words, exchanging saliva, attaching and detaching themselves like remoras on sharks. Flashlights and drinks made their way to and fro as the house filled up. In the middle on the dim dance floor stood a wilted bunch of half-naked go-go girls, their bikinis awkwardly held by slack shoulders and blade-like hips, their limbs graceless in the absence of music, their faces looking sullenly out at the inarticulate general stirring of the room. The band came out and took up stations at the equipment behind the girls. Red floodlights bled onto them all and began strobing. The bare-chested drummer raised his sticks, hit the snare's rim three times, and on the fourth beat the room exploded in a deafening blast of heavy metal that shook the table.

The noise was momentarily all-encompassing, reaching into the brain and clamping down on it like a hand, like silence, in that it voided everything else. It swallowed the sensate murmur of the rest of the house. Walter made an effort to think through the invasive metallic wah-wah pulsing through his brain like a throttling heartbeat. There was just the band and their table in a tunnel of flashing red light and noise, and the dancers throwing their mad bodies in as many directions as they had moving parts.

A flashlight appeared with shots and beer Al had ordered. Walter pushed his shot at Al, who happily tossed it back and ignored the dirty look Walter gave him. He leaned forward and yelled something. "Get it? Tinkerbell!"

"You're not funny."

"What?"

"Not fucking funny!"

"Yeah! Ha ha!"

The Stone slapped Walter's arm and pointed at something—one of the girls, a spiny, emaciated thing who looked flayed alive, her scant coverings wanting meat to hang onto, revealing only ribs and bone slats—was flailing in particularly violent communion with the music. Her long hair shrieked out of her skull when she jumped. Her eyes rolled white in their sockets and her skin pulled from her buck teeth and cheek bones like an ecstatic fright mask. The Stone gawked and beat time on the table after yelling something to Walter. "...that one! Really into it!"

"Oh Wow" Walter imitated, but The Stone didn't notice. The song stopped as suddenly as it had started, leaving a ringing in his ears and a buzzing in his head that had an uncertain source but that terminated in his teeth. He hadn't heard the song as music but as an interval of bedeviling noise plucking at his nerves as his anger at Al and his stupid pranks rose in pitch.

"What do you think?" Al said.

"That you're a jerk. What the hell's the matter with you? What are you trying to prove?"

"Geez Schmerz," The Stone said, "don't nothin' satisfy you. What're you pickin' on Turner for? We're all here ain't we? We're havin' a good time ain't we?"

"Yeah," Al said. "Ain't we? Relax Walter. You must learn to relax. Why can't you just go with it?"

"Oh come on! What's with that whole spiel, and the speed! And *my* name? *Mel*!"

"Just trying to show you something. Trying to dispel your demons. You gotta face it down. Basic lesson in life, and you're the biggest sucker I ever met. Besides, I could use a major buzz. Aren't we entitled after our bout with the sea? Ain't we brother Stone?"

"'At's right, man!" He slapped at the table like a drummer, but without any beat. "Gonna go crazy tonight!"

The band started up again, this time some sort of love ballad, the words to which seemed scraped from the singer's insides like a throat culture as he hung his head in dejection, and the drums thudded and guitars clanged an adolescent dirge. The dancers, too, hung their heads and swung their arms, twisting slowly.

A flashlight came with more drinks. Al and The Stone were getting there, going to Fred. Walter jumped when a gentle hand pressed his shoulder and he saw Al turn around at the same time. It was a vampy looking woman in a tight wraparound black dress, collarless but with long sleeves that called attention to themselves in the heat, especially with the bracelets sliding up and down her arms. Her dark hair was built up in an elaborate bun with carefully disheveled strands tickling down her face and neck, many of them. She wore a heavy base of white makeup with rouged cheeks and exotic lines of black mascara snaking around her eyes. And thick red lipstick.

"Hello sophisticated lady," Al said.

She bent confidentially close and said to Walter in a husky voice, "You want speed?"

"No. Not me. They do."

"Wow, how'd you do that?" The Stone said. "Picked us out like that. In the dark with the crowd and all."

"Well done indeed," Al said. "You comin' from Johnny?"

She took her hand off Walter and put it on Al's shoulder. "You are Walter?"

"That's right." He reached his hand around her narrow hips, but she peeled it off and held it by the fingers in a friendly, or at least patient, and familiar way.

Walter felt with rising panic that he had stumbled into a waking nightmare and struggled for the brakes, for control. "That's it," he said, attempting authority and finality, taking both their hands in his. "I refuse to get mad and I refuse to play along. I am Walter and I do not want any speed and I am not really with these two."

"*I* am Walter," Al said, "and I can prove it. I serve on the Cox with Hasty James and a prick called Mallory." He lifted his eyebrows at The Stone and gave him the hi sign.

The Stone woke up and said, "Oh, me too. I'm Walter."

She was a very cool type, clearly used to having the upper hand. She didn't like being put on or put off balance, and she bridled at this silly predicament, at being made awkward. She snorted. "Never mind then. If you don't want."

Al stood up, wiping off his smile. He looked in her eyes. "I am Walter, radioman first class. These men are with me. I am their boss. He pointed at Walter. "*His* name is Schmerz." He looked at The Stone, who nodded. Now not so fast, *mon petite bourgeois*." He took her hands. "A silly game. Forgive. You see, we are a kind of club, if you will, and in the interest of deception—we have many enemies, as you might guess—we are forced to take such precautionary and seemingly childish measures. These guys won't even call me Walter. Do you have something for me?" Walter said nothing.

"Cost fifteen dollars."

"Odd sum for an even number, but what the hell." Al and The Stone pooled their cash and paid her. "Will you join us? And will Johnny be joining us?"

"First I have some business. Maybe later. Why? You like me?" She slipped him a glassine envelope, then bent over and kissed him on the lips, leaving a faint stain of read. "You're cute. I like you."

"I like you too, but your breath smells like dick."

She slapped his head, hard, and swished off toward the door into the darkness, her chin held high in feigned anger, but her sinewy back and shoulders articulating aggressive play, and her small but mobile behind saying follow me if you dare.

"Shake it," Al said. "Hope she comes back. I *like* her. She's cute."

"Too skinny," Walter said. "She got no hips. Since when do you like vampire types, anyway?"

"I like 'em skinny too," The Stone said. "I wanna talk to that one that dances wild. Man, if she could get into music like that imagine what she's like in the sack."

"We'll be doing a wild dance of our own in a couple of minutes.

Here, start with two of these and we'll work our way up the ladder. Sure you won't join us Walter?"

The band began a second set and returned to the screech and howl variety in full amplification, and Walter was glad to be silent and try to think. He still owed Al for the black eyes, as well as all this. He couldn't beat Al at anything. Perhaps the best revenge would be to cut him off, disengage, detach. Maybe that was what he couldn't stand. Walter could only change himself.

When the set ended the band took a break and Stone rushed out and grabbed the cadaverous bikini. Her name was Maryanne. She was from the province. She always dreamed of being a dancer.

"You're a great dancer!" The Stone said. "Ain't she? I just wanted to jump out there and dance along with you. Could you feel me? I was gonna snatch you up! Hey Maryanne, wanna get high with us? It's okay, we're cool. We're not narcs or nothin'." He lifted his bandanna to show her his emblem of cool. "We're a secret society of the baddest, toughest sailors. You're safe with us. We're all friends here. Wanna be our friend? Wanna be my special friend? I really like you. I was watchin' you dance and I said yessir, that's sure a special lady. You're so pretty. And you dance so good. I could tell you were a professional. Whew, it's hot in here. Well, you wanna?"

He ranted on like that, saying everything that entered his mind, and talking fast. Maryanne looked nervous and turned back to see the stage as though hoping the band was setting up again. "I don't know. I don't think marijuana is too good for you. I have to go back to work soon. You can buy me one drink?"

"I'll pay your bar fine and you don't have to work no more. You can dance with me, and we'll drink the house dry. I don't wanna leave Subic with any money in my pocket. Anyway, it ain't pot, it's these, just to pep you up and make the night last." He showed her the bag and her eyes lit up. Bingo.

"Yellowjack?" She smiled. "For me?"

Al laughed out loud. His eyes were bugged out and sweat was trickling down his temples. "You see that? Stone, looks like you just made yourself a special friend. You just pushed her button. Candy. Sweets for the sweet. Now you know how she keeps that dancing edge, maintains her trim form. You like, huh?"

She smiled at The Stone. "I like you. You buy me drinks? Take me bar hopping? I do things for you, baby."

Al and The Stone looked at each other and connected; they were together defying gravity. "Hey Schmerz..." they both began, then burst out laughing. When they came to they looked at each other and doubled over again, hugging themselves and stomping their feet on the floor. Maryanne licked her overbite and tried to cover it with her upper lip, then smiled impatiently. She had a lazy right eye and a nervous left eye. The right eye roved around the room involuntarily, then slowly crept toward the left one to see what it was doing, and when the two spied each other they jumped and she jerked her head around to try and find something to fix them on.

"Go ahead," Walter said. "Help yourselves."

When they recovered their breath, Al slapped four pills on the table before Maryanne. "Here you go, baby. Do them all at once. On Walter. Man, I gotta see what this thing is like fully loaded."

She now took great interest in The Stone, locking her arms around his neck, giggling into his ear and occasionally speaking to Al and Walter in quick, breathless phrases. Al approved; he seemed to find them a delightfully amusing couple. She had swallowed all four pills in a gulp with only a whiskey chaser and was off and running before they got down her throat, as if her adrenaline was aroused at the thought of what was coming. The boys followed by taking their remaining two each. They were all thrilled with the turn the evening was taking.

"So nice to meet you," Maryanne said for what seemed the fifth time. "You nice boys. I like you the best," she said to The Stone. "You are too sweet. Too handsome. You will be my boyfriend?"

This was too much for The Stone, who jumped up and hooted. "Yahoo!" He cupped his hands over his mouth and yelled across some tables at a waiter, "Where's our drinks? Keep the beer comin' man, and bring some lady's drinks for my girlfriend!" There was laughter and jeering from the tables around them. "Yahoo!" The Stone said, then sat down and hopped around in his seat like a kid pinching his penis to hold it in. They doted on each other, she nibbling at his cheek and pecking his neck and mussing his hair and wondering at his tattoo and fussing her hands all over his body, telling them how great their friend was; he having their picture taken, buying her chewing gum and flowers, asking them if they didn't think she was great, laughing out loud at his happiness and good fortune in finding an alcoholic with a speed habit, the while pouring drinks into her—not lady's drinks but straight whiskey. She was done working for the night. They pawed at each other obscenely, climbing out of their chairs tongue first and licking mouths.

"Why don't you just do it on the table," Walter said.

"Yeah," Al said, meaning it. "Do it. Get it on, man. Give it to her all the way." He'd been watching them like a show, rapt, smiling upon them.

"I swear to god, I love this woman. Fuckin' love her."

"Tonight we get marry," she said. "Tonight I be your wife, baby. You pay my bar fine, we do it all. We go dancing and bar hopping and then I be your wife. I do anything you want. Everything, baby."

The Stone buzzed off to pay the fine and claim his wife for the night. He was already staggering, but not in a heavy way, as though he was floating up and his feet couldn't get a firm purchase on the ground, his upper body moving deliberately, even gracefully, but his legs reaching spastically for the floor.

"What about you," Walter said to Al.

"Tonight's the night."

"Meaning?"

He breathed deeply a few times, seeming to tremble when he exhaled as though trying to control some excitement. "It's early. I am going to do so much, so much tonight. And I'm not going to sleep. I'm staying up for the convergence. I'm just going to do and do and do. I'm going to take it new places. I'm a Mark forty-eight torpedo doing fifty-five knots at five hundred fathoms straight for the midship of Iranian sub. Blam. High explosive, baby."

"Have you ever done this before?" Walter said, meaning the drug.

His face was sweating heavily, and he had a smile screwed tightly to his mouth. "Been here before, my boy. I invented it. But never so much as now. Now! you understand. But even now's not enough—just a hint at what's to come. There's a lot cooking here, and I think you know what I mean. But that's okay—for now I'll just bask in the *is* of it, in the...*potential*. I'm all potential. God, Walter, I never felt so powerful. I'm going to do everything tonight, whatever that is, whatever I want. Lookout world, I'm going to Fred! Nobody better fuck with me 'cause I'm full of mischief. Understand? Hey Maryanne, I'll give you a dollar for a hand job under the table right now."

"Nasty," she said, then seemed to think about it for a second, then laughed in case it was a joke, then twisted around to look for The Stone, then untwisted and ping-ponged her eyes back and forth between them. "So... we all go dancing and bar hopping? We have a great time. You want to meet some nice girls? My friends?"

"Look at you," Al said. "You're flying. You're all the way up. Yeah, I may want a piece of you before the night's over."

The Stone came back, clucking and clapping his hands together. "Okay, it's a done deal. Maryanne costs *beaucoup* bucks but she's worth it. Ain't you worth it, baby? And we're gonna have *beaucoup* good times. Hey. Hey guess who I just saw up front at the bar with that lady, the one that was just here. Chief Parma and Mallory."

That was all Walter needed to hear for motivation. He had once been swimming in a Cape Cod bay and could feel seaweed tickling up against his legs. Then tickle became tingle, and he knew he should get out. Jellyfish. The pain lasted for untreated hours.

"He coming this way?" Al asked.

"I guess he will be. They're talkin' nose to nose at the bar. You s'pose he was coppin' too? S'pose he gets high?"

"Probably begging for a date. Maybe that was his dick on her breath. Remind me to ask him, though I shudder at the thought."

"Well," Walter said, "it's time to leave you all to your own devices. It's been real. I'll just file my report with him on the way out."

Al got to his feet. "Hold on, Schmerz. Just a toast before you go." He raised a bottle of beer. "A toast to the Jizz Jaw."

The Stone laughed and said to Maryanne, "That's what they call The Chief behind his back on the ship."

"Long live his majesty King Jizz Jaw," Al practically shouted.

"Long live King Jizz Jaw," The Stone echoed.

Al drank, then hitched his pants up and puffed his stomach out over his belt. He flared his eyes wide and shook a finger at the table in rage. "Turner," he said, "Turner you better come down off your high horse. You don't know as much as you think you do. You think too much. Turner, you're an idiot Turner! Just remember it's my radioshack. It's mine! I'm King Jizz Jaw! I'm the fisheye and I'm gonna make you regret ever getting orders to this ship! You're gonna regret ever crossing the brow. Listen to me Turner—"

"Siddown Jizz Jaw, you asshole!" someone yelled from a table in the haze behind them.

Al spun around, holding the bottle like a hand grenade, spilling beer on them all.

"Who's gonna regret crossing the brow?" The Chief said. He was standing at the table with Mallory and the lady in black.

Al turned again, facing The Chief, still frozen in the throwing position, again sprinkling them with beer. "Well speak of the divil. In comes himself. Here we was just havin' a libation in your name."

"So it seems," he chuckled.

The Stone clinked a shotglass against a beer bottle four times to gong The Chief aboard. "Chief Parma, arriving."

"Well, lookit all my little sparkies having a fine time and harmless laughs. And The Stone. Hiya fellas. Mind if we join ya?"

"And so the gang's all here," Walter said, glaring at Mallory. "You can have my seat. I got a date. Oh, all conditions normal. Nothing to report at this time, over. Schmerz off to Parma. Bye."

"Hang on Schmerz. Don't run out so fast. You could at least stick around for introductions. Where's your manners? This here is Brenda."

"Hello," he said. "We met. Goodbye."

"Lovely lady," Al said, "it is a pleasure to see you again. Are you two lovebirds? Is there a marriage in the offing. Is there still a chance of your showing me a good time? And speaking of good times, this is The Stone's new girlfriend, Anna Rexia."

"Not Anna," she corrected. "Maryanne."

They pulled up chairs and the seven of them scrunched together absurdly close in the gauzy heat, The Stone and Maryanne fidgeting and petting and giggling, Al swelling with bravado, turning his attentions to Brenda next to him. The glands under Walter's tongue prickled at the palpable taste of bodies and beer. He swallowed the queasy juices and made another bid to leave.

"Not yet Schmerz," The Chief said, gripping his forearm and locking his dark eyes, dead serious now, on Walter's. "Don't let's do anything anyone might regret. Let's just relax for a minute and enjoy. Now I said I didn't want you goin' off alone and I meant it. Too dangerous. Don't cross me son. We got a long cruise ahead.

Mallory says he saw you talkin' to a driver who looks like he might be one of those punks. Bad idea. Thought after we checked in we'd make sure everything's alright."

"I don't know, "Mallory qualified. "These Flips are all clones to me."

Walter yanked his arm free and almost followed through with a punch, his fist mid-air, his words measured in suppressed rage: "*I...don't... belong...to...you!*" He felt Al and The Stone closing ranks behind him and he hung for a moment, stuck between the threat of that "long cruise ahead" and losing face if he gave in too easily. "My personal cop? You can't control me; you can't keep me here."

"T-tell 'em Schmerz. Attaboy. Go go go." The Stone was having trouble with his tongue.

"Guardian angel?" Al said to Mallory, "or spy? Are you trying to keep our friend from his beloved? His date with destiny?"

"I don't need you troublemakers startin' up with these guys again. I'm so sick of your superior shit. Pretty boy. You even talk like a sissy."

"Now hold your fire everyone," The Chief said. "This is not what I wanted. We just came to say hello and see how you all are doin', not to start anything. Turner, I heard that little bit about me when we came in, and that's fine. I expect that as chief. You're entitled to have your little fun, let off steam, and Schmerz, I'm not gonna keep you from your girlfriend. I just want you to be careful, son. Take someone with you. Now everybody just calm the fuck down and make nice. Mallory wasn't spyin' on nobody, and I want you guys to quit pickin' on him."

"Amen to that," Al said. "No hard feelings. Too much of the night left to be bickering among ourselves. Mallory, I shouldn't have called you a guardian angel; you're just alert, and that's as you should be. I would be too if I was you. Besides, I can't help it if I'm both a well spoken and good looking sonofabitch. You shouldn't hold it against me." He put his arm around the back of Brenda's chair. "Now you, on the other hand..." He took a deep breath through his nose. "You know I didn't mean what I said before—just going for a reaction. Like with your friend The Chief, here. On the ship they call him Jizz Jaw, but he takes it in stride. All in fun. Ain't we magnanimous." He winked at her, then stuck out his hand at Mallory. "Make it unanimous." They shook, squeezing each other's knuckles. He returned to Brenda. "Really, you're quite charming, like me." He breathed again. "And fragrant."

"Easy does it," The Chief smiled. "How do you know each other?"

"We don't, that's the problem. And you?"

"Picked me up outside the club. I couldn't resist."

Brenda pouted a bit, and showed some anger, then indifference, but she seemed pleased with the attention, and Al didn't have to batter too hard at the gates of her resistance. If he had found her attractive before, the fact that she came in with The Chief now made her more important than sex. She was a goal, a coup, a prize. He closed in on her with all his speed-enhanced energies, washing over her in waves of words, his voice rising and falling with successive flatteries to her, and of course, himself, the while stirring in a counter current of backhanded compliments at The Chief—the advantages of old age, the mellowness of ripe cheese and soft fruit, the prestige of being owned by a man of rank, the ease of listening to dull talk, the comfort of a soft body and a good night's sleep.

She pouted prettily, offering the obligatory reproofs, touching his knee with her fingertips. The gauntlet was thrown with a clever, happy smile, and with a smile The Chief let it lie there, as if to say it was all in fun.

Maryanne's eyes rattled in her head and The Stone flew around squeaking like a bat and the bat roared like a waterfall and then the waterfall was the crowd in the process of enunciating one long, eternal, falling "Schmerz" while Al's babbling was punctuated with "baby" and "mama" and Brenda parted her red lips and Mallory crushed butts in the ashtray and The Chief kept demanding "what do you say Schmerz what do you say Schmerz."

He had to get out of there, away from it, from all of them. He had to make it be different. Nightmare—the shards of his dreams arranging themselves into this oppressive, haunting nonsense right there in the middle of his waking life. Bits of all the moments in his life converging in a crisis with time. He tried to run but he was glued to them all—the lips, the eyes, the words—all stuck to his skin like tattoos, stained through to the bone, holding stubbornly in place and stretching obscenely as he tried to pull away, and then snapping him back as though their claim to him was greater than his will to be free, as though insisting that they and his flesh were one contiguous fabric. He was panicked. "What do you say Schmerz what do you say Schmerz."

"There's no air in here and I have to be somewhere."

"Sure," The Chief said, again grabbing Walter's arm and showing his teeth. "Sure. Relax. And I know where you're going, where you can get all the air you want. Up in the country where you can just sit on your dock with your girlfriend smokin' your dope. But don't let's break up the party. Why don't we all go?"

"No!" Walter said, damning himself for waiting, now longing for Vivien as though she were his salvation, his peaceful answer away from all this.

"Sure. What do you say, men? Ain't you supposed to stick with each other, club rules or somethin'? Subic City's downer and dirtier even than anything you'll find here, if you're not afraid to get down and dirty." He motioned at Maryanne with his chin. "Better women too. 'Sides, they don't appreciate us here. Ain't no one crawling on their hands and knees begging to suck our cocks."

Mallory laughed, and The Chief raised an eyebrow and chuckled good-naturedly at himself. "Yeah, it's funny alright. Come on, Brenda, we're goin' up the country with Schmerz."

The Stone had stopped talking in words; he was now expressing himself like a baby, cooing and giggling and humming, all but drooling. He was turning in on himself at some private wonder and amusement. Maryanne was clawing at him desperately, asking him to dance, talking fast about the heat and air as he had done earlier, laughing out load to prove she was a good time. His eyes were all pupil, black and unblinking, rapidly scanning the scenery without apparent effort, without squinting or peering, without even moving his head, until he turned to Al, who was grinning hotly at the game of chase with Brenda. The Stone took the cue. He stood up with Maryanne knotted around his neck like a sweater. "Here we go," Al said, rising to follow The Chief. "Where we stop, nobody knows."

The Stone's face was red with excitement; his stifled giggling thinned to a trill wheezy whistle. "Take me with you take me with you take me with you," Maryanne hissed at his back, her voice climbing in desperation. "You pay my bar fine already so take me goddamn with you. You don't get me high and go away." He giggled louder. "Goddamn you Stone! Goddamn Stone butterfly! Go ahead, get the hell out! I hope you all get disease. All Subic women dirty!" She clapped her hands together; Al turned around and bowed deeply.

Mallory and Walter got up last. "You could follow us," Mallory said to Maryanne. "Maybe if I'm drunk enough later and you ask real nice I'll let you go down on me." He ducked ahead to join the others as she tried to hurtle the table after him, and Walter realized too late that she'd settle for what she could catch, her skeletal face and long gnashy teeth seeming to pull an elastic neck ahead of her spindly arms and legs which were still caught up in the business of berserking through an entanglement of toppling bottles, table and chairs. The room whistled and cheered as she caught him—standing there like a stupefied rear guard as the others slipped out—first slapping and kicking at him, then sinking her spidery fingers into him, latching on, seeking his groin with her knee and his neck with her fangs. Some bouncers pulled her off him and someone with a flashlight spirited him out through the maze. He could still hear a struggle as he passed into the hallway, and he pictured her fingers and toes and arms and legs and hips and breasts and eyes and teeth and hair all blasting madly outward from the bouncer's hold. The room hooted.

The group was waiting in a jeepney outside the club like a leering, cheerful ambush. How had he wound up following them to his own date? "This is your trip, Schmerz," The Chief said. "Pay the man. Ten pesos." The driver turned around and reached a greasy, upturned hand toward him—the man who sent Brenda in with the speed, he thought.

"No," he said. He took the driver's hand and squeezed it. "No. I don't think so. You all have to pay if you want to come along with me."

"Allow me," Al said, "as I am in a liberal and giving spirit tonight."

"So what happened to the ugly bitch? She like to kill somebody back there."

"She blew up," Walter said, thinking that he'd been present at her last stand when the sappers set off the charges beneath her feet and she rained back down on him in rent, chunky gobbets of Maryanne.

"Wonder what she'll do for a living now."

The Stone giggled in some secret merriment and said nothing, apparently far into the drugs, his face flushed dark, his black eyes shining at something beyond.

Soon they had snaked their way along Magsaysay and were rising above the shanty outskirts of Olongapo, climbing above the salt and metallic smell of the sweating city. They were stepping along the same khaki mountains he had seen from the bay, now dark in the night light, blotting half the sky with their shadowy mass, looming around them like the lap of a numinous, aggregate presence—watching, breathing.

The jeepney banged and jitterbugged its way along the rutted mountain road that winds its way in and out of the sharply creased hills. The road is primitive and in disrepair, subject to washouts and landslides. Much of the way is along steep cliffs with crumbing shoulders, jungle in the climbs above, and jungle leading all the way down to the thin beaches lipping the bay. Across the bay is a mirror image of mountains decked with sporadic lights, rising out of the water. Far below them fishermen made their way in the silence of distance, their boat torches merely flickering points of gold. Fires burned in the mountainsides where farmers were clearing fields.

Drivers know each stretch of the road and its condition, and theirs took it at breakneck speed, tossing them around like a roller coaster as they hung on and sprawled into one another, jerking around hairpin turns, gassing it down stomach-flipping drops. Mallory banged his head on the ceiling and cursed the man, but Al spurred him on, cheering like a cowboy: "Yahoo! Com on, gun that bitch! Whee! Wheehoo!" The Stone smiled on, his eyes rigid, one hand gripping the seat, the other beating time on it. Brenda tried to look composed and dignified, cool, as her body bobbled. "Wheehee!" Al said and she gave him a cool smile from behind her mascara and black tendrils. The Chief watched them. Mallory smoked and flicked his red sparking butts behind them. The Stone beat time. Walter thought, I am through with you all. I reject you.

The car tracked slowly up the last steep hump and the sky unfolded its secret of stars like points of phosphorus spilling into a night ocean's current. The air tasted like wet nasturtium blossoms or the promise of snow, portentous and substantial, nipping the tongue like pepper. He had made it, lifted above the screams and sullied smoke of town. He drank the air in thick drafts and it cleared his head of the terrible absurdity that seemed to poison every moment of the last hour, that feeling of dread that nothing made sense, nothing fit in time or place or purpose, that a life was a disjointed collection of impressions blown about as if by the beating of great, ominous wings, arranged into a random sequence of patterns like patchwork dreams. He had broken through to the other side, ridden it out. Again he felt the mountain's presence, like the accretion of all life and time itself, holding him up to the sky. Yes, he thought. I am of this. He looked at the others again. I am not one of you.

It was a short steep spill from there to Subic City, past the cabins and shacks that began to huddle closer together with their stick fences and bare dirt yards with chickens and bony dogs and naked children and shirtless men on front steps or working together on boats; thatched houses and houses tiled with tin and plywood and boards and faded advertisements for soda and candy; women gathered at a natural pool washing clothes and fetching fresh water; women walking along the road with their loads, children romping and dancing and shouting along, or dragging at their mothers' heels, cranky and whining. They hear the jeepney approaching and step aside, oblivious to Walter and their accession into his life.

The Jeepney driver let them off directly in front of the Seaview. As Walter was the last one on, he was the first off, and he strode right for the bar, leaving the others to gather themselves. He elbowed the bar as he had fantasized doing, though no one seemed familiar or particularly glad to see him. It was a quiet place, despite the fleet's arrival. Most of the Subic City action was up the street where the lights were brighter and the music louder and there was dancing. Here it was more relaxed, and the American customers seemed like regulars rather than gaga liberty hounds. A clammy pair of hands clamped over his eyes from behind.

"Vivien? That you?" When he turned around, she hugged him, and he just held his hands flat against her back. They hadn't done this before, and it felt odd. Now what?

She stepped back and took his hands by the fingertips. She frowned and gently traced the bruises on his face with her hands, then smiled in a way that surprised him. Her eyes were reading him, and they were alive and open, and she smiled in a way that surprised him, as though she knew him and missed him. Lovingly.

She wasn't beautiful anymore, or even sexy in a sex's-sake way. She was older and younger in her lack of guile and subtlety, in the plainness that now struck him as so unexpected. She wasn't a seductress or a working woman now; she wasn't acting, and she didn't try. She didn't seem anything but happy to see him, wearing blue jeans and a blue and white striped T shirt like an apache dancer, and her hair tied in a ponytail and cut in even, girlish pony bangs. She was so much plainer than he remembered, with so much less pathos and mystery than he had endowed upon his image of her. She was just glad to see him.

"I'm glad to see you," he said. "You look so nice."

She swung his hands back and forth playfully, her face shining into his. "Only nice? Not beautiful, Prince?"

"Yes, you do. I am. I mean, I missed you. I thought about this moment many times."

"You are still strange. How can you think about a moment before it happens? I am glad you are so nervous. That means you care enough about Vivien to be nervous, maybe. I was afraid about meeting you, too. You seem different, too."

"What do you mean? I'm not nervous." He felt like a boy on his first ever date who's expected to kiss the girl on the lips, maybe even a French kiss, which seemed a gross and difficult operation. "Different?" Why did she seem so relaxed and happy if she was nervous?

She took the palm of his hand and held it against her cheek. "Umm, sweating." She kissed it and gave it back, then shrugged, having nothing else to occupy her own hands. Maybe she was nervous. "So, you want a beer, strange man? You can tell me about your face."

His face? What about his face? "Oh. Yes. Yeah, a beer, and I'll tell you about my face and you can tell me about yours."

There was a commotion up the bar as the crew pushed through, and he again felt like that panicked boy, caught red handed, ready to renounce his new girlfriend, ashamed of his secret sweet feelings and doubly ashamed of his exposed awkwardness and inability to stand up to it all, to play the proper part, others be damned. It's easier to swagger with the boys. "Here comes the source of my facial condition now. Ignore these guys. They're jerks. They're not my friends. Don't listen to whatever they tell you."

"Your friends!" she almost squeaked as she hopped and clapped her hands together, turning to greet them.

"Oh Great."

"Here they are," Al said, leading the pack. They surrounded the couple. "You can't get away from us, Schmerzy, old boy. Well, let's get a look at the lady." He stuck his face in front of them, suffused with an even red like a sunburn, sweaty, his eyes burning an adrenal fire. "Yes yes, this is Vivien alright. You look like a Vivien, madam. Do I look like an Al? Don't you think I'm better looking than your boyfriend?"

Brenda shoved him from behind and he lurched forward. Walter pushed him back. "Yes, so sweet and innocent. So you're the source of those midnight jerkings, ah, jottings. The Lady of the Letters. He gets drunk and talks about you. He told me he's mush about you. Mush ado about nothing. Yes, so sweet and innocent looking. Pure as the driven snow. Pretty—yes, you're so pretty. You'll make some Walter a fine wife someday. Never been touched, I bet."

He must have been going too fast for Vivien to catch the drift of what he was saying. She seemed thrilled at the attention of these leering faces.

She was beaming. She took Walter's hand in hers and squeezed it. "It is so nice to meet you all." A weird coming out party.

Walter held on to the hand—it was his and his job to defend it. He would protect her from these people. He and she would show them their faces and then retreat. He'd beat them back if he had to. "Well fellas, this is Vivien, obviously."

"Lemme see," The Stone said, pushing Al aside. They were his first words in about an hour. He grinned—not lasciviously—but in enjoyment, or appreciation, it seemed to Walter. "Heh hummm," he approved.

"I *will* drink beer now," Walter said. "Stone, how bout fetching us a couple of beers?"

"Uh huh, uh huh." He did, just like that.

The circle tightened around them. Vivien drew right up against Walter, and he put his arm around her. She rubbed her chin lovingly against his shoulder. She was intimidated by the close inspection, but the attention seemed to make her happy. What a fuss was being made over her, and she must have imagined it was because of the big buildup Walter had given her. And they, in turn, showed an inordinate interest in Vivien. Yes, they were looking forward to giving Walter a hard time and razzing him about being too interested in a hooker. But he thought they were surprised by what they found. She was inconspicuous and exceptional. *They* would never get such an honestly warm greeting from a woman in Subic.

"Not too shitty, Schmerz," Mallory said. "Hey Chief, maybe you were right what you said about bein' appreciated here."

Only Brenda seemed bored by the scene at the Seaview, pouting behind Al, sultry and sluttish. She had made her preference for him plain, as though he—as she seemed to see herself—was the prize of the litter and she was used to getting that. She stood with her fingers hooked into the back of his belt and was not about to let go. She understood his competitiveness and seemed to share it.

Walter couldn't read how The Chief felt about this development, assuming he'd already paid for Brenda, but he too was now assessing Vivien. "Yeah, you're alright. So you're the lady that dragged us all the way the hell over the mountain. Sure, there must be somethin' special about you. Horses couldn't keep this boy away. She's a cute little shit alright, but I don't know. Must be somethin' special, if ya know what I mean. Ain't that right Mallory?"

"S'right, Chief. Cuter'n poop. Got any more Viviens stashed around here, little miss?"

"That's right," Al said. "Cleaner than poop, too. Ooh, you're so squeaky clean, aren't you? The way Schmerz likes it. And everybody likes Schmerz. And everybody likes what he likes."

"Yeah, everybody like Walter, too, baby," Brenda said, "And Walter like everybody. Now come on, baby." She gave him a firm but patient tug, like a mother to a child before a candy display.

"Do you know what the something special is that they're talking about?" Al continued at Vivien, then pointed his chin at Walter. "Sure you do. But he doesn't yet. I know all about that—his failure, as it were, in bed. Just between me and you, he *told* me. Ssh. Maybe he'll find out tonight. The things that wives do. You want to be his wife, don't you? And he'll make a fine pet. No, you don't look anything like a whore…tonight. Or *ho,* as we say."

Walter could feel her stiffening. Good old Al. I'm going to kill you.

"Listen, Schmerz really is an innocent. A saint. A mere babe. But you and I share a lot in common. We could share even more. He's my best friend and we're supposed to share. I got a cute little babyface too, but I assure you I can get nasty in the most delightful ways."

Brenda had both hands in his belt now, and she leaned back to haul him in. His upper body leaned toward Vivien as he pulled back. "Don't make trouble, now. She got a boyfriend. And I got you. You got me. Everybody happy, baby. You can get nasty with me and I give you a good fuck. Don't make me angry so I have to cut off your balls."

"See, Madam Vivien, we all want a piece of me. And we all want what Walter's got."

"And we got each other, baby," Brenda said.

"Now fuck off," Walter said.

"Ohh la la."

The Stone brought them the beer. "Thanks buddy, Walter said, feeling suddenly warm toward him, a kind of craven face among his enemies, bullies, jackasses out to spoil his time.

"Um humm," The Stone said, standing before them, smiling as though waiting for his next assignment, or at least a tip.

"What the hell are you all standing around gawking about?" Walter said. "Find your own good time." Vivien clutched the beer The Stone gave her and had backed up to where she was almost behind Walter, his arm still on her shoulder so that he was twisted awkwardly to one side, reaching around himself to hang on to her. "I told you," he said to her. "These guys aren't my friends."

"And I told you," Al said, his face grimacing in a violent smile, "I'm going all the way tonight, buddy, and I'll go right fucking through anyone who gets between me and there. And I told you once to drop that corny holy shit. We're the same, pal o' mine. Hey—corny holy, as in cornhole. That gives me ideas." He jerked around and grabbed Brenda's ass with a slap and dug his fingers in hard enough for her to let out a yelp. Then he shoved her toward the bar. "She's with me, by the way. Obviously. Come on Stone. We got drinking to do, brother. My BAC levels have slipped intolerably low."

"Yeah, well where the fuck is 'all the way' s'posed to be?" Mallory said.

"Who knows," Walter said. "Who ever knows what he's talking about? Lookin' for the heart of Saturday night."

"Well let's you and me get some beers and mingle with the ladies," The Chief said to Mallory. "Don't know why my sparkies are actin' so weird tonight. You got a cute girlfriend, Schmerz. Don't blame you for insistin' on comin' out here. Really, little darlin'. Sorry if we embarrassed you. And sure we're your friends. Now you two wanna be alone and I don't blame you. Look, I ain't even mad at that crazy Turner for stealin' my date, long as he pays me what I already put out for the bitch. Lots of sweet ladies around here. Good idea comin' out here, Schmerz. Nice 'n peaceful."

Walter paid Mamasan for Vivien's bar fine—she knew she had him, so the price was jacked up and Vivien begged him not to argue but just relax and make nice—and they retreated topside. They sat on the edge of her dresser looking not at each other but down on the veranda and out over the bay. She had taken him by the hand and led him there as soon as she saw that the others really were trouble. The walls were close in there and grimy with smudge marks in the places that weren't covered with taped-on curling pictures of fashion models and movie stars from magazines. The musky, lurking smell of her body was pervasive. It brought him back to the last time he was there, and he shivered.

Vivian put her cool hands over his eyes again, this time more gently and seriously, as though to comfort them. He stood there letting her rub his temples, as he breathed her in. On her dresser there was a large, dull looking mirror in a wooden frame leaning precariously against the wall. He thought it looked washed out because the uncovered low watt bulb on the ceiling provided only a faded light, but up close he saw the reflecting material had separated against its lead-gray background like ancient paint, leaving a myriad of tiny crack lines fragmenting and interrupting the images it cast. There were snapshots stuck all along the inside of the frame. Some of them were pictures of American men; some were pictures of Vivien, including a copy of the one from the beach that she'd sent him.

When she saw what he was looking at she snatched it, pulled the dresser back from the wall and put the mirror on the floor behind it, facing the wall. "You don't have to look at that," she said. Usually they were quick to show off the competition.

"I don't mind. Of course you have boyfriends. Don't you want to show me your pictures? I saw the one you sent me there. Anyway, I just wanted to see my face—what you see. Sorry I look like shit. I forget how messed up it is. God, my eyes are so red." They looked like rats' eyes.

She climbed up on the dresser and sat cross legged where the mirror had been. "Never mind about the pictures. Tell me what happen to you. Here," she patted the dresser next to her as though beckoning a child.

He hopped up beside her and briefly described things to her, about Al and how they could be friends and not-friends, about how they'd all followed him. He tried to tell her about the time since they met, started to wax morose, then was stricken again with shyness when he wondered who it was, really, that she expected.

He tried to cheer up and rubbed her shoulders like pizza dough. "Well, you saw what those guys are like. Even my best friend's gotten weird on me. I'm sorry. Why don't you just tell me to shut up. Anyway, I'm glad I'm here," he tried again. "I really did miss you." He wanted to mean that—he *did* mean it—but he wanted to *feel* it, and searched through his nervousness for the clarity of that feeling he once had. He touched her hair. "You got a new haircut. Tell me about you now. Tell me about your dreams and fantasies again, my sweet."

"No. That is only a stupid game. We don't play that now. You have to relax now. You are such a shy boy. I did not know. You are so different from the boy I expect."

"I'm sorry."

"No. No worry. Only I did not know. Maybe I like you better now. Before you were too high, maybe? I think there is something mean about you, then. I am glad you are here. Oh, look at your poor eyes." She leaned over and kissed them.

So they took each other's hands and sat cross legged on the dresser—front row seats in the darkened room—and looked out the open window at the veranda below and the bay beyond and watched the Subic night unfold.

The screen door slammed and Al walked onto the veranda arguing under his breath with a very little man who was all motion, tugging, cutting images in the air with his hands and dancing around Al's feet like a man trying to get an elephant's attention while avoiding being stepped on. Brenda followed them silently and stood back a couple of steps, lingering in the shadows cast by the two potted palms against the tiki lights. The man was deformed.

"Renaldo," Vivien whispered to Walter.

"If you say so."

"A bad man. Very nasty. Very dirty. You better tell your friend to stay away. He does business with the sick girls."

"No way. He's going to play this out by himself." To hell with him. It was over between them.

Renaldo was talking in a cajoling whine: "Good dope, man. Thee best focking dope inna whole worl'. Come *on*, man. You wanna get high this is thee best smoke for you."

And Al gave what sounded like a spooky old refrain: "And that's fine, my dwarf, so get us some. But we want *speed*, is what we really want. Now I happen to know that this whole place is crawling with yellowjackets, and I know where to go if you won't come across, so just be a good dwarf and get us some. Can you run along and do that?"

"Okay, sure man. What else you wanna buy? This place is so *boring*. You want some excitement, right? You wanna come with me? This place it stinks." He pinched his nose. "You like movies? You wanna see a movie of a girls gets fucked by a pig? Huge pig, man. Plus I got girls that do anything you want, man. Live show. Get it on with each other. Pee on each other. Short time, long time. You wanna short time? I got girls let you do anything to them."

Brenda stepped out of the shadows, black silhouette against the black bay, and lashed at him with a vicious kick under the ass. Walter had forgotten she was there for a moment. The kick literally lifted him in the air, and he yelped and limped around on the dock, whimpering and holding himself preposterously with one hand in front and one behind, meeting between his legs as though they were trying to hold him there in the air when he hopped.

Renaldo carried himself off, brushing past The Stone, who gave him a grit-toothed smile, then wandered down the ramp to the water's edge where he squatted, surveying the bay.

"Wow," Al said, "you're dangerous. You really are the jealous type. Hope *I* don't piss you off. Well, you can protect me from The Chief when he makes his move."

"I don't like her," Vivien whispered.

Now in the torchlight, they could see her red lips moving in her white, mask-like face with the dark eyes that appeared still against the black mascara background as she spoke. "Your ass in mine tonight, baby. Just you and me, all the way. Brenda always gets her man." Her voice sounded more like a low growl than husky sexuality.

"I don't like her either," Walter said. "She's mean. She's a bad guy. Sounds like Darth Vader. I like Renaldo better. Think he'll come through? Hey, this is fun up here, don't you think?" He didn't quite mean that, but he was drawn to the voyeuristic quality of watching these bizarre people from the vantage of her darkened room, and he was still delaying, awkward about being face to face with Vivien.

"No," she said. "I don't like this. I don't want it to be like this."

"Hey, Stone-man," Al said. "My fellow knight, c'mere. You see that byproduct of incestuous breeding?"

The Stone flew up to them. "Aw, aw, aw," he said in a high voice, imitating the hurt Renaldo but sounding more like a wounded crow.

"That unfortunate gene mutation went to get us some more ammunition from the get-high arsenal. More speed. Smoke-dope, too. We're getting up there, boy. Getting out there."

"Aw," he said, dancing around the veranda with his arms outstretched in flight.

"That's right, we'll be flying. Just be cool around the others. We got to watch our backs with The Chief and his pet dog. Schmerz too. I mean we got to look out for him. Boy can't look out for himself. And I think The Chief got something up his sleeve for him, too. Remember, all for one. He don't know that we know that he don't know, etcetera."

"Aw haw," The Stone said, now pursing his lips and smiling like a baby that knows it's cute.

Vivien gasped and Walter covered her mouth with his hand before she could say anything. He let go and knocked his shoulder against her playfully. "Hey, that's us. This is great. Isn't this fun?"

She did not think so, and now she was angry, but they had her attention too. She whispered more quietly but with urgency now, her breath in his ear. "Make them go away. I do not like these people. Why do you bring these people? First you are crazy and now your friends are crazy. That ugly woman. Why do they want to do something to you?"

"They are all jealous," he said, kissing her cheek. "Because I have something that they can't have."

"Here we go," Al said, and disappeared beneath them—her bedroom jutted out slightly over the porch, forming a ledge under which there was an old jukebox and a small unused bar sitting up out of the weather. The jukebox started up beneath them and Al let out a hoot. "Here we go!" Procol Harum was singing "Whiter Shade of Pale" in such a scratchy and warped rendition that it sounded as if it was coming over some high frequency radio speaker—a durable but poor fidelity form of communication good for vast distances—and the originating station was thousands of miles away, putting out a signal that ghosted through the airwaves, almost as though it were taking the static of the intervening years since the song was a hit. It seemed that the jukebox hadn't been changed since that time.

Renaldo reappeared. He couldn't have gone farther than across the street. He was still limping slightly and yammered in high angry tones, but what can you do when you've got a sale?

"Here we go," Walter whispered, pulling Vivien close to him. "I've had enough." But now as he felt her ribs wriggle against his fingertips, it was she who resisted.

"Bad," she said. "I don't like this."

The four of them moved off the porch and down the ramp toward the water as though that provided some cover of secrecy. In fact, though their voices attenuated over the water, the onshore breeze carried them back to the bedroom, rising and falling in pitch according to the bay's fluctuating exhalations. They huddled together and did their business. The couple could see Al and The Stone taking more pills, and they all smoked a joint of "thee best focking dope in the worl'." Some of that, too—a sour, moldering, burning—wafted up to the room.

Al threw his head back and staggered. "Holy shit! Head spin."

Renaldo giggled. "See?"

The Stone stuck his arms out with fists at the end of them, flying again, walking quickly around the ramp in a low crouch, dipping his wings, then hopping on one foot, incredibly, maintaining his balance.

"

Purple Haze" was playing on the box now, and Brenda began to writhe to it. Al made some jerky motions in her direction as though to dance, but he staggered again, and his jaw dropped as he seemed to be saying "oh wow." Renaldo clapped his hands in time to the beat.

Stone had hopped up the ramp, all on one foot, and Brenda moved in front of him for an unlikely dance partner. He jumped to his other foot and folded the idle one—"Flamingo dancer" Al yelled—his outstretched arms teetering for balance, then pulling in so his elbows did the funky chicken. Brenda circled him, gyrating her pelvis and juking her chest, raising her arms and fingertips into the air and shaking them so her bangles jingled and shimmered in the moonlight. She vanished under the ledge, then reemerged by the palms on the deck with her small purse in her hand, making obscene gestures against their trunks. She hid her face behind the fronds, then stuck it through between the trees, snaking her tongue out of her mouth and sliding her head back and forth on her neck like an Egyptian.

Even The Stone stopped what he was doing to admire her next move. She took that red lipstick out of the purse—the whole while her eyes rolling back and her body undulating in some kind of ecstatic sexual trance—slithered out that long cobra tongue and began lipsticking circles around it until the entire business end was painted. The she followed it toward Al, her mouth gaping and lips pulled back, face scrunched into a hiss, her wrists vibrating the bracelets and her body still moving in liquid waves. She touched his face a couple of times with the tip of her tongue, then she started licking it until finally, with her tongue fully distended, she was practically wiping it off on him, up and down, back and forth, top and bottom. He just stood there with his eyes closed as she backed away, his lips moving as if he were talking to himself. The smeared lipstick looked black in the night, streaked and swirled on his face like camouflage paint.

She kept dancing backward until she was out of sight under the bedroom again. The music stopped; the last quarter had played. Out of the silence and shadows Brenda leaped forward and kicked Renaldo hard in the backside for the second time. "Ow, shit!" he said. "Hey!"

She laughed and continued dancing without the music, circling around him. "What?" he said, trying to back away and stepping his foot into the water. She lashed out and slapped his face. "What?" he said. "Cut it! Stop!" She laughed. The Stone was smiling on at the game, almost chuckling, but it came out from so far in his chest that it sounded like a deep hum. "That hurts!" Renaldo said. He was frightened. Both his feet were in the water.

"What are you doing to my dwarf?" Al said.

"Who needs him? She danced before him, blocking his exit, and The Stone waded onto the ramp beside him and slapped the back of his head.

"Come on," he said, "please."

The Stone pushed him and he fell to his knees on the slippery planks beneath the waterline. "Hmm," he chuckled.

"You're all wet," Al said. "What're we gonna do with you?"

The dwarf sputtered and shook his head. "Please," he said, "be fair."

"Fucked with the wrong people," Al said. "Don't wanna mess with this Brenda, man. She's a trip." He seemed to think hard for a second, then said, "Are you in my way?"

"Please man, lemme go. I go away."

"Are you in my way?"

"I don't know what."

"Why does it feel like you're in my way? Don't wanna get in my way tonight. I feel like you're…interrupting us. Are you giving us static? Seaman Stone, this man is interfering with operations. Take hold of him."

The Stone pulled Renaldo out of the water and held him from behind as he struggled and pleaded. "Whatchu want to do with him?" Brenda said.

"Oh god Walter!" Vivien said. "Stop them Walter! They are crazy. They are going to kill him." Walter had forgotten where he was. He had forgotten that anything could be done. It was as though he'd been content to simply watch the scene unfold, mesmerized as in a dream. Vivien woke him to reality.

"Yeah," he said. "Yes, Christ!" He leaned out the window and yelled "Hey!" They didn't seem to hear him. Al and The Stone were holding Renaldo in the air by his arms and legs, swinging him. He was screaming in terror. "Hey!" Walter yelled. "What are you guys doing? For god's sake put that man down!"

"Help him! Help him!" Vivien was yelling, and Walter was aware of the music inside the bar stopping and the bar noise changing as people began yelling and rushing toward the back, already swarming onto the veranda.

They flung him out over the water. He screamed through the air and exploded on impact like a human water balloon, then thrashed his way back to the dock. Everyone was yelling at them, surrounding them and getting right up in their faces. Al raised his hands and told them to calm down as though it was all a silly misunderstanding. "Just fooling around," he said. "All in the name of fun."

Mamasan was livid, carrying on about "her neighbors" and "her place," slapping at Al's shoulders, and he kept saying, "There there, there there now. All better?"

The Chief pushed his way through and helped Renaldo out of the water, who seemed too flabbergasted to say anything, and perfectly willing to let The Chief whisk him past the murmuring crowd of concerned onlookers, especially after he jammed some crumpled bills into his soggy pocket.

He returned without Renaldo, and Mamasan was trying to shoo the three gamesters off the premises. She gave Al another shove and he reeled completely around. "Whoa, head spin."

"Out out out. You no good for business."

Chief waded into the fray, the even-handed arbiter, the picture of unflappable amiability. "Here now, Mamasan, what do ya mean bad for business? After all, that guy was hornin' in on your business, not these fellas. He smelled like a pimp. He is, right? And your girls are the freshest sweetest things I ever see in Subic. You teach 'em to be like that? or they just learn by your example? You already got one of my swabbies to fall in love, you foxy little matchmaker, you!"

Walter could feel Vivien looking at him. They were standing now. Having been caught between the urge to lean out the window and run down the stairs, they were in stasis. She leaned over and kissed him hard on the mouth. He kissed back and then pulled away. He wanted to see this. "Yes," he said, "but hang on for a minute. Let's see this. Something's going on. He's up to something."

"Why do they want to hurt you?"

"Shh."

Mamsan let herself smile for a second, then folded her arms and frowned. "You, okay. You giving me the business, but I like it. You stay. But these," she said, waving an upturned hand at Al and The Stone and Brenda, "they make too much trouble. They get out of here. Got to go."

"Well, let's be serious then. Yeah, I'm givin' you the business. We all are. Drinkin' your booze. Datin' your girls. that's business. Look, I'm these boys' chief; I'll keep 'em under control. They go, we all go, an' I'm gonna have to take Romeo with me too. You like me? So why don't ya let us stay? Here," he took out his wallet and handed her a bill, "I like you too—this much. Twenty dollars American, for business sake."

She examined the bill and stuffed it in her bra. "No more trouble." She patted the Chief on the cheek and nodded at Mallory, who was being unusually quiet, as though studying his boss, or perhaps he was ordered to keep his mouth shut as part of the plan. "You are nice men. You stay here. I get you a free beer on the house."

As soon as she was gone The Chief grabbed Brenda's wrist and jerked it. "Uh oh," Al said, "I wouldn't do that."

"You're starting to cost me a lot of money, Turner," he said, but he was talking into Brenda's face. "Getting' very expensive takin' care of your ass."

"I'd let go of her," Al said. "Could prove dangerous."

"I'm tryin' hard to make this night work out right," he said, still holding her wrist and glaring into her face. "Be our last one for a long time. Why is everybody tryin' to fuck it up?"

Brenda pulled her arm free and said "Okay," scowling back at him.

"Is this it, Chief?" Al said.

"What?"

"Like it or not, she's with me. She wants me; she chose me. So is this it?"

"What are you talkin' about, Turner?"

"The big showdown. You've been gunning for me a long time now.

Here's your excuse. I just stole your girlfriend. She likes me better. They always do. So what are you going to do about it?"

"You been smokin' them funny cigarettes, haven't you, Turner? You're paranoid. I'm just tryin' my damnedest to take care of you guys, bring the crew closer together for a change. Why're you tryin' to start up with the ol' chief?"

"Sure you are, ol' Chief. Well, I'm ready for you, Chief. Isn't that so, Stone? Watch it, Mallory—boo! Anyway, I'll pay you back for Brenda."

"Yes you will. But will everybody just calm the fuck down for a minute? Look, it's a beautiful evening, don't ruin it, is all I'm tryin' a say. Here." He sat down and hooked his arms around his drawn-up knees. "Sure is a nice peaceful spot. Lots of nice, hot little mammas here and we gonna get us a couple. Ah, speak of the devil.

Two woman came out carrying trays full of beer bottles. They put them on the deck in front of The Chief. "First one free. Mamasan say, for you," one of them said. She apparently meant themselves as well, for they paired right up with The Chief and Mallory. "Can we stay with you?"

"Why of course, little sweetheart. I insist. You see," he said to Al, "no problem. Sit down, you guys, and beer yourselves. See, it pays to be nice. Will you be my date tonight?" he asked the girl. She giggled.

"Do you like me?" the other one asked Mallory.

"I love you," he said, "no bullshit."

"Yes," Al said, sitting down cross legged and drawing close, with Brenda and The Stone following and completing the circle around the beer trays like campers around a fire. "Yes, we all love each other. Brotherly love and sisterly love and the love between a man and a woman. Let this be a night of great love, of unity and togetherness. Yes, I feel a delicious oneness with all things right now, with all creation. I greet life with open arms."

"Yeah," Mallory said. That's why you're into dwarf tossing. At least you could've drowned the little fucker. So how come you ain't got a girl Stone?"

From Vivien's window The Stone's eyes looked hard and shiny-wet, like black marbles. He face seemed to burn with a mindless smile. "Caw," he said.

"Brother Stone doesn't need a girl to love," Al said. "He's self-sufficient."

"That boy's too far gone," The Chief said. "What exactly you guys been doin', anyways?"

"Getting ready," Al said. "You know, like the Boy Scouts say, always be prepared."

"Boy Scouts, alright," Mallory said. "So what're you getting ready for?"

"We're getting ready for the night. Whatever it brings. For all its joys and pleasures and tribulations. For yo' mama, as Bum might say. Actually, we're ready for you. For a showdown that isn't coming."

Liberty Call

Vivien had tired of the show and slipped off away, saying only, "Enough. These men." Walter heard the rustle of clothes but was afraid to turn around. Maybe she was mad at him for putting off her advances. Maybe she had given up on him and was going to bed. He was embarrassed at his fascination with the scene below, all that time practically ignoring her so he could see what the others were doing, watch them continue to make jackasses of themselves. But something was up and he was dying to see what would happen next, to find out if he was going to be in any way involved.

He was blowing it with her, right from the start. It just wasn't going right. She was disgusted and was probably beginning to find him repulsive too. Then he realized that she must always have to put up with seeing and hearing the goings on beneath her window.

"I'm sorry," he said, still looking at the others below. "I've been a terrible guest. Let me try again. Let's start all over."

He heard her strike a match and he turned around. She was lighting a green coil of mosquito incense on the floor, naked. She climbed onto the bed and kneeled facing him, her eyes surprising him with their ache, her lips pouting out in dolorous words: "Do you love me?"

His voice failed as he studied the beckoning sulk of her eyes, the slow, devouring sex of her mouth in the dark, salt scented room; and her body—the color of skin, the light on her round shoulders, the fold in her stomach above the dark pubics, the bumps around her brown nipples and smooth breasts, the shine of thighs and knees—looked like everything he'd ever wanted. He gaped at her, unable to move, thick as lead and slowly melting into the mold of her mouth and dissolving into her eyes. He sleepwalked into her and gave himself over to the erotic dream of sinking and surrender. Finally, after what seemed ages, his mouth spoke for him. "Yes," it said, "I love you," and meant it. Why not?

She held her arms out to him. "Now," she said.

He crawled to her from the end of the bed and she lay back against her pillow, motionless, still with that mournful look in her eyes and mouth. He kissed the mouth and rubbed his against it, licking at her lips, then reaching through them with his tongue and licking her teeth, running it along the sharp ridges and then the sides where her smooth gums met the hard enamel lobes of her molars; then he found her tongue and licked that, sucked it into his mouth and squeezed the tang from it, opened his mouth wider and pulled at the air in her lungs.

She still lay there with her hands at her sides, her body limp and unresisting. He pulled back and looked at her. Her face was wet, and he smelled their saliva. "Oh, now," she said. He kneeled there for a moment and touched her, all of her, running his hands down her arms and legs, over her chest and stomach, shoving them under her to feel her back and squeeze her ass. He put his hand on her puckered crotch, then worked his fingers through, watching flesh unfold, the inner pink skin yielding and sticking a bit to the fingers as they moved. Her hips were now lifting and reaching toward him. He pulled out the fingers and attached his mouth to her, the taste practically stinging his tongue, numbly glancing into the source. He'd found the hidden room within the room of shadows and mirrors, the essential one from which everything there emanated.

She grabbed his hair and pulled hard. She grunted. Now she was moving; now she was clutching at him. "Now, ohh. You too. You too." She was trying to pull his shirt off with one hand and was reaching under to his belt with the other.

Walter sat up and pulled the shirt apart, ripping it. "Wait. God, you're beautiful. Wait, just like that—I'll be there." He was rolling over, trying to kick his shoes off and peel his socks with his toes at the same time as he was wriggling out of his pants and underwear. "Just like that. God, just wait I'm coming."

He crawled back on her, flesh to flesh now, rubbing his chest on hers. Her eyes were closed, and she was kissing at the air with her mouth. He slid in and she made an "ohh" sound, almost like a "thank you, how nice," but sweeter and quieter and sweatier, coming from somewhere in her arched throat. He jerked up till their pubics ground against each other and she flinched.

And then he watched. He didn't know why, but he was distracted—not away from what they were doing, but by what they were doing—as though he'd suddenly come out of a liberating and pre-conscious drug condition at just the wrong moment, to find himself waking from a state of physical primacy, one of consummate communion like a baby connected to the big tit of the world, to that of self-conscious adult in the strangest place, where his mind began to remember and inventory its surroundings, began calculating and abstracting. As with when you realize you're awake—this is my pillow; this is my bed, that's my ceiling with the dirty footprints from the time I got stoned and climbed a stepladder to put them there—he was paying too much attention, his curse. It was mechanical, groin to groin. He was straight up on his arms, looking down at Vivien's pained face, looking at her body and looking down between them at their groins crashing together, and *thinking*. He was a third person, looking at them from the outside—from the ceiling—even as he felt the pleasure of fucking. He thought, is this the way I expected it? Well, it certainly is nice. I can't believe I'm finally in her. It's great. I hope she thinks I'm good. Seems pretty turned on. I think she really likes me. What a lovely woman, great body. God, this room, though. It's so hot and the smell so strong. What a life, and all the shit that goes on out the window. All the shit that goes with her life.

He became aware of the voices on the veranda again, muffled now that they were away from the window, the obscured and drunken give and take of high and low utterances like the dueling notes of a blues band on a distant radio, men and women, sailors and whores, friends and enemies.

Her eyes were open and looking at him. He smiled lovingly and began pumping with renewed vigor. "No!" she said and stopped moving. She grabbed a handful of his face and dug her fingernails into it. Then she punched the inside of his elbow so it buckled and she wrapped her arms and legs around him and squeezed till she shook, making an angry, disapproving growl in her throat. He didn't know what she was up to, but he was still deep inside her with her legs locked around his waist, and even as she held tight she was slamming him back and forth in the clamp with short, sliding-bolt strokes—it wasn't over. She was trying to bring him back to the place from before he started thinking. Whatever she was doing he would give himself over to it. "Oh baby," he said, "whatever you want. Do it. I want what you want. I want you. You've so beautiful. Do it to—"

"Shh. No, shut up. Shut up." She rolled them over so she was on top. "Don't move." She covered his face with her hair and grabbed his own with both hands till Walter thought his scalp would rip, and when he started to moan, she said, "Shh, don't move. Don't say anything," as she rocked their pelvises back and forth. She sucked his lower lip till it ached and suddenly bit it, and as he jumped, she mashed his face down with her lips against his. Now she was ravishing his mouth and they tasted like sex and spit and salty blood and his head was spinning; he thought he was falling through the bed into a black hole at the same time as he was falling up into her. And his body buzzed with something, pain and more, electric burns from his scalp to his feet, burning into his cock and making it grow painfully huge—he thought it might burst; he thought it might burst and scald her badly with whatever was swelling it, or grow till she cracked; she was already so tight around him. then a slow, final, obliterating orgasmic wave began at his sides and ran inevitably to the place where their nerves were locked—her nails scratching deeply along his body to his hips—and she reached between them, grabbing him there. He tried to warn her as he felt it welling up from some place beyond him but she crushed his mouth with her open mouth, and he didn't know if it was him shaking or her shaking or both, but then it surely was him trembling, then twitching uncontrollably as the thing began to explode and burn them both and he screamed into her mouth and down her throat into her lungs and the bowels below. And he followed his scream as though it were a rock shackled to his heart, pulling him inside out as he sank, fluttering along the blood dark lining of her insides to the diminishing waves of their orgasm.

He opened his eye and was outside again. She kneeled above him, sweat running down her neck and stomach. She threw her head back and laughed.

"You too?" he asked.

"Oh yes."

"What did you do to me?"

"Love, maybe. Smile now, Walter."

He didn't want to smile. He wanted to scrabble back in her.

The twisted sheets were damp and rank, spotted with bits of his blood. The room pulsed—Walter pulsed—to the metered respirations of Vivien's nostrils. Her eyes were closed; Walter's were aware and did the seeing for them while she did the breathing—into their bones and blood, into the bed, into the walls and ceiling and the window and dresser which were now just extensions of their our dumb flesh, all pulsing a gentle current, all fused. The part of him that normally breathed was tight, compressed and submerged under the weight of the Subic air, warm and wet as bathwater. Their wall warped under it, their ceiling groaned under it, their window gaped dumbly as it washed in, lifting the bed and stirring it slowly around while Vivien slept and breathed and he saw for them. Lungs and eyes. Discrete functions of an integrated whole. He didn't breathe and he waiting to die but it didn't come. Another kind of release did—the unlimited freedom of *being*. The tiny throb in his left temple—he could somehow see that, and the mottled sheets that were beneath him, behind him, growing out of his back, the bed, and billowing in the salt air. His shoulders bulked and burgeoned, hoisting the expansive ceiling of his head as his arms wrapped around and contained them in a square. The window was the vent through which he saw infinitely inward and outward, the two-way access to the stars and to the steady ticking of his capillaries, to the ocean and to the heap of organs and limbs growing out of the bed like a mass of hydroponic tomatoes. And Vivien was the gill that processed and renewed them, that metabolized and exhausted and sustained them. It was all one, and he didn't need to breathe.

Walter had gone to her again; this time they exerted less effort and energy as their bodies assumed one another's shape, spiraling around each other like the involutions of a snail shell, home and occupant. Finally, they crawled into each other one more time, but Vivien closed her eyes, so Walter curled around her. Now, an hour later, used up, he let her breathe and sleep for him as he lay there mindless, only a dumb sensation, all aware but not alert.

Gradually, he felt a disruption in the pattern of things, as when you're dreaming and a phenomenon from the waking world begins to influence the dream, say, an itch in your leg or the sound of a baby crying. All was still on both sides of his window—he had completely forgotten about the voices outside; they had ceased to be, for Walter—but now his walls caught a minute shudder and his floor hummed in his ear like tracks singing a train onward from around the bend. The implacable clacking rose up from below and he knew somehow that it was heading right for them. It churned around the corner, picking up momentum, moving with purpose. The walls were shaking and the bed vibrating at the violence of motion approaching the room. It reached a peak right as it was on top of them and then stopped with a silence that was equally violent for its suddenness. He thought it might be his crashing heart, that maybe it would burst from not breathing after all. And almost the same instant that he became aware that the voices had snuck back outside and grown louder and harsher, it hit, smashing into the door, and shrieked a sound as familiar to his mind now as his own heartbeat, a personal summons to some terrible inevitability that always awaits. "Walter! You in there? Let's go! Let's move! Walter!"

The Stone.

He sat up, his head spinning. Vivien groaned and mumbled.

"Walter!" He was banging on the door. "Let's go! It's here!"

Walter teetered on his feet as they hit land after finally adapting to the ocean's capricious flux and lunged for the door. He was almost prepared for the white blast of Stone's rolling eyes as he grabbed him and shoved him inside the room. Up the hall a couple of girls peered out of their doors. Walter grinned at them and put his finger to his lips. Shh.

The Stone and Vivien froze at the sight of each other, then he turned to Walter as he closed the door. "Let's go!" His pupils looked like ground zero. His face was a mask of happy terror, resolved to the kind of unnatural hazard that the thrill seeking successfully converts from dread to excitement, anxiety to anticipation. He carried it in the reek of his alcoholic sweat. "It's here!"

Walter turned the bulb on and the play of shadows from the yellow light somehow made Stone look freakish and small, his forehead shattered, cracked in the shape of five feathers, his compact muscles shining, his bare chest heaving at the impediment of air, his heart—so Walter thought—tattooing his chest from within. "Moment of truth!"

Vivien gasped as she pulled the sheet to her throat, perhaps seeing him as Walter did, then got control of herself, of her room, and hissed, "No it is not here. You! Go away from us. Get out—now!"

He ignored her and got so close that he sprayed Walter's face as he yelled, his voice slapping the walls and dying there in a curt, tinny echo. "You know what I'm talking about Walter. This is really it."

"Shh," Walter said. "Stoneman calm down. Keep it down." He feared that he did know what The Stone was talking about.

"It's all coming together Walter. We got to act. I see everything now. I see it all clear. God it's so easy, all right there in front of us! Now do you see it? See what's happenin' to Al?"

"Shh, slow down. Listen to me buddy. Carefully. You are very, very high."

"God, man, don't you see it? They're all in on it together. It's all comin' together. They fucking planned it, man. They're makin' their move, all of 'em, an' they're comin' down on Al." He stomped his foot and raised his voice with the "Al." "Chief and Mallory and that skuzzy Brenda." Walter tried to shush him as he got louder with each name, his face a slapdash succession of emotional extremities, now practically crying with urgency, now laughing at the prospect of action. "Condition fucking red. We got to act Walter man. Now. All for one. Al'd do it for you. Time to make *our* move."

He smiled and reached into his front pocket, pulling out a switchblade. "Kill 'em."

"Christ," Walter said.

"Kill 'em all. We gotta make our move; we gotta take 'em all out. Cut 'em up before they hurt Al. It's fuckin' war. All for one Walter—you swore!"

"I'm going to scream," Vivien said.

"What we did, we did too much shit. Can't come down off this shit so you gotta go through with everything or it'll kill ya 'cause you can't get down. See? See? I stopped drinkin' so it cleared up, but Turner's all kinds of fucked up."

Walter slapped his hand over The Stone's mouth, pulling him into a headlock as he slid around behind him, and pulling him up from the floor to control his leverage, squeezing with everything he had—he'd squeeze The Stone's head off if he had to. Stone stopped clutching Walter with the knife hand to bring it into play, and as the blade flicked open, Walter wrapped an arm around his and pulled it close to him, Stone's wrist working the blade around as if he were trying to bore a hole in the air.

"Vivien!" Walter hissed. "The knife!" He knew he couldn't control that manic strength for long.

She pried The Stone's fingers apart and gingerly picked up the knife when it dropped. "Listen to me Stone," he whispered in his ear. "Listen to me! We've got to be quiet. You're waking the whole fucking house up. We can't let them know we know." Walter jerked his head toward the window, though they stood in the middle of the room. "They're right outside, listen." The Stone wriggled and Walter was beginning to tremble with the effort of holding him. "Listen, goddamnit! We can hear what they're doing from here if you'll just be still." He held off struggling for a second, though still tensed against Walter, his nose snorting hot moisture onto his hand. The voices below were loud and unchecked, engrossed in their own struggle of drunken defiance and accusation, men's sounds punctuated by the exclamations of women. There was a crash of empty bottles as if someone had kicked a pile of them, and all the voices rose up together. The others apparently hadn't heard the commotion in the room, and there was as yet no angry knock at the door. Maybe it was a magical room, providing invisibility, anonymity to its occupants, a two-way mirror. They hadn't noticed them the whole time they had watched like flies on the wall. But The Stone found them.

"I need you to tell me what happened," Walter said. "We have to have a plan, but we have to do it quietly, secretly. We'll help Al, I promise, but we do it my way. All for one, but we act according to a plan. I'll let you go; I need you Stoneman, but you got to follow orders. Are you with me?" He hummed against Walter's hand and nodded, still breathing furiously through his nose. He needed air. "Okay, then." Walter let go and The Stone bent over to catch his breath. He looked like he might faint. Vivien gave Walter the knife and he pocketed it.

"It's so clear, man. The whole thing fits together. You're in it too, ya know. Ain't none of us safe until we kill the motherfuckers. I tell you Walter, we gotta take 'em all out."

"If we have to kill them we'll kill them," Walter said slowly and deliberately, savoring each word, as he figured he'd never have another chance in his life to say something like that, like ordering a four star meal with no intention of paying. He was serious, even though he couldn't mean it.

"No!" Vivien said. "No, this is too much crazy. Stay here Walter. *You*, get the hell out of my room. Go now."

Walter gave her a look that tried to make her know it was a game, then said to The Stone, "Tell me everything you think is happening. What's going on."

"Not think—*know*."

"Tell me!"

"It's a set up. Get it? It's so clear. It just came to me, like my eyes opened up for the first time and everything became so clear—flash, bap. That Brenda's evil, man. Evil for all of us. Can't you see that? It's all a plot and we gotta stay one step ahead, gotta move fast, get the jump. You better see it 'cause she thinks he's you, maybe."

This was getting spooky, but Walter kept in mind The Stone's state and enthusiasm for giving himself over to twisted visions, and it was up to him to unbend the contortions in his thinking. "Get him out of here," Vivien said. "I don't like this."

"Go on," Walter said.

"Just now when me and him went to get rooms on the beach, there, she kept giving him this sly kind of look. Now who paid for her? The Chief! Who brought her along? The Chief! They're out to get all of us, but they'll start with Al; it don't matter to them. Let's *go* Walter, come *on*."

Vivien tiptoed to the window with a sheet wrapped around her and peered out. They were still there. "I'm scared," she said. "Make them go away."

So was Walter. There was a certain worst-case sense in what The Stone was saying. Al always played the game by anticipating two moves ahead and was as good as anyone at changing rules as he saw fit, but then he was getting beyond the point of no return hours ago. Now he was the one out of control—you could hear the spittled lisp, the slurry anger in his speech, rising to the window—and it was The Stone who had leveled off, whose voice returned to him, but who was seeing things from aloft where they were warped out of proportion, as if he were looking down into a fish tank filled with mercurial Subic air.

"I see what you mean, Stoneman, but easy does it. You're not exactly making sense. It's not quite the way you remember it."

"God!" he said. "God! You don't see. First she starts cuttin' me off, like she's puttin' up this wall around Al, but he don't notice nothin', but I'm watchin'. I keep my eye on them. She keeps lookin' at him like she's gonna eat him. And her and The Chief keep smilin' at each other. They all think I'm gone, like if I'm not there or somethin', don't see. So they all ignore me. Everybody's watchin' Al, moving' in with their knives and forks, slobberin' and lickin' their chops. They're wearin' fuckin' lobster bibs with Turner's picture on it. Ha.

"See now Walter? They all got together in Olongapo and planned it. But I got the jump. We got to go all the way. We got to fight and kill. Enemies."

"Make them go away," Vivien whispered again, standing in the middle of the room, her eyes wide. He wished he could. Go away and really do kill each other off, just leave us alone.

"I will." He sucked a lungful of air and grabbed The Stone's shoulders. His eyes were somehow vast black and vast white, filled with wild possibility. Walter had never looked in a face that was eager for homicide before. It was guileless. "You will listen to me and follow my instructions word for word." He had no idea what he was going to say.

"Yeah Walter. Let's rock."

"Listen to me Stoneman. There are secrets to this business you don't know yet. You have to trust me. I know what I'm talking about."

"What."

"We're going to go down there and get Al out of it, but it'll only work if you keep your mouth shut and do exactly what I say. Exactly. You don't do anything, just keep your eyes open. Just watch. Understand?"

"Yeah yeah Walter, but what if—"

"If there's trouble we defend ourselves. You see me go in my pocket for the knife, then you jump. Otherwise, nothing. We're not going to kill anyone, unless. Swear you'll do what I say."

He looked away.

"Swear it, or you'll never be one of us again."

"I swear," he said, disappointed. Walter wondered how he could control The Stone's energy and for how long. He had no idea what would happen, but now that he was acting and giving orders, he felt he had some control and direction. With each line he ad libbed, he felt more confident that he could handle contingencies, that if he followed his impulses they'd somehow deliver him at last to where he was meant to be, even if it was different than he expected, the way he was finally delivered to Vivien, the way each sentence he uttered to The Stone worked; each step he took brought them closer to resolution.

"Come on, Stoneman. Remember, not a word. Just follow my lead."

"Goddamn you," Vivien said, "don't come back."

"Please," he said. "Understand. All I want is to come back." She stood stiffly and looked away when he tried to hold and kiss her. He whispered in her ear, "He's gone psycho. I have to defuse him. I'll be back."

She shrugged Walter off. "Don't bother. You go with the crazy people. You like trouble. You choose them. I can see who you are."

Walter tried to think about what he could say when he got back to Vivien while also preparing for the puddle of craziness which he knew was spilled before him. Mallory was laughing, a har har finger pointing kind of laugh. He was sprawled among a mess of discarded beer bottles with a girl rubbing his shoulders, laughing at Al. Walter descended the last step, feeling The Stone behind him as an unstable shadow, and stepping onto the deck he and The Stone saw The Chief getting to his feet, an arm around his new girl. Al was standing, draped around Brenda like she was carrying him from the battlefield.

"What's so funny?" Walter said.

"Where's the slut?"

"Probably listening from the window up there, plotting your demise. What's so funny?"

"You been spyin'? You were listenin' to us?"

"Trying not to. So what's up? What's the plan? You guys came all this way for some game. What's your next move?"

The Chief slicked back some disorderly strands of greasy hair that had fallen forward from his temples when he got up. "Hey Schmerz. No game. Just some straight up communications between radiomen. Just warnin' Turner here about the treatment."

Mallory snickered. Al growled and lurched toward The Chief, but Brenda held him back. Walter turned sideways so that he could keep a corner of his eye on The Stone and looked up to the window. He wanted to do this well. "Al—"

"Obstructions!" Al yelled. "Can't stop me. I'm better than you. I'm more than you!"

"Too bad about the treatment," Chief said. "I tried to put the breaks on the chiefs."

"I stole your girlfriend! I fucked your mother!"

Mallory shook his head, smiling. "Boy, I'm glad I ain't you."

The Stone nudged Walter and said quietly, "See? See man?"

"Alright," Walter said, "what's with this treatment business."

"I told you about the treatment, Schmerz. Seems the chiefs wanna revive an old tradition. Seems word is gettin' around chiefs' quarters that Turner lives in his own navy. I told them I didn't think so. Told them about his mother 'n all, to make him look good. Brenda don't think he's weird, do ya honey? Well, what can I do, he's prettier than me. Anyway, they're gonna run his ass right off the ship. Nothin' I could do."

"Do you have a place to stay?" Walter asked Brenda.

She pointed up the beach where there were a number of bungalows on stilts. "We got a room there."

"Get out of here then. Get Turner to bed and make sure you get him up in the morning so he can make muster."

"Man, *no*!" The Stone said.

"Orders, Stoneman, remember the plan…"

"The fuck are *you* Schmerz?" Al said. "Don't get in my way, man. I'm going ballistic!"

The Stone tugged at Walter's arm, who spoke quiet and fast. "Follow. You got the watch till morning. Guard the beach. You can tuck him in if it makes you feel better." He wasn't going to sleep anyway since he'd stopped drinking, but Al could pass out for a few hours. This way he'd be out of trouble and could straighten up nice and peacefully with the rising sun over the bay. He turned to the others. "And there is no treatment. Game's over. Go to bed. We got work tomorrow."

"Well done, Schmerz," Chief said. "You'll fill Turner's shoes alright. You sound like a real sailor with leadership qualities."

Al broke Brenda's hold and lunged for The Chief's throat, but he could hardly stand, and The Chief easily knocked him down. Walter grabbed The Stone and held him back as he tried to fly past. Brenda picked Al up. The Chief pulled a comb out of his back pocket and ran it through his hair. "Wow," he said, "See that? That's serious criminality."

"You know nothing!" Al yelled as Brenda began dragging him off, cooing, "Come on baby, come on baby."

"Easy pal," The Chief said.

"You are nothing! Mere obstructions." His eyes were rolling back in his head.

"Go on, now."

"In my way. You're all in my way." Brenda practically carried him away as he looked back for a moment with an eye of uncomprehending wonder, held open by the last remaining thread of consciousness.

"Baby baby baby baby."

The Chief and Mallory sat back down on the deck. The Stone relaxed in Walter's arms and he let him go. "Hope you learned something here tonight, Schmerz," The Chief said. "That was the idea. Part of the job of chiefing is to be a teacher." He took a swig of beer. "I can reach anyone. That boy's been got to."

"Go to bed," Walter said. "You're bothering us."

"Still givin' the orders, eh? How'd you like the treatment, too?"

"There is no treatment."

"No. But oh man. Oh wow. Wait'll he gets to the real joke! Almost forgot in all the excitement. Talk about queer!"

"Brenda!" The Stone said.

"What did you do?" Walter said.

Even Mallory perked up, surprised. "What is it?"

"Well, wait'll he gets to his bungalow and wants a little tender loving care 'cause The Chief's so mean to him—that's if he's not too far gone to try—and he goes to bury his face in the pussy he thought he stole from me... and pulls down this chick's pants...Ahh, ha ha ha!"

"You mean Brenda's a dude?"

"A transvestite!"

Mallory roared and they both rolled in uncontrollable laughter. Walter looked to the window. The Stone, he knew, was waiting for Walter's order to kill them, and he kept checking his hand to make sure it wasn't going for the knife. It wanted to, as if being fed by The Stone's impulses. They laughed convulsively, sitting with their legs straight out, slapping each other's palms like kids playing patty cake. Walter imagined killing them—a satisfying fantasy—slicing them with the butterfly knife and being splattered by the slow motion pulse of arterial blood, or bludgeoning their heads and being splattered by the slow motion spray of gray matter: a Sam Peckinpah movie. He liked thinking that The Stone and his hand were waiting for the signal to kill them, that Vivien was waiting for him to sweep them away.

But then, here at last was Walter's revenge on Al. He would do nothing. He wouldn't unloose The Stone. He wouldn't warn Al of the game's surprise. He'd let him stew, let him bring whatever happened down on himself without any guidance or help from Walter. Hell, he thought, he's probably gone enough to sleep with Brenda, and I'll always have that over him, no matter what stories he concocted after tonight. That would be more than revenge enough. That would humble him.

The Stone sprang away from Walter's reach, crouching with his hands up as if to fend off any comers, and began walking backwards.

"Don't bother," Walter said. "He should be finding out about now."

"That's right," Mallory said. "He knows, but maybe he don't know we know."

Parma was still squeezing a few sniffles of laughter from the joke. "Picked her up in Olongapo. Paid her fifty pesos to come along and do the job."

"On who?" Walter said.

"Who else?"

"You know she was working with that driver, a dealer?"

"And now she's workin' with me. Workin' with your buddy Turner too, it would seem."

The Stone screeched a high "caw" like a movie Indian and vaulted over the side railing onto the beach and disappeared into the darkness. Mallory laughed. "*That* boy's gone, too."

"Goner than you think. Better sleep with an eye open tonight."

"Meaning?"

Walter let his hand move into the pocket and caress the knife. He'd said enough—let them think about it. "Meaning you are a fucking pig. Both of you are fucking pigs."

"Watch it, Schmerz," Chief said.

"You took it too far tonight."

"Too far? Look at Turner! You know what he's doin' right now? I thought he'd come back but he don't know it's a joke. He's with that drag queen from hell. But he's not comin' back. You say I've gone too far?"

"I don't give a shit about him or any of you."

There was a "caw" out of the darkness up the beach.

"Too far. And the night's full of craziness—evil spirits. And there isn't a soul out here that likes you. Just Miss Dark and Miss Lonely." The Stone howled again, this time more distant but more chilling because human, a frightening, agonized wail that seemed to catch itself up short as though the darkness up the beach snuffed it—probably a shift in the breeze. Maybe Al found him and shut him up. They looked at each other. "Yeah, I'd stick together tonight if I was you."

Mallory rose to his feet, swaying. His head was bent, angry, sunken eyes looking up from under his thick brows, sweat shining on the creases in his forehead. "Oh yeah, bitch! That a threat? Think you're up to something? Well you and your faggot friends make me sick. Why don't you go join the party. You're the one that's not wanted around here. I said beat it!"

He leapt at Walter from a few feet away, his second step landing on a beer bottle, and the world went out from beneath him. His head thudded on the deck at Walter's feet and he was still. Parma walked over to examine him. "Out cold. Might as well leave him here. He'll need the air when he wakes up. Boy can't handle his liquor. None of yas can."

"Tough guys," Walter said.

The Chief looked at Mallory's girl, then at Mallory, and smiled. "Scavengers. Bottom feeders." He pulled Mallory's wallet and things from his pockets and crammed them into his own. "Hoy, scat! No more. Nothin' left. Beat it, now.

"C'mon girl," he said, taking his girl by the hand and walking past Walter without looking at him. Then he stopped and turned around. "I feel sorry for you, Schmerz. You have failed to recognize the authority of a superior. Big crime. You see how Turner couldn't get away without payin'. Had bigger plans for you, but you just can't fuck with The Chief and get away with it. Law of the sea.

Yeah, seems like everything's changed. I'll have to get rid of Turner—"

"He's comatose, for Christ's sake! None of this counts. It isn't real."

"And I'll have to deal with you. The rest of the division'll know I'm comin' down hard because of you and I'm sure they'll resent it. Then there's this thing, this...animosity with Mallory...and your...unhealthy relationships. See, it doesn't matter to me as long as the division performs well. I don't have to live with you guys. I'm the boss. But someone could get hurt. You have to smell each other's funk, get it? It's really a shame, Schmerz. I thought we'd make a damn good communicator out of you."

"Did you actually plan to get rid of him?"

The Chief turned and walked off toward his room, and Walter turned toward Vivien's, leaving the stars and the whisper of the shore to Mallory's unconscious bulk.

He waited for dawn with Vivien breathing in his arms. When he had come back she slid over to the edge of the bed, still angry, and he couldn't blame her, but he'd make it better soon. For now, he'd wrap her in his arms as a gesture of tenderness. The ease with which she fell back to sleep seemed an acceptance of an offering.

The rest of the night had been still, silent, as he watched the blackness out the window dissolve to the color of water, the static before his eyes taking incremental definition until it was officially day. Without sight of the sun or the contrast of clouds the sky seemed a haze gray void; day, a mass of clay wanting effort and responsibility. He thought he knew what to do with it now, knew who he was and who he wasn't. Despite all that was out of his control, he felt vaguely that he knew what to do with his life.

He freed his arms of Vivien and rolled over for a cigarette from the nightstand. In fact, his arms and legs were like lead welded together at the joints. His head buzzed with dizzy sleepiness. Another year in the Navy before he could even act according to his conscience. Would he be expected to kill? Murderous pirates. Muslim insurrectionists. Taunting Iranians. Communists. Russians. Mutineers. My country's enemies. A year, and the hell of that ship and the players—all the ships and all the players the same. Remember the luxury of youth and a future? When living felt like practice? And if it eludes your grasp, you'll just get it on the next try, like fielding grounders.

There was a knock at the door.

Vivien groaned and said "No." What now? Walter pulled on his pants and took the butterfly knife in his hands, ready for whatever craziness was visiting them this time. It was Parma and Mallory, looking glazed and hollow, ashy faced and red eyed. Mallory had an angry looking lump rising from his thick brow and remained silent.

"What do you want?" he said.

Parma looked at the knife without expression. "Wake up call. Let's go."

"How considerate. Great service around here."

"Come on. We gotta get goin'."

"I'll head for the ship directly. Bye."

"Come on Schmerz. It's roundup time. Let's go. Game's over."

"After everything?"

"Gag's a gag's a gag. Now quit playin' cute. Game's over. We got work to do. Get any sleep last night?"

"No. Too busy working on the plan, up plotting all night."

"That's good. Now where's your buddies?"

Walter looked at Mallory's swollen red knot. "How's the head, tough guy?"

Mallory seemed to make a conscious effort at manipulating his jaw. "Fuckin' mule kicked it."

"That's nice. That gives me a sense of accomplishment."

"Where's your buddies?" Parma repeated.

"Not my buddies."

"Fine. Now quit bein' cute. Gag's over. Everybody learned their lesson. You don't fuck with The Chief. Turner'll understand the joke better'n anybody. We all get some laughs and we got plenty of material for stories underway. You need that kind of stuff. Now we're all a little tired and the worse for wear, so let's get goin'. Like it or not, we're still shipmates and we got work to do, lots. You can't hack it, fine. We'll deal later. Now get dressed and we'll go collect assholes number one and two. They're at one of them tree houses on the beach."

Boys will be boys. Here Al was a timebomb, a man on an irreversible, one way game of brinkmanship with the rest of the world, playing chicken even with himself when there was no one else around; and The Stone, the lost aviator spiraling and sputtering into ether, finger on the trigger and mad eyes frozen to the gun sights, squeezing off rounds at phantoms above. *Laughs and stories.*

"Unbelievable," he said. "All one happy family again. All for shits and giggles. Let's go then, by all means." He bent over Vivien and kissed her head. "I'll write, a lot."

She looked at the door. "So go."

"I'll make it better. I'll write. You too."

She pulled the blanket tight around herself, her back to him, her body kinked into a final closed parenthesis of mute exclusion.

"Let's go, loverboy," The Chief said, "lead the way." He did.

They crossed the courtyard and turned up the road toward the beach adjacent to the dock—a wormy and colorless little stage in daylight's reality— and he glanced at his company. They looked weak and human and...white. He pictured Al and The Stone rocketing through the night and never coming back from Fred. "Yeah, some night. I wonder if they'll dream up some joke for you during the IO. I suppose Al'll have a wild story to tell. Yeah, you guys look tired. I think if you just go to sleep for a little while it's worse than not sleeping at all."

"Oh shut up."

"No, really. I learned a lot last night."

"Uh huh. Which one of these is Turner's?"

"How should I know? Look for the one with The Stone on the roof. I told him he had sentry duty." Having said that, he literally began to look there. They were small out-buildings, really no more than bedrooms on stilts, their weathered gray woodsides revealing themselves beneath the cracked red paint. The beach was quiet and the air still in the early morning, the bay barely breathing against the sand.

They did look around for The Stone, but there was no one out, so they walked up to the first bungalow and stood dumbly by the side. "Knock on the door," The Chief said to Mallory, who looked in turn at Walter, who folded his arms and smiled. Mallory glared back, then went up to the door and banged with his fist, and it yawned open.

"It's open," he said, as though reporting on his mission and awaiting further instructions, the while backing out.

"Could be an ambush," Walter said, amused by the look on his face. So they weren't so sure about what the morning would bring.

Mallory banged the door open and disappeared inside. Some gulls cried and a dog cantered by.

He stuck his head out again. "Nothin'. Nobody home. Fuck it. Let's get back."

"No no," Walter said. "This is interesting. This is fun. Let's see what's behind door number two."

"Yeah, Parma said, "C'mon." He sounded distracted and looked as though he was thinking something through. "You know, I kinda expected Turner to come back last night. Boy was fucked up. We all were, I suppose."

"How'd you know about her, anyway? Brenda. You know The Stone got it in his head that it was all connected—I mean, life or death. I wonder if he's come down."

They were coming up on another bungalow. "This is a simple place, Schmerz. I saw you guys with them, asked what it was you were doin', then put in my order. Told the bossman what I wanted and for who, and voila, made to order. Oh, he loved you guys. Acted like I was doing him a favor."

"So it could have been me."

"Don't be such a turkey, Schmerz. Could only of been Turner. You got your girl and Turner got mine, as planned. Try this one Mallory."

"Yes, try it Mallory. Maybe Stone's there too. He's out there somewhere. I mean he's really out there—going, going, gone goodbye. Got it in his head that you're trying to kill him. Well, he's probably straightened up by now. Knock on the door and see if he's home."

"Shut up Schmerz! Go on boy. Hey Turner!" he yelled, hands cupped over his mouth, "Wakeup call!" His voice was swallowed by the silence of the beach.

Mallory moved toward the steps and stopped, turning his head to the side. "What's that?"

"What?"

"*That.*"

They stepped up along with him and stood still. At first it was simply the water pulsing its gentle biding rasp upon the countless and ageless grains of Subic beach, but as their ears settled in like eyes acclimating to a shift in light, they picked up a tenuous but deeper sidetone, a low drone of more character than the benign wash, of some intent. The sound grew closer and more focused than the diffuse gargling of stone in the inlet's mouth. Organic. It came from the shack.

"What's it supposed to be?" Mallory said.

"Check it out and see," Parma said.

"Ain't air conditioning?"

"There's no electricity."

Now that they were aware of it, it was clearly a buzzing.

"Sounds like TV static."

"I said there ain't no—"

"No," Walter said, feeling his skin tighten into goose bumps and realizing that the clear morning air felt chilly. "It's living." They were frozen there in a tableau of statues, half-crouching, arms akimbo, heads tilted toward the birthing east in attitudes of apprehension.

They looked at each other and listened to the living sound without moving. The shack waited, humming. A dog trotted up and sniffed around the pilings, then whimpered. A slight breeze rustled the palms and Walter thought he smelled the almost imperceptible hint of shit.

Mallory straightened up. "Well forget it. Obviously they ain't in there." He sounded worried. "Let's try the next one. We gotta be getting' back. What're we doin'?" A slight, pleading whine insinuated in his voice.

"Sounds like someone humming," Parma said.

"It's lots of bugs, man. Just bugs in some slob's garbage. Let's get outta here already."

Walter picked up a chunk of driftwood and threw it against the side of the shack. The report made Mallory and Parma jump; the dog dodged and barked; then the noise intensified. "Better go check it out," Parma said, still balancing himself like a man caught in a minefield.

"Oh shit!" Mallory said, detaching his feet from their spot and kicking at the sand as if to prove that it wouldn't explode in their faces. "What're we doin'? I told you it's nothin'." He stomped loudly up the steps and banged on the door. "Hey Stone!" The bungalow droned back at him. He grasped the knob and thrust the door open.

A black wave burst from the sudden opening and ripped through the serene morning air like a discharge of shot. Mallory yelped, flailing his arms, and jumped from the steps. It was screaming flesh flies, stirred by the noise and maddened by the sudden intrusion of sunlight, swarming from the darkness inside and descending on them, a living, buzzing mass of palpable frenzy with a foul smell on its shit-eating breath. The cloud quickly dispersed in the fresh air.

Mallory scooped up a handful of sand and threw it wildly in the air, cursing. Parma crouched to his haunches, eyes bulging and panning the sky, mouth gaping. "Oh wow. Oh wow. What the hell."

Mallory walked slowly back up the stairs, kicked the door and ducked as a fistful or so more flies droned by. He turned sideways toward the door and stuck a foot and arm in ahead of him as though sidling in the dark and sending his limbs out as scouts feeling for obstructions, while one hand was fanned in front of his face to protect that.

"Eyooh!" he blurted in that comical involuntary shudder people do when they touch a live current. "Yooh!" Walter may have even started to smile until he staggered down the steps and fell to his knees retching.

Parma's face was a gargoyle, eyes bursting, fangs bared in a grimace. He rose and started walking backward. "Alright," he said, retreating. "Alright. Shit! Okay. Okay? Get up, goddamn you, it's just a bunch of fuckin' bugs! Let's go. It's getting' late."

Mallory rolled his eyes up at him so that only his whites showed under his beetle brows, then convulsed again. "Christ!" Parma said. "Jesus Fucking Christ! Alright, what is it? What's going on? Never mind. Never mind about it. Forget it. Gotta go…gotta get out of here…back to the ship. We have to go now."

Even then he wanted to make it something that hadn't happened. But Walter already knew, and what he felt was something other than surprise, as though he somehow knew it was coming; it already felt like an integral part of some inevitable pattern. "Never mind," Parma had said, but by then they had all long known.

Walter was cold, as if he had known for so long that he wasn't even moved anymore. So cold that his gooseflesh had twitched to shivers and his teeth chattered, as if a valve opened in his brain letting all thoughts and emotions escape to his skin and muscles where they dug in and tightened, hanging on to his rattling bones blown cold by his doused and unstoked mind.

His body moved toward the shack and his tunnel vision eyes registered first the gargoyle, then the beetle brow, then sand and clumps of grass at the base of the wooden steps and railing. His hand was on the rail and he watched the steps, dipping slightly in the middle and worn smooth from the procession of feet entering and exiting through the years, feet of lovers and one-nighters; first step, second step, third step, fourth step and the landing and the open door with the hollow metal knob—it, too, smooth and dispainted from the touch of men and women who are anxious or loving or dispassionate or businesslike, and then sad or guilty or angry or contented or happy—and the darkness within is hot and foul and crawling and now he's sweating and still shivering.

Brenda had really done a job on him. Why torture? Why not simply execution? Mixing business with pleasure, perhaps. His wrists and ankles were tied to the bed posts. His throat had been cut clear through to his spine. His head hung back over the bed, lips and eyes open, teeth clenching a bloody gag. The slash was busy with life, host to the shiny movement of fly and, already, maggot, opportunistic bugs generating merrily in their warm new niche. They go to work fast in the tropics.

He was naked and butchered. His stomach had been hacked open and his guts pulled out and slopped on the floor, hence the nauseating reek of offal, and it may be that he had already begun decomposing in the heat. His genitals were cut off. There was blood spattered on the walls and the floor was slippery with it. The pools were still black with droning, drunken flies, absorbed in debauch. Geckos ran up and down the walls, their reptile eyes darting about nervously at the orgy.

There was a little globular pyramid, something knobby and yellow, sitting in his gutted midsection—a pile of gelatin capsules fusing together, rising out of and melting back into his cavity. No waste in the message—they were clearly empty.

Something large, animal-sized, moved on the floor jolting Walter out of his wonder with an electric thrill up his spine into his temples, and in the tick of a second that it took to shudder "ooh!" he fumbled for the knife against the phantom flying out of the darkened corner at him.

Nothing happened. Still hopping backward, ughing and oohing and shuddering in frighted revulsion, he looked again toward the motion. It was The Stone. He looked at Walter. Walter looked at him. He was gagged. His feet were bound with a bandanna. His hands were tied behind his back to some abandoned plumbing project leading up out of the floor and just ending midair above his head. His knees were drawn up, resting his chin. He was humming, singing with the flies. Had Walter confused the two? His head rocked slowly to and fro, perhaps in an exhausted effort to chase the flies that walked freely on his face, lips, and eyelids. There were specks of blood all over him. He looked at Walter.

"Oh. Oh Stone-man. Hey in here! It's The Stone! He's alive!" Walter cut him loose and dragged him out by the armpits.

The others were where he had left them. "Give me a hand with him. He's okay, I think. Al's dead. Here. Bring him to the water."

He wasn't alright. He made no attempt to walk, his entire body balled up and rigid. When they removed the gag, he kept humming. Mallory held his jaws open while Walter fished out the pieces of dead flies that had squeezed through his lips and been chopped by his clenched teeth into his still living mouth, just because they could. He looked at Walter but there was nothing there, no expression, no recognition, no hint. Whatever happened through the night had been too much—the blood, the taunts, the bugs, the air, the hours, the murderous treachery of it all, so intimate and so impersonal. It got him, and he kept it a mystery. Why didn't Brenda do him too? Maybe she just liked the idea. Things don't have to make sense—what we do to each other is madness. It was their secret. Brenda's torment of Renaldo flashed in his eyes—his eyewhites with his limbs stretched out above the bay, his cries about drowning. Walter had seen the pleasure that's taken in playing with your prey.

At some point he gave up thrashing. Perhaps he saw with horror that he was reaching his limit and burned out like a light bulb; perhaps it was with relief that he passed beyond endurance. Walter imagined it, the blow by blow insults and indignities, the shock and then the shutdown. Picture army ants circling animals and then moving in, a sting and then another sting as it dawns on the startled armadillo or lizard that the worst thing in the world is happening and it's too late. Like that. The knowing is what's so horrible—the brief lifetime between the first bite and the paralyzed last instants before the devouring column.

They dragged him through the sand to the water and scrubbed him as best they could. They got the blood off his face and unbuttoned his pants to rinse the water through. He stank. Parma's mind was beginning to calculate again, faster than he could get the words out.

"He'll be okay. Sure...kid's gonna be fine. Look at him. Had a rough time, though. We have to have a story, you know. We have to do something... get out of here...away from this." He looked toward the shack. "Have to have a story. We didn't have nothin' to do with this, but we'll look bad. People will think...there'll be an investigation...lot of questions. I'm going up for Limited Duty Officer, ya know—lieutenant. Oh Christ! Why did this have to happen? We gotta go. Act like we didn't know nothin'...shit! Make him stop hummin' like that!"

Mallory rose up, glowering from behind his bulking shoulders and lumpen skull. "Turner's dead. That Brenda chopped him up. Go take a look. He's split wide open. What are you talkin' about? LDO?"

"There were pills on him," Walter said.

"What?"

"A pile of yellow pills. On his...stomach."

Parma was panicked. "What's that supposed to mean? Don't you look at me like that. Don't say it like it was my fault. How could I know he would do that? It wasn't my fault. I didn't know. You think I don't care? I care, but what can we do now? He's dead. We have to think for ourselves and you're talkin' about pills. What are you talkin' about pills? What's that about?"

"Oh, I don't believe this," Mallory said.

"Oh no you don't," Parma said. "No you don't—don't even try it. I see what you're gettin' at. Not my fault. No fucking way in the world." He looked at Walter as if an idea came over him that offered a ray of hope, a way out of the mess. "You," he said, pointing a finger, "you're the one. Your fault. It's your fault. Don't you see it? Started the whole fucking mess."

"It won't work. Come on, give me a hand."

"Hold it! Hold it right there. Where do you think you're going?"

"Back. To the hospital."

Walter and Mallory were holding The Stone under the armpits, but he was easy to balance, inert and rigid. "Aren't we gonna call the cops?" Mallory asked.

The idea seemed absurd. What cops? Which cops? Local constabulary? MPs? Who were they? What would they do? It was all too late, and the locals were owned. The killer was gone—anywhere, in disguise, behind a mask, in uniform, changing, transforming into an inconspicuous speck of background color amid a jostling of elbows or a rustle of leaves, just an innocuous piece of the scene, only incipient violence and horror. The MPs would come, and Naval Intelligence, to conduct an official investigation and file everything in its proper slot and make it all legal and correct. They'd ask questions and reconstruct the entire night and beyond.

Something like that went through Walter's mind, and the only concern at that point was getting The Stone to help, and the fastest way was by taking a jeepney immediately, not waiting for official handling. "Call them if you want—one last joke. We've got to get him out now. I'm taking him to the base."

"That's right," Parma said, grasping for desperate hope. He was following them as they dragged The Stone toward the street, his machinations breaking down to a clattering babble. "Schmerz's right—what a joke. What can they do? Could be anybody, for all we know. We'll tell 'em when we get back to the base. Important thing's getting' Stone to safety. Report it all we want once we get there. Give us time to get our story right.

When you think about it it's Turner's fault, really—well didn't he walk into it? Look, it's too bad and I'm sorry for the guy—terrible—but didn't he ask for it? Always a bad influence—look what happened to Stone, here, his best friend. Gotta make it reflect on him...I mean, it's awful but he's dead and we're not.

"He went off—took Stone with him—found the kid this morning like this—no Turner—we'll have to pay the girls to keep quiet. Shit, the fucking girls!"

Mallory jerked around and almost tore Stone's arm from his socket in the process. "Shut up!"

"Listen to reason!"

"Shut up! Did you go in there? Did you see him?"

The street was quietly stirring to life with the drowsy motion of early risers padding barefoot out of doors to the sound of someone coughing or a baby crying within, roosters scolding in the yards, the still chilly breeze shaking the last of the night out of the dry nipa fronds, the odd dog yapping. The mundane rites of a new day and old errands were set in motion. On the street a sailor tucked in his shirttails, his chest spilling out from where the buttons should form a closure; further up a woman gathered bags about her for a trip into Olongapo; a motor started up; a madman hummed in Walter's ear. The jeepney rolled slowly up the block and stopped next to them. The driver smiled. Mallory studied him a moment, then nodded to the others. They climbed in.

Mallory gave the driver some pesos and Walter told him to go straight to the base, fast as he could.

"No no. Go slow. We have to take it slow so we can figure out our story."

"Fast as you can," Walter repeated. "It's an emergency. Our friend's real sick."

He nodded.

The woman shook her fist as they passed. The driver smiled.

Walter sat on one side with The Stone cradled in his arms, humming his blank song. Walter embraced him stiffly, holding his head off as far as he could get it, not wanting to feel the touch of him or breathe him in, not wanting to get too close to it—the personal touch of something disgustingly damaged. Mallory collapsed on the bench opposite him and Parma sank down by the open back.

They roared up the hill in a cloud of roadside dust like a parting blast at the village, knocked backwards and then hanging grimly on as the driver kicked the gears. Parma stared out the back at the street as it pulled away behind them like an endless tongue sucking throat-ward as they spun their wheels in stasis, maintaining but unable to gain distance from the slavering mouth of the world. He turned around to look ahead and mark how far they had gotten toward the doom at the other end, his great eyes wide in panic and the effort of figuring a way out, the eyes of a man who knows his life is hitting a wall.

He looked up the road, now liquid with motion, rising and falling and bucking them forward. If you look straight on a point ahead then the objects passing along beside you melt and blend into a solution of indistinguishable shapes and shades in a continual, self-renewing pattern. Mallory maintained his silence. They advanced, out of town, away from the people and up into the hills. If you blink and keep your eyes on the discrete splashes as they spill by you can see them before they're gone, before you're shooting past the gray bars and bungalows, beyond the shacks and thatched huts, the sleepy children, the water buffaloes, the fishermen heading for their boats.

Walter's eyes lost focus and everything went green, a great waterfall of living jungle green cascading all around them, roaring now. They lurched around a curve as though being turned sideways by a wave, but the green was constant, screaming in his ears as if to deafen him. The noise built like cymbals inside his head, about to make his heart burst. Was it the car, the green, or was he himself screaming?

He covered his mouth with a hand but found it was closed. He thought of Al, his buddy, reduced to the mess they left there to be cleaned up. The room, the body, his blood screaming at Walter. He put his hands over his ears and heard himself groan. "Oh god."

"Mmm..."

Parma shot his head around again. "Why does he keep doing that? Make him stop. For god's sake it's unbearable! I can't think!"

"...Mmm..."

"Shut him up! Shut him up Schmerz, do you hear me? I order you! Cover his mouth."

"...Mmm..."

He lunged at them and grabbed The Stone by the collar. "You snap out of it goddamn you!" He shook him. "What's the matter with you, shit!" He slapped at him and clamped a hand over his mouth.

Walter held The Stone with one hand and punched Parma in the face with the other, then leaned back and kicked him away. Parma was in a panic, running his hands mechanically through his hair—his fingers and wayward black strands trembling to a vibration accelerated by the shimmying of the car—and he looked as if he was going rattle apart into a heap right there on the road. His voice was strung high and out of tune, struggling to find the proper pitch through his fear. "Look men, this is my life here. We have to slow this thing down and work something out. We'll say we couldn't find Turner. Don't know where he was staying. This is my career."

His voice sprang out of control as it found itself pleading, the words hard to make out above the commotion of the road, still casting about for the right story to tell. "Just found Stone on the beach this morning, doin' like that. Drugs for all we know. Nothin' about last night...the joke. Act ignorant. Won't look for 'em right away. Time to pay the girls...give 'em some money. C'mon fellas, let's make him slow down?"

Walter watched the back of the driver's head, but it registered nothing beyond the business at hand of negotiating the road. Even the back of a man's head can be a mask. He must have been curious. Walter wasn't sure if Mallory was even listening, whose big face, frozen in an expression of unreserved anger, never changed. He was radiant with malice. He glared at the desperate man, then tapped the driver on the shoulder. "Faster goddamnit."

"Hey, easy goes it, okay buddy? It's a bad road."

Mallory opened his wallet and shook the bills onto the passenger's side of the front. "You make this fuckin' thing go faster! Floor it!"

For the first time Walter caught the driver casting a dubious eye back in the mirror. "Okay Joe. You got trouble?"

"Just shut up and drive."

Parma resigned his attention to the road disappearing behind them. The truck snarled and jumped forward. Dust flew as they clawed and skidded around soft shouldered cliffs. The few cars and pedestrians that were about scrambled out of their way.

Walter tried to concentrate, to keep a foot in reality and climb outside himself to see the whole picture. What did it mean? Where was he in all this?

He dreaded getting back to the base, but the place that they left was bad, bad. The base would be bad. The base was still. If only they could keep moving. If only there was some place they could run to. Maybe he was the one who was doomed.

He thought about Al. Could it really all have been connected? Impossible. The universe couldn't take such special interest in them, in himself. Maybe when you put it all together there is no picture that makes any sense, no meaning, just a dance of shades. It was all an absurdity that sometimes bore the illusion of a meaningful pattern. That's what Al thought he knew, why he was so intent on blowing everything to pieces. Nothing but Al, the piece of the picture who refused to fit anyone else's concept, the thing itself that no one could have, not even himself, no matter how fast he chased.

They rocketed on, tossing about as if the jungle itself was rolling beneath their wheels. A hand slapped on Walter's thigh—Mallory, feeling the knife in his pocket through his pants. The hand raised and presented itself to Walter, palm up. Give, it said. They locked eyes, and the hand jerked, insistently repeating the gesture. Walter's eyes went to Parma's back. It seemed to be sobbing. He pulled the knife out and placed it in Mallory's hand.

Now they were on the highest stretch of road, the farthest from the water. The pavement narrows here. Beyond the shoulder is a drop of about thirty feet, and there, with open arms and gaping mouth, grows a fulminating shock of tropical green, its intent pure, its violence unhampered.

Mallory turned around and peered up the road. Then he stuck his head out to scan the road behind them. Parma was muttering something like "okay…nothing wrong…not my fault," as if by floating out those feeble words like bubbles he could try to buoy his sinking self from under the weight of what had happened and was happening. As they approached the inversion of an "S" curve, Mallory rolled over onto his back and drew his knees up, holding his thighs with his hands. At the middle of the turn he tapped Parma's back with a foot. Parma turned around and gasped just in time to see the big feet coming at him. Mallory grunted and slammed them into Parma's chest full force. Parma never had time to yell before the impact took his wind and blew him up and out the speeding tumbrel backwards, flipping twice on the road, and over the ledge, into the hungry maw below.

When the driver realized what had happened, he slammed on his brakes and brought them to a skidding halt.

They all—save The Stone—ran back to the approximate spot where Parma went over, and they looked down for a sign. No movement, no sound. Their driver began stamping in agitation. "Holy Jesus. Hey man. Hey man, that guy's probably dead. He fall out? someone push him? Sweet Mary, I never see nothing like this! You guys are trouble. Why you want to go so fast for? You don't ride with me no more. I gotta get out of here and tell what happen. You go down there, see you can find him. I get some help."

"The hell you are. You got our money and you're takin' us back to the base."

"Not me, man. Too much trouble. I don't need to get in no kind of trouble." Mallory, outweighing the Filipino by about a hundred pounds, quickly spun him into a choke hold. As the one stood there, sweating and struggling, the other growled in his ears. "You know, I could break your neck. Or I could just squeeze you till your head turns purple. Or crush your fuckin' throat. Or I could throw you over the side with him." Then Walter saw the flash of the knife as he brought it into play, pressing it flat against the man's face, the point just below his eye. "Cut your fuckin' eyes out! You wanna die? Think I never killed a Flip before?"

He snorted, pleading no with his eyes but not daring move his head, standing on his toes reaching for slack.

"Good. I didn't think you did. Now you're gonna take us back like we paid you for. And you ain't gonna tell nobody nothin'. If anybody does ask you, just three of us got on and that's all. Understand?"

He gurgled and tried to move his head back in a half nod. "No one wants to die. That fuck Turner didn't want what he got. Our friend in your taxi there didn't. That guy who's not here? Who was never here? The one who didn't get in your jeepney with us and isn't lyin' at the bottom of that gorge? I fuckin' killed him motherfucker! Was easy, isn't it? Nothin' to it, huh? People, they just break, like anything else. You should know, shouldn't you, killer? Murderer.

"You got Turner, didn't you? I saw your fuckin' smile. I recognize you. Brenda? Johnny? What're you called now? Oh, you did it. You killed this one too. His name's Chief Parma in case you're interested. He's my friend, you fuck! We know you did it. We recognize you." Walter understood it all.

The man's eyewhites were blinking through his tears and the trembling of his face against the knife drew a spot of blood to its tip.

"Enough!" Walter said. "Let him go. He's okay, it's not him. Leave the guy alone." At some point they had all lost their minds and got caught up in the cycle, the noise. Paranoid and deluded, unable to distinguish the real from the imagined, casting blame and finding enemies, oblivious to their own motives and consequences, they went off in each other's faces.

"Hurts, don't it? Oh he's our man, alright. Yeah, we know you. I could cut you now or I could kill you later. See how it feels to be afraid? If I suspect you ever mentioned this, I swear to god I'll get you. If they lock me up my friends will get you. I got your license number too, and I never forget a face. What do you care about one American sailor? Fuckin' Flip. You're all the same, all together. You'd love to kill us all, wouldn't you? Well, don't you worry sweetheart, you'll never get in trouble…unless you tell." He let go and the man collapsed onto the dirt, sobbing.

Mallory reached into his sock and pulled out a wad of green. "Here," he said. "Here's my last hundred pesos for the rough trip." He stuffed the money into the captive's shirt pocket, then frisked his prone body. "Good," he said. "Okay." He took two measured steps back, hopped forward and strode into the man's ribs with his boot like a place kicker. The man screamed, then howled, surely more from the pain of fear than from any bones that might have cracked.

"Ow!" Mallory said, dropping the knife and hopping on one foot and sort of half-laughing in mockery at his own folly.

Walter looked up the road both ways; both ways the road bent into the obscurity of the hills, a gentle breeze caressing a low sough from the trees. Something was about to round those green corners; something would emerge from the screen of their white noise. It always did.

The driver wormed himself into the fetal position, whimpering. Mallory had circled him in a holding pattern but was now homing in to tee off on him again. Walter pounced on the knife and jumped beside the hurt driver. "That's it! Stop it. No more."

"I paid for this! Move."

Walter held the knife at eye level and cut the air between them. "No. It stops here. Now. Listen, we have to get Stone to the hospital."

Mallory looked at the jeepney and it seemed to remind him of something. He looked at the road, remembering where he was.

"Come on," Walter said. "We're done if we stay here."

His shoulders sagged as if the hate had leaked out of them. "You're the man," he said. "You got the knife."

"Don't be an idiot." Walter folded the knife. "It's over. Let's go."

"Yeah." He bent over the driver and slapped his shoulder. C'mon old hoss, get up. You still owe us a ride." He pulled the man—still whimpering—to his feet and slapped hard at the dust on him, then helped him toward the jeepney, Mallory limping slightly, the driver bent over, clutching his wounded side, sniffling miserably. Walter pocketed the knife, took one last look down the precipice, and satisfied himself that Parma was gone.

Welcome

Of all the stories that came from the citizens of Subic City about that night—the random brutality that the visitors had rained on them; the heroics, fears and suspicions in the face of such terror—the worst was the interview with Vivien. She told it the way it really happened with Walter. They saw it all from her window—he wasn't with the others most of the time; he didn't bother anybody. He was with her. And she was convinced he was in some way involved in the murder of Al Turner and the disappearance of Chief Parma. The inquisitors were confused. She screwed everything up, but she was very interesting.

"What is this man to you?" they asked. He had been locked inside her ribs. He had breathed through her throat, swum in her blood.

"He is my customer."

"He paid you for your time?"

"Yes, he paid for me."

It was after her story corroborated Walter's that they suggested there was something special there, and she was getting into trouble by covering for him.

"I like him good enough. Not now. You can put him in jail if you want. I don't care. He is no good."

"What changed your mind about him? Did he hurt you?"

"Not me. Those others maybe. I think he hurt somebody. I tell him not to go but he goes with them instead of stay with me. They all want to hurt each other. The little one, he is loco. He has a knife. He wants to kill the other ones and he says the other ones want to kill him and the dead one. They all fight. Walter too. He goes away with them in the morning. Don't trust him. I would never trust him."

"So what do you think we should put him in jail for? Did he do something with the knife, maybe to Chief Parma?"

"I don't know, but he has it from the other one. He is bad. Don't you put bad people in jail?"

"Didn't you see a crime? Did he say what he was going to do to Chief Parma?"

"He tells them he is staying awake to think what he is going to do to them. He says he has a plan. I don't have to see anything. But I know. I know men."

The Outland pressed a patchwork gang of emergency replacements into service and sailed for the Indian Ocean late, its communications division decimated of its veterans. The pair were blamed for that too—realignment of ships and schedules so the Midway would still have a proper submarine screen and the battlegroup could still get near Iran in time for whatever was planned. The ripple effect. They'd bumped everybody's schedule a little off kilter from Yokosuka to Washington, maybe even Tehran. Could be they even touched you somehow. Where were you in nineteen eighty when Walter Schmerz made the news? Where are you now? He knows the world works that way. From his little stunt to international politics, it makes you feel at once insignificant and delicately responsible. When he reads the news about disastrous military adventure and atrocity, he's sickened by the world's surprise. It sickened him into poetry.

Subic had taught him everything from the beginning to the end, and in every direction he found always himself; in the life and death of the light and heat, in the patient presentient wisdom of vegetative existence, germinal organization into the functional glory of external and magnetic beauty—color and sight and smell; in the orbital motion of rocks and stars and tides and the geometrical lines of time and speed and the magical vehicle of memory and sympathy and imagination that permeates the ectofilm of objective reality, traverses the two-way aperture of the eyes of man; in the joys of fools and cruelties of lovers, the agonies of beasts and the appetites of gods.

Dennis Doherty served in the Navy for six years. Before his honorable discharge, he experienced life on shore and sea all across the globe, some of which was during The Iran Hostage Crisis.

Doherty is also the author of four collections of poetry (*The Bad Man*, *Fugitive*, *Crush Test*, and *Black Irish*) and one book-length critical study (*Why Read The Adventures of Huckleberry Finn*) in addition to individual essays, poems, and stories published by various literary presses.

Having directed the Creative Writing program at SUNY New Paltz, Doherty now teaches literature and creative writing while living in Rosendale, NY.

Contact the author or read the full bio on thmaduco.org:

For any related live events or collaborations, please contact The Mad Duck Coalition through its contact form.

Author Recommendations

Dostoevsky:
Crime and Punishment

Melville:
Moby Dick

James Baldwin:
"Sonny's Blues"
(one of the best stories ever written)

Seamus Heaney:
The Collected Works of Seamus Heaney

Cormac McCarthy:
The Road

Tim O'Brien:
In the Lake of the Woods

George Saunders:
Lincoln in the Bardo

Joy Harjo:
An American Sunrise

Tracy K. Smith:
Life on Mars

And the special works of his fellow mad ducks.

I would once again like to thank Mark Delluomo for his help and gorgeous artwork.

Concluding Note

Thank you so much for purchasing this work! Your support allows us to continue to avoid resorting to anti-consumer DRM practices and encourages our authors, not just this one, to continue following their passions and producing intellectually stimulating works. It also enables us to provide special programs for supporters like you!

One of our programs is a special discount for reviews, positive and negative! We believe that even negative feedback is vital feedback, so you should say what you really think. For more information about our review program, contact us through our contact form and select the appropriate category. In short, if the thought of supporting the authors and our jolly little coalition isn't enough to move you, we offer 5% off your next order for each review you post, with limitations obviously. So send us a message!

Information about our other programs and offers can be found on our website, including but not limited to: complimentary copies, contests, and collaborations.

Please reach out for further information. If you couldn't tell, we like to...*quack!!!*

The Mad Duck Coalition

The Mad Duck Coalition publishing house is a group of innovative intellectuals who want to publish what they are passionate about without compromising themselves or their work solely in the hopes of being published.

As such, The MDC publishes quality works that intellectually stimulate the mind, not necessarily the pockets. We wholeheartedly believe that quality and commerciality are two different things and that quality is far more important.

Check us out at thmaduco.org: